J.F. Mamjjasond

and

Fafnir Finkelmeyer

HOPTIME

AF085678

with a new foreword by

Fafnir Finkelmeyer

edited by

Walter Smart

Sagging Meniscus

© 2016 by Fafnir Finkelmeyer
Book design © 2016 by Sagging Meniscus Press

All Rights Reserved.

Printed in the United States of America.
Set in Adobe Garamond with LaTeX.

ISBN: 978-1-944697-30-3 (paperback)
ISBN: 978-1-944697-09-9 (ebook)
Library of Congress Control Number: 2016962205

Sagging Meniscus Press
web: http://www.saggingmeniscus.com/
email: info@saggingmeniscus.com

For L.C.

Contents

Foreword

Although J.F. Mamjjasond and I began work on *Hoptime* in a square-lined composition book which contains on its first page another unrelated Krinstian fragment, it was viewed by us almost immediately as a "work of some length" with a place outside of, if aligned with, the traditional Krinstian canon. For us, its truest and perhaps only appropriate audience, it had and required no title; it was called simply, and as much reverently as mockingly, *The Book*. When it was time to unveil a part of it on the Institute of Krinst Studies website, the name *Hoptime* was chosen (from Frog's line in Chapter XI, "It's hop time for yours truly"). As I think we were both well aware, giving it a name was in some sense an act of desecration, as for us The Book was a living thing and not an object: intensely profane, horrifying, unrelentingly sophmoric, a work of folly and vice for which no apology or justification could ever suffice, but still a kind of scripture. And yet the temptation to reify it and name it, to present it as if it were a literary accomplishment, as I am now doing, was strong and also an inherent part of its frame. That the book utterly fails to meet the criteria necessary to be any adequate or coherent thing, and yet must be something regardless, is an essential part of its identity, and part of why it could play such a vital and intimate role for its creators.

For a period of several years, we met every few days, and for some intensive periods, daily, sometimes in motels while travelling, to write together in the graph paper notebook, printing in block letters with ink. The paper was thin and the pages took on a palimpsestic appearance as writing from the other side shone through. Despite writing in capital letters, our handwritings were distinct enough that I can still tell who wrote what, although that can usually be determined by the content and style as well.

The rules for composition were simple but strict. Intoxication with marijuana was *de rigeur* (despite a brief dalliance with sobriety towards the end of the second notebook, which did not really feel right). After smoking, we sat in silence near each other in intense, if narcotically altered, concentration, and took turns continuing what had just been written by the other, passing the book back and forth often without looking at each other. Sometimes we would come out of a reverie to notice that the book and a pen were held outstretched by the other's hand towards us, the other's face looking away into the distance. We were not allowed to change what the other had written, and could only append new text at the end, of any length, long or short. Sometimes in a turn one of us might add just a single word or a character (a period, say), or he might add half a page. A typical entry would be three or four lines. Whether to finish a chapter was likewise a decision made by whomever held the pen at that moment. Very often the book would be handed back with the text ending in the middle of a sentence that demanded completion; equally often it would be returned with a continuation that changed the direction implied by what preceded it. Part of the process was accepting the frustration of the mischievousness of the other.

When the evening was complete, two or three pages may have been filled in, and they would be read aloud. Then we would part.

I don't know exactly when we started the project. Neither of us thought to date the manuscript at the beginning; towards the end of the second volume, when we met irregularly, we did begin that useful but self-conscious practice. But work must have begun in 1990 or 1991, and most of the first volume was written in the first couple of years, before I moved from New Jersey, where we both had lived, to Upper Manhattan. By 1994, most of the second volume was done, but from now on the pressures of life and life and work made our meetings increasingly infrequent. The last dated entry in the second volume is April 8th, 2000, shortly before J.F. moved to San Diego. We met only once after that, in California in 2001, but were not able to write on that occasion. For a brief period we did pick up writing in a similar way online, but it was a less satisfying experience and not much was done. I include that document here as a kind of postlude.[1]

For the two of us, I feel that the Book was a kind of imaginary life we had together. It was a life of great intimacy and a kind of chromatic and emotional repleteness, even if it consisted primarily of childish play. That this intimacy was predicated on something absurd and impossible did not make it any less precious. I know that we both took it seriously as something fateful and necessary. And so, despite everything about the artifact that resulted that is unacceptable and embarrassing—the repudiation of form and sense, the sexual violence, the forced vandalizing purplization of any poetic impulse—I claim for *Hoptime* a special place in the world, not only because it has in fact some inherent virtues in the small—its poetics sometimes strikes home, and I can never read it without laughing uncontrollably—but more importantly, because it was a way for the two of us to love each other in the only way we could, willingly and totally entwined in each other's foolish, ugly, wise and beautiful words and fantasies, which we heard, supported and forgave. Perhaps the sympathetic reader will feel the spirit of this rapport beneath the noisy

[1]As Book Three, *Idylls of the Chicken.*

surface of this cast-off part of a living thing, this enormous and dreadful basilisk skin.

J.F. Mamjjasond died of pancreatic cancer in 2014 at the age of forty-nine. None of his old friends knew that he was dying; only one knew that he was sick, but he did not know how seriously. Neither did J.F., it seems; when a doctor finally explained that he could not hope to recover, he became so upset that he had to be physically restrained. A few hours later, he was gone.

We spoke rarely after he moved and I had not spoken to him for months when he died. We were both rather depressed and unsatisfied with life, and reluctant to make each other feel worse. Having shared a pipe and a quill with him, twenty years and more ago, leaving these traces behind, is not one of my regrets.

Fafnir Finkelmeyer
December 29, 2014

A Note on the Text

The first 22 chapters of *Hoptime* were published in a now rare Institute of Krinst Studies anthology by the authors (with technical assistance from myself and the late Merganser Dawlitt, J.S. D.D.S.) between 1992 – 1993. The IKS edition is the primary source for those chapters here, as it intentionally differs in some details from the original manuscript, mostly in typography (such as the formatting of the very first paragraph of the first chapter into verse). We generally silently follow the IKS edition when it differs from the manuscript; when we do not, or when the discrepancy is worth calling to attention, we add an editorial footnote. Overall, the IKS edition version was very faithful to the source text, and that precedent does not encourage the current editor to take many liberties, especially since one of the authors is no longer here to clarify his intentions.

We present the work divided into three parts, in accordance with Fafnir Finkelmeyer's wishes. During the 90s, the authors spoke of the book as consisting of two volumes, corresponding to the two notebooks in which it was then written. However, this division into volumes had little if any structural meaning; the first notebook was filled right to the very last line, and the final chapter it contained continued into the second notebook (for just one sentence), chapter numbering continuing uninterrupted. This second notebook was never filled, and the third part, written some years later online, in a shared document, has an ambiguous relationship with the main work; the authors had no definite idea at the time of writing it whether it was a separate work or a continuation, the characters for the most part are different (with the exception of the omnipresent Bunny) and the chapter numbering starts over afresh. The names we've given the three parts were chosen by us from the text, with Finkelmeyer's approval.

Speaking of chapter numbering, the authors' original numbers sometimes went backwards, as whimsy demanded, or to suggest that the scene or environment of a previous chapter was being continued. We use the original numbers, in roman, as chapter titles for the first two volumes; the third volume's slightly different and also misleading scheme we leave as is. For ease of use and reference, we also provide a linear numbering in the header and the Table of Contents.

Walter Smart
January 2015

HOPTIME

Part I

Silt Waffles

I

That walking erosion,
silt waffles eager to badger.
Hey beaver.
Bay leavers pray on pigs,
always ready with a cleaver.
Always on its way,
but only in the mirror
is the parliamentary wrapper flagged
and quiverously nearer
to the deepest needs articulated by
those found to be inferior finds
for our people's innermost celebrated dinner host,
Necrophilia.

SUDDENLY the telephone rang thrice like metal studded shrimp sewn in the flesh of my albino mummy leopard-skinned nightcrawler and his carnivorous axioms. Pockets beget geld. Merrymaking is as silent, but not as transient, as gerrymandering. A pity.

Whereas that immortal barge, a wafer carnival conical in odor, texture and appearance and resembling a target, was contained by a concession stand throughout the latter half of the evening, even later than needed for a standing ovation, my impermissible ingress into chaotically harnessed horses made a suggestive connexion where we desired to brand our family servant, Jodhpur, with heated floss. Ouch! My riper tones know surface tension like dwarves delving into rich caves have taken backward steps. The sun over October's mind pains me rightfully. I rubbed my beauty to a shiny gloss before.

Simply to exert control on my hemisphere leaves me blameless. My ducts accept a certain burden of lifeless forms in pudgy vessels upon a green spongy carpet, the moon blessing's bank (wisely at a major convenience). Remember to worship that witch you have forgot, or sometimes called up on sultry forlorn and confused moments for washing. No amount of detergent would deter the dirt. No amount of detergent would balk before failure. No amount of failure could cleanse me from my bathetic mirth.

My pincers seek the nougat that they will hold and yet hang from, loose translucent ribbons and steel flowers. Containers of toothpaste tumble from the shelf, crestfallen. Do not feed them. Vertical spaces play haphazardly with the reality of the subject.

I refused to open it long enough, and it leaked out. The service was lousy, the population of bacteria in the sink was frantically investing. There is so little time; play. The cup was only half full, the matron declined to offer another.

Or you can put it this way: "Don't be in such a huff. You will exchange eyes with the one you watch. Sleeping colonels flopped in cribs of corn. The sky's new spots echoed a hearty *Hello*. Now fantastical objects are general, and stealing them will result in a punishment which is corporal. You got it; how would you prove it? Look at it again. It is not a mirror unless there are people on either side. Lucy knows this probably better than anyone. Sadie knows those rows of Sharon 'better than any pet [can] tune ya', she would say."

An army of men convinced by beauty to recline gracefully backwards expand into turkeys, trotting a measured mile in a New York minute, beside themselves and others waiting breathlessly in a hole. An army of men convinced by their agnosticism to tie knots into a frog examine various methods of foreplay, just pretend that it means something is amiss in mystery, clamp down on their hard lozenges of guilt while sampling cheese under the open night sky. Changed backwards by a statuesque griffin, I would pensively scratch while taking a billiard shot from the Empire State to the Rio Grande, or, alternatively, soothe various penumbras' shadings in a to-and-fro manner, or, perhaps, clink glasses and sing old songs, eh? The right brothers float on foil and gold leaf in an attempt, or a motion towards attempt that was foiled from the start. So what if your foot is being sucked in a quagmire between beaches? Something landed on my elbow. Will you please refer me to another Simple Simon Signature Series? And that isn't my only objection, either.

The banks of time never close—there is nothing between them—but the taste of chicken is like the vibration of empty space itself, except that it is, unfortunately, full of a zestiness no one can afford. I devolved on pork, and came to know God from behind. Decreased by its contact with divine excreta, the shimmering rod swam lopsided as if wallowing in gelatin. "Your characterizing yourself as a leper is one thing, but equating me with a prostitute I deeply resent," I intoned, caressing his product. Besides mistaking light-years as units of time, I always dated losers.

Plumed and spangled, but not too hesitant to further instigate an emotional coup d'état, my slithering precious bodily discharge hastened to the call. I swept across the plains in a dinghy just large enough to have pride oozing from every crack in its clucking little body. Couldn't I notice how to prevent myself from foraging around for a twig or a leaf in the middle of the woods where a fissure in the desert floor looms alpine on all sides and giants tread above from time to time? Roe and ambrosia, bagels and dreadlocks, all are conniving fools. I felt like three men among them, what with my straw hat and my special chili, what capers I could pull off, what barnacles I could scrape from cactus and pine.

A nuance immortalized in steel by zealous creators lived better in Brooklyn-based authors' homes among raging scandalous ties to meant-offspring affixed still to their respective gonads and wondering aimlessly among the fissures whose greatness is indistinguishable from their immateriality but, anyway, is passable to the stony scrutiny of reason. Say, shells, easy to pick up along the stormy bottom, fill easily with the yeast derived from reversing the baking process of only those types of bread which I eat. Imagine the shock of witnessing infants popping out of pumpernickel.

While you are shrinking, don't forget these items:

1. a dozen eggs

II

To cater exclusively beyond the urge to entirely redecorate, one's whims need seriously to be fudged before one has a self or two. Smiling window-dressing and concealed indecency expose one to an almost uncertain channeling of strong desires through the sieve of public humiliation, and cows fly. We rely on traditional sandwich form to replace our particleboard-like awareness who is sliced and pressed for our panes. The ardor which replaces zest denudes our descant whirling a down helix a bit too quickly to avoid being pricked by a long tine and found succulent, though not ultimately, by famished chickens perched on kitchen stools piled in heaps around a small Central American altar. Why shouldn't its windows be blackened by the kind of grime which seeps more than it pours onto and around untold surroundings' feathers, making them crumpled and gloomy? Samson bopped me with a kola and I fell dead. Man, that infinite void ain't worth nothing.

I held a daffodil gently and wept into my left side pocket with an almost elfin inanity before mounting the donkey. It shot forward as if shown a carrot on a string, precariously balanced but otherwise entirely edible. Before it could reach, now it could only bluntly gesture towards its swollen reddish-brown tide and its somewhat sullen mauve-gray cheer. To toast with a cracked cup is to assassinate the idea of "Beauty" for which one sacrifices for the idea. For the bad idea, "Beauty" is toasted, which sacrifices the idea and assassinates one for no reason. If this is as things should be, then why now more than ever do you think?

It was too quiet to hear noise. Din was easy; could soil ever erode due to deficient D-scale modal systems that punch and flutter in tactical squirm postures? Lamb chop dinner for supper caused an impatient motion, tough as the universal mind rind, to agitate and break, enabling stillness to contradict the general state of inanity in spots chosen for their stews to escalate wildly. Did pucked dollops flick a square tee to teething children saucy to the squeeze-nosed tweed daffy luckless simian, escaped halfway into a bargain-basement freedom and halfway below that where the shaft lifted a vibration which one could get, rigged by the raised eyebrow on the sheer inscrutable face that falls deep below where you stood so long?

Dilated juice was crammed and therefore meant something swollen to diapered sages just and fell by winding expressly for purposes of helically snakelike movement and its many health benefits. Calliope-playing pranksters added surgeons to shoeshine boys and obtained diamond. Its many edges came to visit you one day. Do you remember? Sweatshirts soaked to overflowing with the by-products of filth just streaming, just streaming out, and your hair in the moonlight. We rode camels down to their butts and sang nude in the sand: "La-la." Then, after too many orange squashes in a white suit come up to me and say in a loud clear voice with a mustache, once actually an entire being but now only included within fluffy mashed potatoes washed by rivulets of mucus, "What's it when your problems take your body out for a midnight spin, like what happened with Jethro or McGee or that Philips head guy or the toenail clipper? I'll tell ya: momentum. *Momentum* is what all those guys have in common. Can you beat it when that rhythm washes over your bed as it rolls through a deserted town, past rows of silk-enshrouded Bugattis and skeletons counting coins, and you holler yourself into a knot with a graceful, yet imprecise, frenzied whirl? No, and stay there, sailor, because I have something here to tell you and you need to hear it squawk. And like it will really hit the Richter for a bloody bullseye next to some slightly-out-of-focus cauliflower in a saucer dripping gore on terror-stricken matrons and rust on demented art-lovers and other lovers of art, the salt of the earth's sauce of the galaxy's sweetness," something happens. That bony finger always staggers 'em on the street, with its musky, enchanting smell and its ineffable smile getting laudatory mention in several various differences of an uncollected Spartan menu that sputtered and raped a nearby nut, I think a Brazil, with a sort of muted flourish, nonchalantly chewing someone or other. It flaunted its appetizers brazenly whilst tempting various patrons with (just) desserts.

It tumbled long and emerged later still wet to ravage continents where they don't speak English. That's why you're here when you are. Splitting atoms couldn't tug me to the place where our kindred fellows were mutated into pure cholesterol and danced in rings around the sun, all the while melting sadly and wailing copiously into trick little cups that let out onto your faces in rare blessedness as often as you can get it, see? Like, take the analogy of the blistered insect next to the nasal profiles of various former presidents becoming morose and crawling into the lair of the enemy and stripping naked and passing gas while sitting in a puddle on the living room floor just like yo' mama.

III

WHERE do the layers meet and why aren't you beholden to them any longer? When you've eaten a sufficiency of your surroundings and sat down with a roomful of pudgy half-grown goslings, swimming in the pools of Beelzebub towards an arch and consumed with an overweening pride like snooty doormen keep tucked away in their leather boots, you'll know what it's like to just-be-alive. Don't fret about how many sheets or how much lasagna you wanted nocturnally, since you would not only be exposed to layers of varnish at a time, but behemoths would liken lichen to Fritz. And you wouldn't much care if my army of ruthless and cunning sprats became absolutely frustrated and sat down on rocks clumsily in despair. You'd go right on in a straight corkscrew, narrow from the neck down, just a few more times as always as never; anyway, besides jiggling frantically I'd say several things at once. The great rainbow-colored sky shook like a jelly roll quivering with laughter and delighted at the choice of matching color in the picnic arrangements planned by the wise men for the benefit of relatively few children. Most are obliged to look on from a distance at the straw baby in a box which is worn as a phylactery while using snowshoes to surmount a large drift, otherwise an obstacle to intimate familiarity with the contents of crimped-shut woks all lying in a large field in Pennsylvania that has more significance for you personally than you'd like to acknowledge. Candied, his face was anything but supple; he gave up (or "renounced") changing his name to Mr. Marzipan after several frightening encounters on the sidewalk in front of his house with a boisterous mouse demon wolfing down cheese with impunity, the swaggering blackguard! and what a mess whenever he ate too many grapes out there.

Prim oysters couldn't reveal the essence of ilk to just another existence-eker seeking an appetizer more highly prized than so many others of various size that fail to attract one to cosmic extinction, but nonetheless comely in their own capacity to attract so many offers of definition and/or estrangement from the unknown. Take a friendly bite which might longitudinally puncture my abdomen in just the right spot to facilitate my intellectual development and my constant awareness of the omnipresence of Elvis 900-numbers scattered throughout the South. I'm flying like a turgid orb heaving through the soft shitty sky region where it is rotting from where it rested on moist ground. Preferably no one cared whether or not the ancient Mayan king, Eighteen-Rabbit, was a bloodletter. Have a cookie in the meantime.

There is a time a few yards away from your typical convention center when your average saint bludgeons and hacks large masses of bloodstained pus and ulcerous material for the delectation of the press, whose collective pastrami sandwich resembles a squirming octopus salad with regard to exchangeable golems and their solemn and noble, not to say grave and uplifting, task that all admit without hesitancy has the property of descending and ascending simultaneously—that's just the sort of task it is. "Cremate me a diphthong, Percy-Phone," cry the townsfolk; you've won a lifetime supply of mommie again and, instead of turnip, they had a partial berry. It sounded a bit squishy, so I turned up my collar and fused with the gaslamp on the black and white streets of napalm virgins spending facial textures as rapidly as and as insincerely as enemy pussy lapping up stolen testicle purée high in a lime tree in freezing weather.

An aid to comprehension is to seek out intense sourness at the critical times when clocktowers usually will ring. Coughing all the time is not enough. You must pick it out with a handy growth of fingernail at certain times, like I said. You must pick yourself to pick it, which is unfortunate because it feels yucky unpicked.

Faith barnacles me and makes me quiver like clasps of naked steel on the stairs which border on gelatin, tranquil in the moon ring's frayed glance through space's hole of wisdom at little starlets in tights over smooth butts, jutting out over buttes cute as dairy cattle wading in a stream. In that condition I'm apt to steam rabbits on the banks of the river of fire, gloating flatulently over kernels and prostrate nubile darlings sizzling their toes with automobile cigarette lighters.

Preoccupation, walk this way into an enclosure I can't remove so that I will finally be able to remove it. An animal without the freedom to forget must always go around remembering everything. Pacing, haggard, motionless, fresh; every kind of fish.

The only way to acquire salvation is to write away for balm and seek the ends of things and of Thing. The string, carefully stretched out, is shaped like a ball. Get wet in the rain of sound until you are burned and leave smiling from the dark circle with your eyes somewhere else, looking out of your head. The candle is above you. The candle below you passes to the zone of directionlessness directly to the left rear and right rear of your head. Detection: mostly instinctive, but nothing less than an inscription on cliffs or bluffs—motionless, haggard, remote. Conical, looking out for your head, Mr. Maximum ambushes the sulky scarved men and succeeds wildly. Thorns on a rose wouldn't rip so jagged a laceration as that ripped by the Master, the Embryo, the Mighty, the imbroglio infusing the soul like dirt in clay infuses the clay with that sort of ripped-soul that becomes unclean from dirt. Logos' nail lies rusting hulks of sunken ships on the ocean floor like a faerie. Pity the beggar who blatantly blocks the fulfillment of the vise by becoming a machine based on the cantilever, bowing and scraping his wig against forest bark, while several pinwheels which protrude from turquoise spots on his backside begin to spin. To mourn the simplicity so flat was but his first mistake. In the silence, it gleamed from a small red eye amidst a sea of noise waiting to happen; as of yet unlit farts, one might say. About the size of two identical raisins, but purer.

Don't hesitate to call up to his apartment if the door is jammed. His number stands on the shoulders of giants, poised on the brink of stardom: "Hey, Donald, what about the meatloaf?"

IV

In the community of upstarts of which he is a member and frequent speaker, flyers, instead of being distributed, were carelessly tossed around. Trussed up in rope and unable to defend themselves against varmints and critters and dragonfly queens, and round robins, milquetoasts and marmalade skeins, he cleans when he's in the area. Business keeps him on the move. His sunglasses have been around his neck ever since he put them there, sitting on plantains the way he does when they're black and extra long, like Scandinavian winter nights, enjoyed while sitting in the starlit ballroom, sipping tropical drinks and sweating profusely and making the little people dance and liking it a lot. At home, going out ceases to be home to a host of reasons for remaining sequestered; but home is not going out. We can realize the tremendous ferocity of our need, but realizing the need is another thing which often goes unrecognized in one's own country.

Onyx shards could have been flavored somehow, I'm sure, but instead the older generation found other things to do: wrap fraudulent elves in silk, sink tautological rogues with a heavy-clay application, rub bare adolescent behinds on a night which was long and extra black, spill coffee on Grandpa's treatise on bismuth, and, not least, decorate various soldiers' chests with pin-ups of honor. How they strode! Not even a single character or fiddle-dee-dee in their uniformly outfitted mass was able to speak clearly into the telephone receiver and they faded mournfully into mist like a wash of rain slowly diminishing the lustrous coating of sebum on the mons pubis that came in with the seaweed at tide. Someone would not wait on me, and I made such a scene that that someone was promptly fired in the kiln of my suppressed wrath like a tiny mermaid, or a goat, or an obsequious sea creature. The ongoing orgy of fossils was juxtaposed with the sideways face of a halibut who repeatedly was saying, "Ingots are tablets of ease." The painter cannot turn away from his model. You'll note that his smile made people happy, especially the occupants of the pediatrics ward of an abandoned warehouse next to some stubble rising ominously from the gorseseed-shaped embankment near a pile of stone. The cluster of their beings hissed. Look! A fang! One of them had a blister which was immediately broken open and allowed to drain thoroughly; then, the whole company performed a little dance in colorful village garb while running backwards down Santa Crisco Street. Someone said "Mary, will you please come along," and there on the porch he lit a cigar and slowly pressed it into his nipple, completely ignorant of the fact that Neptune, Uranus and the other planets hovered somewhere high above his head. In the remnants of his imagination that still stained the purity of his subjectivity like an ossified crust in an otherwise empty basin he floated equidistant from all tide and cheer. Oblivious to the tableau, he would occasionally reach a metal cylinder which always stood in the corner, and then he and it were both there for a reason. It was at precisely that moment when all-hell broke loose from the realm of Satan, that doddering queen always sitting on her damned throne holding that scepter making prissy-prissy with enormous gums in double-breasted attire and a mouthful of butter. How rewarding interaction with a slab of meat can be a joy or a pleasure remains to be seen.

I called forth my floating wheels so long muted beneath the shrines of elders in a field so long ago noted and bejeweled with song till glittering with fame it burst its goitered vestments and gained aspects of all its worldly investments which catered to slowly rotating carcasses. "Gyro," I repeated, and twiddled my thumbs to make a certain sound which I can sometimes make by trying. The shapes caressingly take the cocktail out of my hand and with a tiny bell-like laugh bring me onto the dance floor whirling defiantly while cannonballs bring down the house and chanting "Allah." Inspiration comes like an insect crawling in your hair; the bushmen haven't one iota of film left in the obscure camera accessory bag out back of their buttocks where the wildebeest roam through a land of fermented youth and carnivorous abandon where the trees are always flowering and building with wood is really a problem because of all the sand which is there. It's much like salivating over rattlesnake back at the ranch: when all that juicy spittle would yield to the heat of the roaring open fire of the bar-"b"-que pit, boy, a sweller time could certainly never be conceived or had by all. Walking about so erectly in that little cloth beneath the trees and the stars, hand in hand, gazing blankly into their own private abodes and seeing furniture, the starlets and the eensy sprigs went to jail so no one could see them. The courtyard was under a certain strictness—it was a haven of pelts. Dust moved. Ravens could be both heard and seen by the west wind, but we weenies sat with faded smiles in the black box of our avionic little lives, sad and spiraling endlessly downward towards a small town but a rapidly growing one, if you mean what I nudge. Pow! Kaboom! Bang-bang! Ouija-ouija! A squeak-toy was occasionally dim but was nevertheless a classy item for dashboards. Why would birds bear any relation to those squat tortoise-like spouses of theirs, only to have the good-for-nothing dump ya' like ya' nuttin'. Marcus slapped the hydra-cephalic monster on his tummy, stuck out his best sundae tongue, and exclaimed, "You big bully. Me no like. Want make like monkey. Bend over, honeycomb. You and me constitute an intellectual community." Need I delve into the myriad cackles scribbled into the sonic surface like clauses lost somewhere in fine print in order to find out what they're saying about me, or for some other reason obedient to a mysterious first cause scoured off of the somnambular surfer: for instance, that god's personal requirements oblige some of us to go without clean underwear for 3 days running? Hopefully not. To live without a view is itself a vista; the balcony is you, my friend, letting out onto what sort of night you'll never know (especially by letting that little man on the other side of the wall both break and get wind of your inner sailboat, wafting like a microbe over tonsil-waves towards you), and you'd better start getting used to it, pal, or there may soon be something somewhat macabre associated with your face, a gyrating whispering orb revolving beautifully in light of its own making, like the feeling produced by passing one's hand across the back of a Surinam toad spawning itself out of a job and thereby having tactile perception of a sea of various lumps with a small band of dervishes who insist on gyrating around and wrecking everything bouncing up and down on top of them. Soft, fair Ophelia took a pill to be her buddy. Across the street, a man with a roundish sort of, well, nose, started to say:

"Jackal on pixie's eye.
Bric-a-brac with a cackly cry.
La!"

and everyone felt a mysterious gap in their lives and began to call it: God. Felt. Syrup. Magpie. Drizzle. Greeks (some Greeks came up with that one). But the figure and ground are just an unimportant detail when the entire left-hemisphere thing happens for the umpteenth time and your eyes roll back in your head and you can feel a plush velour and everyone seemed so nice and, darn it, the drain acted up again today. Don't say et tu, Uttc, purge yourself like a sponge. Wring the changes in yourself, you fox, you. Thrice was a varmint given a sound-thrashing, whereby the ears felt stapled against the side of the head where parasites numbering in the manys of millions have pretensions too many for too long in too tootily a place with too much to do when viewed through blue spools screwed onto the sides of vestibules to return and get that old neighbor of theirs, Mr. Hat, because he needs surgery soon. Yes, I called him a cat-man, and do you know what we called his fæces, we called it cat-man doo. But we were only appellate court judges then and look at us now: natural-fiber clothing makes us itchy, we make love deep in the wild forest like savages, and yet we crave TV's so we can pile them all up in a heap. To give scarcely a glance is a daily occurrence when you live with the serpent and keep your eyes closed a lot. I've said enough.

V

MERRILY surely is merrily surely does. I've grabbed it plenty of times, each time using my hand to grasp it firmly while squeezing with my opposed thumb the digits outnumber. Apples, fragments, fragments, apples, some more of them; fragments of apples. Fragments are the apple of my eye when I, old Oedipus, bask in light coming into my cell from the central courtyard—smell the fruity tree smell! If only we hadn't coveted our neighbors' goods we would have been right up there alongside of those mangrove inhabitants with many legs that come in here on weekends giving us long looks and demanding a steady supply of Darjeeling to go with them. They call it reciprocity but I make the following sound: "Ptui." A man chided his wife because her back legs were soiled with horsehair from her innumerable bronco experiences, which also required so many many gallons of sinus medication that she was forced to change majors. It was a gloomy parade; the sensitive one died battling a trace of infinite blood in the moon lake, in which fish, refusing to swim, just sat there and frowned and were in an ugly mood all the time and griped and bitched like a bunch of stupid fuckers and had a short life span at that. Most fish are like that: incipient Miller drinkers. Where have we come? Where have we started from, man?! Why doesn't gravity work sideways? Because picture-hangers needed to have work shown at galleries and would have been Soviet or shiny, I forget which, but it makes sense to me, myself, and I at once pin it to a certain redness of the skin. The treasures of your navel swept across the great plains, but your penis atrophied to the point of invisibility every time a flame thrower was pointed between your legs and you shrugged, did the vacuuming and the James Brown, and followed the plots of several soap operas, all without realizing that there was an enormous blood stain in the seat next to the ottoman with your feet on it. Perhaps it was from the time you cut your feet off so you could fit in that new machine which was actually a dog-sizer in a very literal sense and you gladly made dinner too and installed a new light bulb. So thrifty! Myopic salesmen with cloying whiny voices, greet with all the warmth you can imagine or buy your new men, after which your usefulness will dwindle and I'll be a pretty ferocious dude by your petty standards. None of the calliopes work, for they are jammed with silt. I look out the window just once a day at the daisies soiled with blood, at the infinite fields whose sun-drenched verdure conceals shorn limbs of babes, and I become a butterfly, daintily straddling my image of shallowness, like a purple gallinule. Do you expect me to skip breakfast just because, or should I have an actual reason?

The surface could use something of its own, while the interior is usually forced to borrow from the aged sheriff who spat thick dirty yellow syrup with such gusto that a polecat couldn't holler in the noonday sun any more than a varmint could whistle between his feet using his shins as a new kind of bellows. Does it make sense to you to say that it's rough to be that deep, or is that a dangerous question? You don't delve for peach fuzz in these parts, Mister Smith does. And Mr. Jones is the one with elbows, and Mr. Brown is at the controls, and Mr. Taylor mans the lookout, and the farm animals fuel several industries at once by not even trying. Those big tubes begin to shake and a forestful of albinos grovel and the big balls roll about noisily in the heavens and all the heaveners revel in togetherness without having to suppress the least bit of din because of the garb they wear. Galaxy-shaped sequins were piled high in large boxes awaiting shipment.

The menfolk sullenly struck themselves in an epidemic of conscience and deserted the village, seeking The Bob's Big Boy they had robbed, in order to return and take the rest of the money and goods and rape and pillage the surrounding area to the detriment of their ingrained and perpetual personal dissatisfaction and to the enlargement of certain glands while hitting 20,000 feet in a turboprop over the Yellow River back in August. Remember Mamie's beadle and how he used his head to reface aquatic zones that have been in the vicinity for an eon with cheap imitation stone and brick, or the time when Jethro hogged all the corn at the state fair? Keeping his long ears wrapped in ham made his proboscis redden and sing by making semiotic gestures toward works of art made by rocket scientists which are beautiful to a Nazi sensibility, but would you care to audit buzzy bugs? "No, that sounds a little boring at the moment." All you fiendish flagellaters out there, all you real bad guys, all you gold-toothed meanies, you are, you will admit, devastating in those tights. Here is an easy recipe for awarding me a sinuous pleasure-dot-like ripply feeling that snakes around the back of my neck like drippy jelly. Don't look at it now—stuff it into your pocket so it shows. The doctor is in, baby. About all your leather: does it also come in apricot-lined albatross, or does jam-down-your-back sound uncomfortable? I'll be the garlic-nosed old waffle iron sizzling your dough as I spend my own destiny on chaw and Felix, while you make the motions of darning something soxy, remember: a suture in the future is super.

A cat's cute efforts to survive are only a feeble attempt when compared with the longevity of those boots and the sleds, the scream in the night, the little pop and the sounds of enormous looming Mother hanging a wet sheet on the clothesline, only to have pigs and hens walk under it constantly. "What are you doing at this time of the night out in the garden, Madame? Are you sniffing the flowers in their sleep and the moist unseen night-dung, and witnessing the transitory gleam of the nut-like raptor spits? Whose turn was it to set the table? We are the angry penguins of yore in your lore. Watch your slippery step! Paramecia like you ooze freeze in the gaze of our rich ball of molten baklava steaming from the ancient ovens, possessing intelligence and capable of falling just like the rest of yous and not just on New-Year's. Dumby bumped into Bambi purely to avoid hitting a canary in January, and now it's May already. By October the bakery will be in full swing and a cat who says 'Meow' will wait patiently for milk by the back door of the kitchen back there. That's the great outdoors for you. Reconsider, dumb bitch that you are."

The slimy Minerva, immediately upon hearing this, hailed a cab. Saying "Too much of a good thing," she left Eden like an untouched burger but she took the pickle in her green dufflebag along with all the tea in China, some coal from Newcastle, and a couple of bags of crawly insects found in the lawn. How does she expect to unload that on us? Oh, but she always does. How much cole slaw must be thrown out with the trash before mankind rises in righteousness and pomp for a few days of brazen discontinuity of spirit: stringing along a hopeful acquaintance until suddenly, "Zappo!"—a war. Then she wears a black mask and rides over the pampas with a very serious-minded horse who eats chilled delicatessen salads exclusively. Okay, sometimes a rum baba.

Foam-rubber cubes, slightly deformed by enormous lead weights which rested on them, why don't you eat zucchini? Delve slices into richly crafted squirrely chaser, daft stallions and 12 years old, matured in oak casks of a certain majesty. Bring forth your wretched and fellate a tiny pixie, sweating near the beach. I'm off again, communing with benign spirits, wearing scarves of eggshell-finish paint specimens, and a shopping list tattoo with quaint prices on my four heads that ache in perfect synchrony with the rolling television picture out in the living room which shines on a brass ashtray and bores me like a good screw stuck in the wall of black night and hanging—what exactly?—on that delicate thread god hangs spiders on, you see, and, well let me put it to you this way:

VI

Oh sailorboy! Sailorboy! Yield to my solitary whim. Don't hold the soy, but give me joy! Cede to my extraordinary limb! In my left hand I hold the bulbous abdomens of one-hundred tiny spiders, but in my clenched wand I like to look at those little metal specks floating in thick fluid—wouldn't you if they forced you to wear this ridiculous cap? I never wanted to create the universe, but Mother insisted on making an obstacle of me. The entire family, including myself, was jerked rockily by a standard wave of vibration, fluid in its motion, like the kali, like the rabbi, like the paneled study or blue funk you get into to do certain, well, confused, ill things with the penis-shaped homing radar device between the legs of a big robot as I indicated before, I thought, rather well and at considerable length. Suddenly I smelled a vapor rising from the cove on wings. Kind of like the big vee of trademark fame. But perhaps that isn't relevant.

Dear hearts, surrender suddenly and the wave of love which pours in will positively overwhelm you. All the little birdies will rip apart vermin and bring you choice offerings out of auspicious entrails as tribute, and much rejoicing gladness, happy little smeared smiles (of four-year-old girls at a birthday party), and just a sort of jolly-style atmosphere-thing there. Come out from behind that hostile tape, you music you. I want you out here where I can hear you, bozo. Without gloves but with my two ultrasensitive mitts wide open like flowers at noon. And while you're not busy, please please my spouse, if necessary, even while you two are going up inside of yourselves like a lollipop commercial embedded in that very hard candy, by singing away your boiling and rubbing a giant Australian earthworm with the calves of many foals, all grouped together collectively until one day, when Jove was jiving yet and there were no smokestacks yet, Alicia coughed painfully and out plopped the nest of a small bird, and what would Johnson guess as being the thing in the middle of the nest? Probably some variant of someone else's view of the matter from a similar perspective, although maybe just a bit more different than that.

VII

O FARMS *and dam, anising the soup*
flavor melting into my honey's liquid pheasant gaze.
"Stormclouds caress moon. Dewdrops sweet
pro patria mori…" *See Jonny get his shoes.*
Set his satisfaction down to
objects dim, sighing suspects obdurate,
A bit hazy 'round the blowhole:
Fuck me again, and sleazy, you know?
…"I surrender."

Now where were we
when the gin 'pon the riverbank puffed its last,
and phenolphthalein solution got sucked down fast
through spirited hose like Cézanne's Wooden Pork.
Deliver to me some zealots, in your sidecar oh, so gleaming,

(if the local fishpeople haven't yet swallowed her boyfriend's semen, they will sell you her removable texturized belly-stickers, reminiscent of those days on the hot farm, making sticky love amidst the peppers)—a swig of maniacal resolve burns my throat like the time I tried to spit from atop the ziggurat onto a school of artists and I found that contempt, with time, helped my aim in the same way that a kernel makes a plant grow. Personally, I can only drive in person, but I've long admired a more rarefied buttery approach, like they keep trying to show me in the Indian shop window; but I don't have the necessary big shiny lens. "If the grape is sour, my wife will sit on it and become really quite wild," the shopkeeper said, filing his face to a point

("To pop her later on," he explained). The man, his daughter, the scapegoat, and several thousand fire ants had finally met, face to face, each one exploiting the other through impersonal arms of their organizations. Which brings us back to the holiday schedule from Troy to Syracuse and the way the train betwixt the two makes my tummy jingle rapidly like the under-the-seas marriage between tuna and skate, and all the marvelous devices, trick bunnies, etc., that attended and no doubt drank too much liver oil and spate upon the earth (which actually had no effect since it was already wet from being underwater). How does three-thirty-eight sound? Will it produce a rich glowing sensation, or will it be time again to hobble off, all dusty, leanin' on ol' Pegleg, your trusty native guide, and fucking pustulized waifs you pick up in Chinese laundries without a ticket? Conical sibling, you can just bet your granny's shoeshine kit that it's the latter, son, the freaking *latter.*

An active night life of this kind necessitates collecting, shall we say, curiosities which, when mixed between layers of silk and taffeta, coil to become a skulky mass said in an abandoned warehouse by unlicensed practitioners or any other dubious ritual involving skulls, the moon, and cheese. In one corner, a robotized belly bulged and shrank while standing next to a table which contained a happy cake. Flying around it was an exceptionally good-natured paraplegic who, realizing the extent to which he was inferior, clung to the idea of a triangular neon elf elected to the office of world leader by a planetary consensus advancing slowly on him from a cheap surprise sort of angle solely for the purpose of forcing him to shake the intelligent hand of a bloody mime who must have been slicing turkey for hoagies but in a heightened way. Regardless, it was obviously one of the more special corners of the room. But does that reduce the intrinsic human value of a kitchenette, or a functional, sanitary and pleasantly shaped replacement for the soon-to-be-Soviet lookalike or what?

All around you, you will observe, are other members of the audience looking at you. Now that you feel unique, reconsider. Post a glandular guard at the peripheries of your biochemical existence and beg it to let you leave. "But I'm a big powerful gland," it reminds you. "I secrete all day long. And further down the viaduct are even more terrifying endocrinal edifices—gigantic frowning testes that will roll over you and reduce you to a bouillabaisse within seconds of reaching the kitchen, all slack-jawed with a pair of wire covers clenched in your teeth and smiling, and oh, forgetting is what I do." You walk past, unharmed? Nor do we wise meander menacingly on open and always leaning lists forgotten forever. You'll find us doing splits at the corner store most Sundays and hoping for free rides in the paddy wagon. Whoopee! Little girls say "Mummee rub my bumee" after they get a father who makes them go scrapy-poo down the laundry chute to my heart.

If you've never received a card filled with much thick paste on Valentine's Day from a tall man wearing obvious makeup exams fastened to his simple sheath, well, you've lived a little. And I'll take a question from...oh god, what fangs! What atrocious smacking smirking lips smugly oozing some muck! Oh viscous visage, oh percolating eyeball fastened on my tasties! Grind my beans, you big bad man! By now, the warehouse reeked of Precious' odor, as well as that of the dour and quite invisible widow, and the contents of an open jar on a window sill, which made us all say "Phew." Take that into consideration before you force me into another confrontation with my god and his big hairy bass-baritone anchorman's voice, not unlike that of Dr. Natarajan as he said "Sally was delicious" to Dr. Jegenathan in the back of the limousine, while Cookie the driver muttered inaudibly to himself something about eggs. Those are all real people.[1] Ninety blocks was still a considerably close distance to live from her, her tentacle-like reachingness a bit too caustic on

[1]Editor's note: in the IKS edition, these names, which were indeed real, were replaced with initials.

the lazy horizon of animal decadence, her snorting feeler making one reluctant to have anyone over. The age of 31 felt like a nice one to her as she nestled her son in the rapturous clutches of incestuous brickwork, her 70 some-odd years being a bit too tutelaged to find a colored freedom between her tongue and upper palette. When he submissively stung her like a wasp and she thrilled to the quadraphony, the symphonic pulse of his venoms, he said to his dazed self's bare butt, all shiny, red and surprised at her young grip, "Why, I've not heard the gynecologist upstairs cry out once today, would you care for a cube of ham?" It replies softly and with deference, "I'm up to my ears in a variety of cured meat but it is catching a disease as we speak. I feel rather like a phosphor tweed wrapped in moisture with a sidecar of leché, *n'est pas*?" "What an ass you are after all," he said curtly and walked out on his hands. Between obviating the skin in which rose his own mortality and surrendering some past conviction to be trodden upon by a fleeting image of a dire utopia, he has his hands full. Together they performed a performance, or a piece of one, entitled fully to one full title (*Waking To Moët*) in which pucks of ice were shuttled to and fro on the donkey-headed one's exposed and recumbent breast. Meanwhile, the mother rose and wiped off a wet soup bowl with a small towel, and then immediately went about vacuuming and dusting with it. What a big noise it made. Woo! Woo!

He abruptly stopped the vehicle, uprooting an elderly maple, and got out, crushing spent fag 'neath boot and singing the word "vehemence" with the innocent soprano of a little child. Nearby, a pharmaceutical company's employees were leaving work for the day. Strings of corn vanished endlessly into the umpteenth fire-sign made within industrial diameters. And it was her fault, the goddamn bitch. His pure treble resounded in a glowing 3-space 'twixt cloud and field, and even the guppies and frogs and lilies in the brook pricked up their so-to-speaks: "Burble-burble! Turbo-Minerva!" Each wandered in his own bit stream, hastening Minerva to the primary grommet, the underlying rivet, or the outstandingly silky elemental vanadium chunk, delicately nestled in thin tungsten fingers of pure mechanical perfection, perched on the boss's desk. At this moment he felt kinship with his previous selves who also regretted having shaved so consistently for years with an electric shaver in his office at noon each day, irritating all those secretaries and hence not getting laid. He spoke with a mouthful of saliva-moistened masticated Doritos: "Gabba fukin waba aybee. Peeda, de dum de oingapluke, oh, see Ma, me mucky oiler-poke, ewgh-ewgh uhhgh, achoo." He could have used a drink, and he had to make a good impression, so it was very lucky when his mom ran over to his office with a freshly baked pie, and doubled up on dew orbs of drippy globular droplets encased in elk-purée with a twist of vex pops. The VPs of Marxist-Leninism and R&D, respectively, sodomized her with their outrageously stout prongs as he convinced her to be reasonable with blows of two different but both pleasurable kinds and ate his pie. The local amphibian came waddling up just then and pushed his sweating head against a softly springy diaphragm of dog skin (from the north-40), causing it to stretch in several directions at once. It liked this, and he liked them to like it. Doc Septerbater pulled up just as the toad was trembling fast enough to emit a shiny low tone, and got out of his pickup, bringing his bag of drums. He quickly set up and improvised a callous little piece, during which a drachma coin was placed between the two lips of a svelte miner who wouldn't be seen in public without a lump of coal shoved up his daughter's tight little girlie-ass. Soon it was time for our hot glowering rods to burn like still-unspent uranium into all the little preparatory incisions we had had the forethought to make. A local character dressed in a Lafayette get-up quickly threw himself down and was immediately covered with acid burns and blisters from being torched with a small propane welding device, while the young girl rubbed bear fat on her pubescent chest and strangled newborn kittens in the fading afternoon light. When, wincing with pleasure, unable to withstand any more, they seeded him, severing his throat and bathing in his red sauce, they heard grateful applause, and, turning, found the king and the prince watching from the royal grove, sucking juice from a bucket of some leftover cells from the bio lab and jiggling their jelly with an armload of glee. The boy's enchanted voice was again in possession of the valley, and it said to itself, "Kill," and laughed a light fluffy laugh rippling through the mist like a smoke pancake.

The girl's young shorts shot an arm out one side out the hole and wailed like a puppy for the dismal viewer of stepped-on candy, he thought, to come hither. That was why, she at last exclaimed, we once bore the fruits through the streets of Galilee, walked through hundreds of picket lines until we reached Rome, bringing swarms of fruit flies unto the plebes and squeezing gnats in their fæces. She read this from a script found in the Italian mother's handbag and then suddenly everything happened exactly the way I wanted it to happen, and all my hopes were fulfilled and my wishes came true.

> "Those blasted toots,
> that blimey whistle,
> oh, hell, that dratted tune!"

sang the salesman on his way out the door. The girl, sprawled on the floor, played tootsie with her footsie and wrenched a plastic strap-on from the hands of a little Guido idling on the rubby carpet. An enormous hand fell to sucking on the whole screen. The room was pulled by its gigantic space-perverting gravity and her buttocks became distended. There was this tendency towards the corner and everything sagged towards it and everyone made excuses to go there. "I left my glasses!" Sure.

VIII

My glycol dynasty was infrared some thirty days when Merv tickled himself between his legs and the limey robot eked out a scratchy argot-based existence under a shell, saying things like "Logger, wipe-a my knee all ye lands."

Itchy.

That archo-copter bragged to the left singularly but ultimately sang out the often belted much like larger-than-life Ethel, but it wasn't dead. The frizzy jezebel paraded around in his underwear, holding something underneath the water for a long time every time gelled spots under a miffed pseudo-haven cupped my lumbar under ragging orphan bastard Johnny-come-latelys; probably kittens.

After a good wash in which all three of us tossed a loaf of bread around and Carol showed us her own private truth, we flossed with a warm feeling of contentment and bit into our gooey sandwiches with frank hatred. I looked at a picture of Elvis and immediately shined a flashlight onto a giraffe's side. Germans crouched down and supped while we changed the set. Almost, too, a siphon carried silt into the unit. It made it break. Then, I "then, I" several people moving around me, normally, but this time.... Right. Under normal.... Right. Right under, to the.... Right.... Right. The normal circumstances, right? Right. But this time.... I think you're.... Right.... Right, whereas.... Right.... Right.... Right. You see, normally.... Right. The un-it.... Right.... Lift it up, you ass.

Happy as a clam, and fit and full of vim, the sorcerer lolligagged a telepathic noodge and proclaimed, "La plus mon coeur marche comme un homard, la plus la viande me fait malade." How did the unusual noise and the powerful bouillon get along so famously, so many breaded follicles clogging their metachronic faces? Well might you ask. Firstly, the phenyl bard of totemic patience and widely acclaimed proximity ran a vanquish-booth at the world's fair expos on military initiative for controlled-pest substitutes. Secondly, and the relationship should be clear and can't be stressed too much, time had found its border and they had both stepped across it into Forever, so they had much in common and never argued about what channel. As a direct result of their lack of indecision, they completely avoided hitting a rocky shoal where they would have surely wrecked the ship had they not been able to avoid it. Then its loudness and her splashy sauces would have been all wet, but as the facts in fact fell, they were safe and went home for late-night pancakes with syrup evenings in between. A man named "Ralph" found an A-bomb lying out on the ground one day and flew high above the earth whereupon he dropped it and blew everything up. *Bam! Bam!* A little lucky, a martyr sucked in the snot in his nose and gently rubbed the sensitive flesh underneath his penis while an amazing act dazzled a leprechaun-shaped urchin who gagged on his own sweet mushy refuse in a sodajerk's flat in western Tennessee, somewhere. But their equipoise was never jolted, so they were called "well-equipped boys" and everyone winked and nudged (or *noodged*). In the next room, a spider the size of a quarter sang a note so high in pitch that it shattered a Waterford crystal, but it didn't do 'squat to the Pyrex. That's 'Merican quality, right there, for ya. It was sheer destiny when they met: one lounging seductively in a saucepan, the other manifesting itself by means of a clanking procedure run on it and a matching lid. Bursts of $x + \sqrt{x+y}\cos(\Delta y - x)$ splintered the icy silence of night like so many scabbed and nebulous brain-meat toaster nixxers like jugular moving cochlea-influenced goober-chomping lawmen from Biloxi or Mobile or Little Rock, even. Penmen and postmen alike got mashed into butter in the ensuing mêlée. We now admire them in coil form eternally adorning the cosmic *smash-a-potat* of the sky—Big Bear, Little Dog, Wounded Knee. They ran around all disheveled-like and got knocked up like the bunch of varminty critters they were; a long-faced collection of the most miserable, low-downest scoundrelly chooch-heads who ever sat next to my sister on the too-soft sofa watching a Bing Crosby movie on television on New Year's Day. They lathered to crooning at all times and in all places, especially in the little monopoly man's sumptuous apartment on the boardwalk, complete with stunning ocean view, facilities for walking around while carrying a steamship on one's back, and a big lovey-dovey bedroom with a heart-shaped waterbed smack-dab in the middle of a pool of continually replenished whipped cream, and a bon-bon fluffy make-out pad strewn recklessly on the carpet, too. Oh coo-coo, my little one, my inflatable ducky, you are oh so smoooooth, let me spread you, my tasty nut-butter. Why not grate the same cheese over alien pasta now and then? In a wink of the eye, his little mustache twiddled-dee-dee in the relishment of plugging his swizzle stick into the lovely lolly candy-apple naughty naughty boopsy-woo of gushing fuss-fuss gudgy-fingered icky-pooberry pie of her munchkin-muff foofoo device whoopee-doo hickey. And a new need was found. "Now, what do you think, honey? Is freedom attained by finding all our possible needs and satisfying them or is it found by eliminating needs?" "Those aren't mutually exclusive, you clod," she retorted while beaning him with her handbag and firing missiles from her attack-bra. "Shut up and eat, bitch," shouted Hamlet, suddenly entering in flapper garb. Somewhere in the distance, and quite out of focus, F.D.R. could be seen strolling with Sam The Drummer and the owner of a huge pet food conglomerate. An eleven-year-old girl cantered past enshrouded in nothing more than a swarm of butterflies, absentmindedly fingering herself while a 37-year-old father-of-three was fitted for his twelfth penis ring while hanging by meathooks stuck into his buttocks. A lion roared. Hamlet traversed the lawn skittishly, waving his scarf in mock-horror's face: "Oh-hoo! A big bad lie-on! Fierce creature, my meat is spoiled, let me go!" Just then, a large carrion-worm leapt out of his chest and into one of the beast's nostrils. A not-so-funny British comedian with a big chin crouched near the lion's back end, sniffing the occasional bursts of gas which emerged from its anal sphincter while simultaneously flapping his arms like wings and changing into a loud plaid jacket. "I'll be late for my dinner," he said just before the animal shat profusely and buried him with instantly digested worm meat. (It's a special lion.)

"Well, Hamlet was in quite a fix! What do you think happens next?" (Points to Suzie, 6 years old.) "Well, I dink…. I dink dat when me an' my brudder take a bath togedder, an' dere's all suds so you can't see under da wadder, dat… that Hamlet is going to be very scared and then…. It'll get bigger and bigger and all slippery…. Whoooo…. An' nobody'll know dat I'm I'm snuggling-in, an' I hope a big spider doesn't come." "That's very interesting, Suzie! Does anyone else have an antidote they'd like to share, or a child, perhaps?"

I still can't help wondering how they made it all work so well, so architecturally. Hamlet, the cheese Danish, the Danish ham, cavorting nude like a bunny on the grass, getting those parents to compete for the privilege of having him rarebite the offshoots of their loins. The lion, suspended in the act of terrorizing them all by the magical mayhem the prince's dong wrought. Gruyère couldn't be obtained in those days, you see, and pennywisdom very often took precedence over poundfoolishness. "Another kingdom too late," remarked the traveler, as he swung over Hamlet and lion, the father-of-three, the eleven-year-old girl, the six-year-old girl, the leprechaun-shaped urchin, the monopoly man, and all the rest, here, on a fun-packed exotic weekend all for you, here on this lovely Saturday afternoon in Palm Springs. And didn't the seats swivel so slightly, didn't the screen shift just so much, didn't we all hate what we had loved the moment before? No one can remember. It is quite disturbing: this mess we have gotten ourselves into here is merely a shadow of lost loves, gross defeats, and rancid shrewishness on the hosts of our congregation, the stinking bunch of good Samaritans; all of them, every one. Fuck 'em.

Having made something from all this, you've really come far. So sit back and let us, your sunny servants, dissolve your will in absurdly powerful fruit punches which knock the proverbial stuffings out of your fairy asshole. If you weren't such a wimp, you'd rub fresh shit into your mother's steaming guts.

IX

O Adolfo, stop it. Stop teasing me. You're making me itch, ha-ha-ha. Adolfo, honey, why don't you bake me in the oven now, at about 350 or so. Will you, hon? Adolfo? Oh Bernice, I'm so sorry, I didn't recognize you with that enormous furry mouth and those cruel, rapacious eyes and that bulging goiter, and the leprosy! Oh! God! Bernice! Oh, honey! Sweetheart, your most recent boil makes me yearn to pleasure myself! Oh darling, make me come! Make me pustulate with desire! I want the oils of your chancre dripped on me like the juice of roasting meat! Listen Dolfy, my sweet, your navel flavor makes me want to control an alien species like that one landing outside in the yard. Look, here they come! Ohhh, juicy!

We'll be able to handle it, bitch. Kiss my ass. The hole. Pack it with oatmeal first. And don't forget the mealworms or the inflatable innertube either. Here, gimme an injection in the tip of my cock, baby.

The aliens are coming. The aliens are coming. News flash. God, the disaster! Spreading like singing aphids over the hills, reproducing prodigiously, sucking life out of our flesh. Sucking flesh out of our souls. Sucking our souls out from our rancid minuscule hearts, our mutual blind-deaf-and-dumbness, till we fall gracefully downward on a spiral towards the molten center, glory be.

Dear, I've had enough of these newscasts. The broccoli is engulfing us all, we don't need to search for far-fetching explanations. Ice already accumulates on our graves. The total bellows-pressure of nautically scruffy old men on our rectal regions would be enough to warn any one of decay.

He sipped coffee, lit old butt, carefully reshaped his lips with both hands, and then, screwing his eyes back into his head and clasping me with his legs, exclaimed, "Can you hold your water for weeks at a time? I can. They call me 'Expert.' They call me 'Champ.' And anyway, what was that about your mouth that hurt me so much last time?" And then Bill found an old sheet of paper stuck in the moulding. He opened it and was astonished:

PLAYBILL

Miles and the Seven Machines

Cast

Ludwig van Beethoven	Mickey Rooney
Franz Schubert	Dick Cavett
Heinrich Schütz	Carroll O'Connor
Galileo	George C. Scott
Herodotus	Michael Jackson
Millard Fillmore	Bea Arthur
Hitler	Phyllis Diller
Uncle Joe	Himself
Zoë Burncock	Dick Cavett
James Joyce	James Earl Jones
Merv Griffin	DeForrest Kelly
Miles Standish	Hervé Villechaize

Why, wasn't this the play Clovis El Tondo made into grand opera, he himself singing lead soprano in the title role? Why, no, rather it's the product of having performed an operation on myself whereby I extended an optic nerve down through my body and threaded it through my phallus, at the end of which I had inserted a miniature eye. In this way, the aliens and I could relate on a higher level, so it was we who authored this play, after all. You see, I'm not quite one of you. I'm only outwardly a smiling father-of-three, a cranky mother-of-two, a cuddly baby.

My lethargic uncles came hobbling up to the hospital to get at me, you understand.

X

AND the orb arose and the budget froze, the little ladies were supposed to scrub it with their cello bows and rub it with their little toes, but those of the harem who were mostly to scare 'em but also to lair 'em to Bahrain and there pair 'em, they chose to pose as lotion salesmen probing the locus of Polish varnishkes-peddling homeboy-Joe little itty-poo Barney ripples piddling woodcut homophobe jumjammers. And the orb, lo, it shook, and the homeboy-Joes forsook all their stuff. Look. Look. A gentle lambasted skipper dabs a simple poi muckily on his barnacly surface. Look. Eat an avoirdupois dram of pigeon filth. Just do it and stop complaining, why on earth can't you just get on with it? With it. With it.

Jesus McGee floated on the mists of Nazareth to a loftier prow in the midst of a chug-a-long harbor, on the coasts of Gollyjumby. Boy, he was proud… and happy. With the confidence of a man who believes, strengthened to a repulsive impregnability by his unshakable faith in his own future on the face of stamps, he first indented a food processor in the celebrated contest of '02, later being responsible for taking the square-root of putrefaction and the inverted mordent of sudsy nickel tub handles all over the binomial expansiveness of about a Grand Canyon-full of muff. Liszt rode a horse, Satie a bicycle, Karajan flew, Ned lay in a puddle, I took the subway yesterday. Quetzalcoatl got sprung from the boobyhatch while fledgling titillaters barked out an oath with moxy verve. Splendor! Oh, splendor be not vanquished from my blubbering eye!

The fringes of our sight are our riches, the jagged edge, the veil. Seek not to blather over quantities of julep, unharried in Achen's relative treble of disinherited twizzled myopia. Make that straining befuddled face you make when you say "What?!" except smiling like an idiot in full glorious regalia with a codpiece instead of eating liver smiling, and moving around a lot, and wiggling impatiently as an adult, or marinading a little bit more out of life each time, or, you know, who knew? Who, Marty, who? And when it's made you'll call it smashing. Naming is death, but who can afford a collection of live butterflies? Oh perfect man o'kine d'ami!

A quacking mutton jalopy driver's sojourn into zizzy freakiness vilified infamous cottontails, proving once again how riding hot meat back into the kitchen is at best just a romantic way of getting there. Morgen replaced nacht as a détente among lipsmacking underneaths made them feel like vehicles by which Muggles snuck the whole roast-chickens and gallon-cans of chocolate pudding out the back door of a church. Today the puddles of spit near the body of Christ are a major tourist attraction.

Mind your beanie and check your coating, it's bastable traction melting the chews of a lumber ox's grudge. Fleck the wing off tootle-Lou's bravo tool in torquey laxative electron jizz-bolt. Tip the attendant and he'll watch, raising brow as if you had something special to pull out. Now here on the right are the recorded tours. Brochure, anyone? Mind you, it's always better to observe records of pressing victual-flakes than to gamble that moments of inertia come tumbling down the happy snowy hill with Lyle and Wendy and all the yummy fluffy oo-oo nick-a-nock-a yummervator of snufflicious pucksy droplets bellybuttoning babies with fabric, textiles, and globular portholes, more than enough of them, actually. In this room we'll gather icily around the diorama and fry ourselves silly. Winging at your neck has never been easier, my giblet; a foxy wealthy babe always succeeded in straining my hamstring for megadollar bucks, man, I mean ¡Mucho dinaro!, you know what-eh meen man? Teddybear Roosevelt, in a canoe with two sad-faced braves and a big stick. Note the electronic mosquitoes—they even bite.

Pandemonium erupts, as it is wont to do. But here in this office, in this mystical minute, in this

...magical moment, carefree evening,
my heart is bubbling,
it meets the requirement.
Ocean of feeling, so
carefree, so listless,
my butterfly darling,
it's right right now.
Up to date—
are you up to a date
with me?

Sarah was rearranging the flowers in her hair and Dr. Kleindienst was hurriedly coiling up a length of good stout rope and shoving it into a big wooden chest.

Three bags of laundry
on a dead man's Sunday best.
Give me ole Kentucky
and you can take the rest!

Found me a corpse
up in the hills a piece.
I never saw a country cutie
match the beauty of the beast!

I rubbed her with thyme,
but I was too late!
No, not the first one
to mate what I ate!

Lazarian in-breeds quenched the thirsts of mangled bumpkins on tiptoes with a leaky flask, a nimble gesture, and a smile. They were gay with the scissors that day! "William Tell! William Tell!" they cried, and with a crunch audible for miles through the cool dry autumn desert air bit to the core an apple agleam before them in space before there was space. It hailed an angular custard for four lonely daisy fluffiness encounter panels, so the mice benefited. Slope, keep increasing! Hall, fall down! Juxtapose a deviled crust of a blubberer with Nome's ever-loving feely resident, younger than a peach-taffeta silk-ivory wearer's bottom corset rung but with pedigree nonetheless and a connoisseur of the arts and cultures generally. He had never had to search for his niche in the ecosystem. He had his fodder and his crest laid out for him in the morning, the afternoon, and the evening, except on Saturdays. Loose me in the square, dialer of burnished yesterday, wiffle country burlap, take a mug shot of garbagy yellow phlegm splotches, or tear rilable menses seekers who hanker for the loins of disappointed moths hovering around the cheese growing on my wheel, my Taurus, and ultimately, my doughnut.

My friendly yuppie mage neighbor looked out of town as Bruckner poured syrup on rock candy and rubbed his hand inside a greasy hot machine. The woman (the one with a leather eye socket) arrested me for living as quietly as my triangle teacher's suitcase lay in the corner all those years. My life was a blot on the town, she said. I didn't know she was the mean type, so I escaped and now I'm here.

And I'm wanted in every state—when I'm blotto, when I'm towno, when I'm upo and when I'm downo. My lozenge! It's gotten itself caught between my chic mother and Tootie's curly tail. What a maroon! We drifted, then we finally landed on a little island—-you know, the kind with one palm tree growing on it. I proclaimed myself a millionaire. "My plantation! My… my empire!" I cried, and immediately subjected the others to my cruel domination. I was great, wasn't I? Well, they died and then I was alone on the little island, and there was just me, the tree, and one little coconut. And I said to the coconut, "Eat me, you great big chunky excuse for chimpfodder!"

It is time enough now, I should think, for us to affirm jointly, rising above our immature shame, that we generals sit in cold lonely tents on the barren windswept hilltop, look out on the fighting, and feel confused, helpless and afraid. Blunderers are we, ignoble as dwarfed cowards bungling yet another nebulous caper of folly. If only we had cable we'd tune to Concord and escape. I dreamt once that mice in outrageous pink suits climbed the rungs of an Irish psaltery in the heavens, all very celestial-like and wonderful. The next time a large cheddar were to get talked to with a mouthful of sherpas' hide smears rapped around their throats, horses wouldn't be able to gallop and France's kissed quiche wouldn't begin to deflate a flatulence of misery, like body gas puffing out a corpse. So I was glad it was just a dream and I got out of bed that morning with renewed appreciation for the aesthetics of the delicatessen counter environment where I must spend the bulk of my time. No, I never had what it takes for a military career.

Total luminous wayward niggardly barstool of a lummox. Put two pieces of toast under the recliner for a double-dip of lovely sudsy nudies pooh-poohing old Zebulot and causing cancer in a frictionless environment of overrefinement. This will cause you to take root in the worst way, right in front of everyone. They'll look and suddenly stop chewing their dagwoods—-jesus, all they do is eat, and do you know what they're paid?—-and besides, they're ugly. Little Polly's Listerine-flavored drops could outclass an Indian with a rosary and a diary. "You gotta d's, I gotta doze." And even that, and even that.

Listen, I'm trying to get through to you, that's all. Something more than all of this is at stake—-our hearts. *Shake shake shake your booty* is a pretty reductionist slogan, and I definitely don't advocate it to today's youth, but I can't deny its validity in my own life. Like the other day, when

I ran out in the street on a rampage-like spree, flashing knives before little 7-year-olds on their ways to school. The look in my eye, the evil glint of light which flashed from inside my mouth, those flared nostrils pushing up from underneath the ground! It is I, the Earth—-and I hate you! You human filth, I will destroy you!

—Don't mind my friend. Let's sing together. Take a candle and a mug o' mead, you dumb fuck, we're off caroling.

> One night our king stepped out to smoke
> and Butch, his son, smoked him;
> jump along, frumpy one,
> clamber whimpering mumpy-mon
> and savor steaks and gravies.
> Weighties! Davies!
> Test the iddle wavies!
> Toss the old bird in the stew!
>
> One morning flesh of my baby awoke
> and rose like creeper towards heaven;
> nestl'd among sweet creatures and their lairs,
> rising planets' creeds and cadences
> boil'd in a soup!
> It's a bobaloop!
> Snabapoop, peepers snoop!
> Go ahead, bite it off!

—No, I'm sorry, I don't think that's quite the sort of song I'd like to sing.

—Well, don't be so hasty, and have a little whiskey, you whimpering cockroach basket ready to spill black beauties like a piñata!

> It was a sore evening which Mitchell dropped dead in,
> a period so trying his wife and sons et him.
> Shake your fanny in an air conditioned version of a
> down-by-law megalopolitan romance on the verge
> of shaking large containers of a frothy liquid

for all eternity, never to open them.

—Oh come off it, you expect me to wander through the neighborhood singing like that? You're crazy.

—Not at all, not at all, they'll adore you for it. Now, let me see you naked.

—You've taken leave of your senses! Mother! Mother! He's gone mad!

—Your mother is unable to hear your cries, my dear, my little chicken!

—Oh, is that all I am to you, some chicken?

—No, no, that was just a harmless term of endearment, really.

—No it wasn't! And if you think you're going to get my mayonnaise, well, you've got another think coming, you masher!

—Very cute, but you don't have a fine thangie like I do.

—Okay, "Chicken" will do. But you're still glossing over the social and political realities, there.

XI

I'VE decided that I am very much in love with my anus. Not that I would enjoy having cylindrical objects forcefully inserted into it, but rather that I experience an intense joy when it loudly belches methane gas, and makes a delicious sticky sound as moist shit is slowly and lusciously squeezed from its pouty little sphincter.

—And that, that is why you refuse to go to school? Listen to your mother! These, these desires of yours just aren't natural for you to think that they are natural enough for you to tell me, your mother, even though they are of course 100% natural, just like the cereal I made you eat this morning, my dearest! You should feel ashamed when you speak to me of your true pleasures. After all, you sprang from my loins and used to suck my tits, and I can assure you that often when you sucked your pleasure from me, I was stimulating myself to ecstasy.

—Remember when you and me and Daddy used to take baths together, Mommy? When we all rubbed that stuff on ourselves and then got the dog involved? Sure, I knew. I remember all of it. Like the time you made me lick the raccoon's little penis till it came all inside my mouth and you would rub your crotch up and down Daddy's face.... I love you, Mommy.

—Well, screw you, dear, too. I don't know if you recall the time I beat your little testicles with a spoon until they bruised, but if you don't stop it with your lip I'll soon give you cause to, so get over and get your mouth working in my bush, where it's of some worth. I'm going to look over the accounts.

—Hurt me again mom, you know what I'm like. A suffering mere-shadow of a combination of Wordsworth, Leika, Moshe Dayan, and Louisa May Alcott. A pruny devil made those toes, and my name is Telemann.

—That's good dialogue, but how are we supposed to use it? The sponsors will pull out. And speaking of which, give me a working over with that peninsula of mine that's overheating in your pocket.... Yes, there it is, and rightfully it belongs to me—see how it approves of the idea.

Nearby, a group of tourists were gathered on the beach of a small Midwestern lake, which gives a clue as to exactly where the previous conversation took place. Grace might like Kenny Rogers, but Boopsy eats all yams with big pleasure. Dracula's margarine was tossed at a British Marxist, with furs. It was aerobic, they decided, to gather pebbles while they may. They griped, but at last mounted their dustbowl chargers and went to do their aforementioned thing in the best place to find the smooth stones wet.

Rhapsodic menses swept over Vichy's pomegranate orchards of misty harbor bay. Strike up a dirge for old Methuselah, poised on wings of lamb, strangling mewling forest animals (bunnies, raccoons, turtles, chickies) for a century's abatement of jangling pocket-change. When the clouds come down for a certain space and take you by the hand with their cold iron grip, and smile, and ask, "Are you now, or have you ever been..." and buy you a drink afterwards, that's when by chance you also notice that the sky is streaked by strange portents, omens and signs: perniciously anemic Pharisees stretching out their glandes so little cattle-minded idiot-savants could double check their moss and cartilage deposits, a mysterious distribution of candies and a trash bin that talks, a *Hollywood Squares* of the gods.

Square with me. What kind of random mean do you suspect presages your vanilla cream filling? The living body of a groundhog wouldn't deliver roasting flank-cut to V.F.W. hospitals, nor would men named Richard link donkey stories told in a frat house with the back label of a package of Lifesavers, unless they thought about it a long time. But the veterans are still fond of their gums and their fruit charms. That's one superficial interpretation of the message God sent to me, and I have many more. We could trade. Do you have any macho? Climb the highest pearl, you sand-grain-sized pinching things, flavors wash over me as obscure Aztec symbols form in front of my face. They call me to battle, they call me home, to a widening ooze of glycerin coming from my tube of toothpaste. Is that on my face?

On the road there lay a squashed form on a bed of snow peas surrounded by a row of cherry tomatoes and little meatballs alternating in sequence. Some Indians (the kind on elephants) had painted themselves and put feathers in their hair and were dancing around the pyre, ululating and generally whooping it up. So, will the widow make bright colors? Go to Parma! That way Gomez will feel his filth through his drawers, and the little plastic bags will sell for big buxom bazoobs and their gazebos of warm flesh wrapped tight like a fruit basket, and the purple sky, as it darkens, will shake, rumble, even make the snaky-waky, do the Charleston Chew and the Chubby Checker. Contort your boobyhatched siblings and yourselves into shapes of the noxious woods, lusty and remote like a singular rusting train trestle spanning a stream through endless barrenness, and willing to learn to fly. Soon you'll chug in your chariot from China to Chihuahua—mind you apply the sun-block! Beware the Jabberwock! Fly neither sharp nor flat! Write your mother! Don't open this special fun box labeled "Oooh! Surprise!" with which I'm locking you alone in this dismal cell for a year, letting myself out of the tower by means of a fancy basket of discarded kidney stones which always takes me exactly where I want to go.

To be:

1. at one with the bubble
2. even with the forces of evil, deuce take 'em!
3. in a green mist
4. redelivered by a magical obstretrician

To be:

1. subservient to causality
2. differentiable with respect to x
3. triplanar in magnitude, squishy with respect to mouthfuls of yams
4. flatulent

and lastly, to be:

5. a symbol of imperial malevolence and architectural cynicism

Well, what do you think of it? I recognize Señor Glandez.

SEÑOR GLANDEZ: *(wriggling in ecstasy with the microphone, sings.)*

Gala, Gala, presto on lever,
Naughty, naughty, naughty with a cleaver,
Poisoned a pie for a poke in your eye,
Dolly, wed me, do.

(Big band strikes up a brash finale.)

If I understand you correctly, Señor, then you are a filthy beast and I know your number and will probably give you a call. Madame Bète Noire, you are wanted in the podium area!

LIZA: One dollop of cream. One. Do you hear me? One dollop, not two. One. Do you hear me??

Ponce: Granted the beast may violate you. But it can hardly style your hair.

(A loud explosion.)

Attention! Cyrus and The Gobtweezers will now dominate you from the bandstand. Their nervous systems are raging electrical conflagrations. It's hard to be their road manager. I do extremely well at the job. I'm a genius.

Willy: Poodles! That's what we all are. Fucking poodles! Don't you see it? What's wrong with you people?!

(Many clicking sounds.)

Clear the way! Clear the way! Behold! The behemoth of all the musical arts and his stubby cohorts: the one and only C*yy*rus and the G*ooo*btweezers!!

(A man, obviously medieval in spirit and abundantly blessed by the creator in the nose department, clears his throat as if to say something.)

Medieval Man: Rrrrrrrrgh!

(Frog with human voice hops on stage.)

Frog: I love you, Medieval Man. You are my morning and my night. You are my everything. Oh! Medieval Man, please do not be led astray. I worship the thongs of your sandals.

Medieval Deity: Rrrrrgh! Rrrrrgh!

Frog: Oh, actually, I prefer you, Medieval Deity! You rully turn my crank with those two "Rrrrrgh"s of yours!

2 year old baby: Er gukick muggley whoo!

Frog: Alice! My cocktail!

(Curtain opens to reveal Alice, a velvety herring standing up on its tail.)

Alice: Waddaya godda wanna maka lika all-a-dat noise? Huh?

(Liza slaps her cheeks.)

LIZA: Whoa! Baby! Like, what a trip! Baby! Double-occupancy all-the-way-to-St.-Croix-*baby!* Big Daddy-Man—hey Babe, I'm talkin' to yuh—watch the talkin' sardine! Heh-heh-heh? Is it salty, baby? Oooaah! Oooaah!

FROG: Or rather, Brekkek-Kekkek! Sardine, I enlarge!

LIZA: Oh baby, it's time to catch a fly! Ooaah!! It's a homer!

ALICE: Wah dontcha goata duh t'ing deh en-uh go up an', uh....

WILLY: That's enough! *(takes out age-old morningstar and mashes Alice until she physically becomes a jar of creamed herring.)*

LIZA: It's good we brought plenty o' balls. Now, serve!

FROG: Forget it, baby! It's hop time for yours truly. Been great. See yah.

(Liza spits and crushes him with an enormous boulder before his frenzied leaping could be effectual re exodus from the area of hostilities.)

WILLY: Liza!

LIZA: Willy!

WILLY: What?

LIZA: I've made it, Willy! I've finally arrived!

WILLY: Promise not to make stew. Please? Promise me, now.

LIZA: Actually, the Medieval Man was going to make stew.

(A loud squashing sound is heard as the Medieval Man sits on Liza, mistaking her for a sofa, and crushes her to death.)

MEDIEVAL MAN: Rr?

WILLY: Now you've done it! Just look what you've done! I'm ashamed of you! Beast!

MEDIEVAL MAN: *(gets up to club Willy, but looks beneath him and detects a trace of Liza's remains.)* Oh Liza! There was so much I wanted to say to you. *(He weeps, gnashing his hair.)*

(Enter the blissful enchanted Fairy Queen, vengefulness and acid showing through her guise of apparent bliss.)

FAIRY QUEEN: Oh, Lovelies! Darlings! Joys of all life! I hate you all so dreadfully much that I am going to have to exterminate you all. Well, good-bye! *(waves her wand.)* There! I've disappeared!

(She sits down contentedly on a rock and knits.)

SPORTSCASTER: And over to you, Narrator.

No, to Newscaster.

NEWSCASTER: Now, Willy, now that you've won the title, do you anticipate a challenge from Tyson?

WILLY: Who's Tyson?

SPORTSCASTER: Hey! That's my job!

You just shut up or I'll bench ya all season.

MEDIEVAL MAN: *(sings)* Let's have another cup of coffee, and let's have another piece of pie.

NEWSCASTER: You rat! I get paid just to hear you squawk! Keep me, Newscaster, from turning yellow and undergoing paroxysmal aortal fibrillation. Back to you, Will.

WILL: Will somebody please randomly test me?

If you would thoroughly think about it, maybe I might. I could subject you to stress beyond your wildest imaginings!

WILL: I question that, Bozo. You big fat clown, sittin' up there on your comfortable plush chair. Without me, you can't do nothin'. Without my cooperation, you is paralyzed. Willy is a jealous will and it digs its power over your dumb bullshit.

(A large pewter corn cob, probably weighing more than 500 lbs., appears on the horizon and slowly wafts over the gathering, perilously close to their heads.)

SPORTSCASTER: Hey! That's my hair!

(The Fairy Queen lifts up her skirt and softly pushes out a large, long shit. She wipes herself with her hand and then licks off the accumulated residue.)

MEDIEVAL MAN: Rrr! Rrr! Rrr! Rrr!

FAIRY QUEEN: Sakes! I'm not invisible! Come, die with me! Raaaaa!!

Once they were all ready, I spun the cob rapidly against my big fancy teeth and the kernels shot off like bullets, penetrating the delicate insides of each member of the cast and popping.

EVERYONE BUT ME: Rrrrrrrrrrr!

TELEPHONE OPERATOR: *(in a nasal voice)* Hello?

LIZA: Oh, that's for me. Excuse me.

(Liza goes into the next room with the Operator and the two of them have loud sex.)

OPERATOR: Oh, Honey! C'mere! Oh! Oh! Ohh!! Toots, you make me all topsy-turvy. You benefit me. Oh!

LIZA: Lov-ely da-a-arling! Oh, you're so luscious. Let me lick you out, but *thoroughly!!*

But that's just talking in comparison to the feats and the feast of their eagerly lapped up labia.

The clouds that were hinted at by the edge of the sea had a dark, bitter cast, but the crew of the ancient skiff was solemn and impassive, uncaring of their fate. Liza and the Operator finally found their ultimate destiny in a strip mall in suburban Delaware. All the rest just faded away, except for the Medieval Deity, who was stuck holding the bag.

XII

LONDON broil never minded being boiled in hot oil before. This would be the first time my groin area was washed in my entire life. I drooled. The ducky had enormous gleaming teeth. It swam towards me stealthily under the water. Quickly I looked for the soap. Only it could save me now.

DUCKY: Quack! Of all the things I thought you might have done, I never thought you'd hurt me like this.

Oh, just because your sores never heal you expect sympathy! Well, forget it, buster. I'm about to fill my mouth with peanut butter! Make it all better! You'd better go get 'er! Dolly in a sweater! All fall down! And so we arrive, recirculated, at the house of Ester and Myrtle, those two notorious Drag Kings, to examine (in some detail, mind you, or don't) the many species of divine waste, dirt and effluvia to be found there.

Myriads of doubt played fungus-foodle with Mrs. Haverstrom's musculature.

MRS. HAVERSTROM: Inside! Inside! The needle pricks, but entices. Love me when I doodle in indelible ink on my bruised region. Please, another portion of deviled eggs, toute suite!

INK DISTRIBUTOR: Ma'am, your ink is fully guaranteed for a period of five (5) years.

Look closely at some gold-like chunks blowing in the wind of light, the wind of time and of space. Why so afraid to pull back and lean forward? If your gaze is stuck, have you not chosen to be dead even though you are alive? And this human stupidity is a crime worse than ferocity.

Mrs. Haverstrom: Why did you invite him?

Ink Distributor: He's all rumpled.

Ducky: He's the host, and he's trying to soap me. Help!

Ink Distributor: Ma'am, I hereby declare you to be your own customer. Shazam!

(Mrs. Haverstrom suddenly takes on the voice and personality of the deceased Frog, who possesses her in an undead form.)

Undead Frog: *(as Mrs. H)* You fetal cads! Zeus! All of you, feel my neck! Here, right here! The neck, see where the pus is coming out? Quickly, you embryonic brutes!

Medieval Deity: Hey, you, Froggie over there! You escaped from my bag! Come back!

Can't you turn around? Where is the second face? Why are you forever distracted? Have you been interrupted midlife by the advent of time, and are you waiting for it to stop before you resume? Where is the heart who says Yes and says No, and both Yes and No are the path of love? Give me its coordinates, you swinish crew, and I'll send someone to eventually give it this information.

My load became like ham, and I winced at the idea of pickling my future like a jar of kimchee or grandmother's box of souvenir testicles or several other things I could mention. Steer me away from the concept of beatification towards the more gnarled surfer-types who never stop the silence or anything or so much so after that or a wizard cheese spread out on a child's white sneakers, for that matter.

So put it down, the sandwich, the film, the book, and now the award-winning cheese, the jeans. It might help if you were all to suddenly take a walk. Anyone who doesn't walk at unpredictable times and in unpredictable ways is apparently attached to predictability, and you can figure out where that gets you. When you are rid of it, there is nothing but the ocean of sadness—but living in that ocean is our only joy.

Have you ever had carnal knowledge of a marine wildlife specimen? The answer is....

ANNOUNCER: Noo!

What could touch a more visceral location could match my synapse-fondness with a certain instinct for making wubbadoo.

INK DISTRIBUTOR: Well, he obviously thinks nothing of what others might need to do with their time besides listening to him gas off.

DUCKY: He bubbles like a diver out of his behind and calls the bubbles "God."

FROG: That's what an ass is.

2 YEAR OLD BABY: Goopy! Goopy! Goo ...pee. Oooeeee!!

FROG: Shut-that-thing-up! Shut-it-up!!

My God, I pray to thee, O sayest I on this, thy day, that thou hast for me mistaketh a sacrificial lamb. The genesis of truth is in spawn. Denieth me not a mechanized sphincter in my time of solace. I liveth for this day, sayeth I, O Lord.

ANNOUNCER: And now for a public service... uh... thing:

The sleeping body quivers a great deal. I sleep very badly, especially while I'm awake. This is a considerable distinction. It makes me sexy. I sell it in quart and half-quart bottles and with the money I've bought a big comfy couch, some slippers and a lifetime subscription to *Modern Succubus.*

A filigree with timpani sounds surrounds motor karma like they used to refer to Skeezicks' skirts, and the fast blowing Bosch used to do on orphans like a liquid sundial knife blade. Euphoria mesmerizes the lectern-standers over nightshades with curls and a bottle of mink oil boiling solid globs of solids on dirty-faced impy gobs of people. That's how rubber is cast into shapes that are normally not possible except for faith healers. Notice that there are discontinuities, shapes within shapes, that the toilet doesn't work in 13A....

ANNOUNCER: We return to our movie in progress, *Woody.*

VOICE: *(in movie)* Okay, here you go: *(counts out)* 1000 Pesetas, 80 Baht, 325 pounds Sterling, 27 Cruzeiros, 3500 Yuan, 5 Yen, 11 dollars U.S., 275 Øre, and 40 Austrian Shillings.

OTHER VOICE: Oh! Ohhh! Thank you!

VOICE № 3: Excuse me, Mademoiselle. Could you spare 17 Moroccan Dirhams? 1700 Lire? A few Kenyan Shillingi? A Sou? Together they would make possible an internationally balanced diet, and then I'd shut up.

VOICE № 4: You promise?

WOODY: You're all shit. My wallet gets fat on your ugly asses. You eat me. Sometimes, in the wee hours, I suddenly begin to sob in bed. Then I take a pill and forget....

VOICE № 4: I'm the bigshot around here! Stop stealing all the scenes. You smell like a liquefied moose.

WOODY: Kneel, bastard. Luckless sniveling lackey from a time gone by. Service me!

VOICE № 4: *(reluctantly)* Yes, master. I'd be willing, I suppose, to take your swelling into my mouth, to scrape your syphilis pus onto Melba toast, if I might characterize the experience so boldly, but I'm already full-up on the frog's (or the lady's) pus secretions.

(Enter Sir Janus.)

SIR JANUS: Do my duty, № 4! Come, see my thangy hangin' out. Diddle with me, honey baby sweetie!

Woody: Guards! Guards! Throw this man down the steps of the Senate!

Guards: No! No! Noooo!

Senators: *(in unison)* One noise stops and the other is immediately stimulated to begin.

That's quite right, immediate stimulation is the essence of divine energy. Consider the case of the collision of two billiard balls. One contacts the other, and energy is transmitted, but this energy is not expressed in matter, rather, matter reflects, and is expressed in, energy. Now consider the case of the collision of two passenger trains. They hit hard, very hard, and explode, causing a tunnel to partially collapse, trapping hundreds of people and a carload of live poultry in a torturous inferno. Outside, one-hundred soldiers had thunderous erections and raised them in salute as Woody surveyed them.

Woody: Finally the missing link, the secret code, the....

XIII

GUY was roped in the west, in a land gone astray, by a fleelined pack of weavers, locks and copious silk cavalcading down Theresa in a glinty dock-spot maelstrom wave. Its whitewashed alleys and whitewalled towers, like the whitewalls on my Mercedes, keep shifting position. Guyogradiencia, its capital, has therefore stirred the waters of the Caribbean and has no map. One day the Capitol dome is across from Guy Park, the next it travels across town into the notorious red-light district, known as "The Windlass at Fox Grove." There, people prayed and struck up conversations and found a pile of severed cloven-hoofs out in the woods surrounding the area. Form was digested, conscience increased proportions of their prefix-pride home-of-the-good-lovin' chimera Texas-ass. The monoliths, slowly circulating around the inhabitants of the town in a way unknown to science, induce a sort of hypnosis, and under their spell they appear to one as a purple fog with a kindly quadraphonic voice whispering, "It sure is quiet in here! Hey, hey you. Pssst! Hey, why is everyone whispering here?" And you reply (in a loud voice), "Why, that's b'cause you're now in 'Whispering Willows.' See, before, you were in 'The Windlass at Fox Grove' and now you're in 'Whispering Willows.' Lots start at $109,999. Can I caveat your emptor, spiff your shoe's shine,—anything?" As real estate director, you'll have to follow the big rocks around all day, reappraising properties on the basis of the city's constantly changing configuration and the resultant rise and fall of neighborhoods. I, myself, whatever the case may be, doorknobs are as much to Mrs. Fliegershorndorf to shorten her name to "Flieg" that many many cold Marches ago through a bitter November populace eating Joycy and her cantaloupes and chicken-fried mella-puff-glomerates all down as can be. Cobbled bitters control lickable magnetic fields around the upper G.I. bleed of the family. Loving, adoring Mother; brusque, chuckly, piqued old Dad; Big Brother's rollicking toaster capers and Rex's tricks, oh!! Was I ever futzy, oh! One spring Aunt Melba got et by a panther, and we put on warpaint and pounded on drums, and my father, with the utmost solemnity, put on his curare-pouch and his darts and took a machete and a sub-machine gun, and I got into the tank with him, my mother piloted the fighter jet, and my youngest sister manned the rocket-launcher, and we went out to kill that tiger no matter what.

The sub-machina came before "119" like a trayful of stuffed cabbage reminded me of life without my skin. Sprinkle dust of ancestral bones, bones burned to carbon ribbons, ribbons likewise wound into young bones before you go west, youngster! We gathered in the main tent and wailed, some of us (the initiated) snorting Aunt Melba's snuff.

Steam engines produced the products of man's desires in a fancy basket out of a hat, then pulled out a rabbit briskly by pulling on huge oily chains to the tumultuous applause of a few geeky leftovers lying next to a largish pile of meatloaf in the drill surface zone. Ahead of lettuce, radish and cucumber ran madly an erratic stopwatch that claimed the role of judge. This is what ran down a hole and is pursued by mystics. Mastication, merely another reality, purged its teflon offspring from the hinges of mass-identity, and surged toward my little nephew, Yutz, like a horse towards grain; that is, to not do so would be against grain. And Yutz.

Mafia ironing boards served well as a sort of "Lovers' Leap" for countless lower middle-class inhabitants who, in a state of grace, would climb up on top of the things and there would be lightning scarring the hilltop and they would come down later with tablets that they could auction and fetch a good price. Bastards fought an army of idiots along the Sudatenland, the Yangtse, Minnesota. They jarred the meat of their defeated foes with sudden news of their own surrender, but that was just a ploy. Soon they got nasty-wrap to finish up the dirty work. Lapis lazuli cheeks flashed instantly behind the curtain. The television flicked wet scraps of rotten material:

> *"Thank heaven…*
> *for little girls…."*

The old set mumbled on its sweet-nothings-of-a-generation with a muff taking it all the way in. Young muff. *Very* young.

That second, a box with two pistols that stay 'em in appeared out of thin air and floated around. Later, the Pope pantomimed a vacuum cleaner while standing up through the roof-opening of his limousine, while a big whale juggled zealots with its tail and ol' Pegleg chewed a roach until it had the consistency of a mushroom.

Boron Mitzie dropped moo-shoe carbon-daters like dead flies make buzzing sounds by accumulating on the trigger of a raygun. Then, in the bush near the fjord, a barroom carder with a raygun was nixxing the neighborhood Johnsons, asking, "A can uh 'deez?" The eyes in our true men rose a welt. Will sun harden? According to the Reverend Moon, a bulge served in Szell's tuba section until a special ceramic wire vacuumed him into exile. Of course no one believed this, but we have to report everything. Your dispatch number, please?

Barking Pfeffernüße targetted a beetle hatchery as a hitherto unknown vortex trigger bunched up a juicy heifer's silk kimono like so much that can be brought for brunch to the offshore oil rig. The concert began inauspiciously. Warped and marred, shelled almonds with little arms and legs stood around sullenly and sniffed the air. Then a monstrous domino fell on them, producing a percussive chain reaction which sounded like maracas to the Woman Talking Upstairs, as the conductor was called. The almonds were scattered about. There was smoke. There was an imitation-scallop dangling a chain from a Byzantine tower. Then a Brazil came onstage and a rich singing tone poured forth from its extravagantly clothed, or carved, body that also cavorted in postures lewd and prissy, profane, sacred, etc.

Finally, the bell rang and it was time to rescue Oscar and feed the birdie. The drug smuggler turned off his beeper and most of the opera-lovers in row 13A had to get up as he shamefacedly snuck past, squeezing knees and murmuring "Excuse me" under his breath like a litany of tirades or maybe it's not like that. When you put your hands in jars a lot, sometimes fate can seem lumpy. Like, getting stuck on nettles services my need for cat meat, like, it's a hang-up of sorts. It costs. He didn't like the idea of riddlin' Oscar through with the 45 just as he was about to sprinkle, the Parmesan cheese!, but the magpie tittered and bobbed its tail and out popped a gory li'l baby—a disgusting little wretch of a thing, all slobbering and helpless. God! What a sight. It required that he master himself and go forth with the assignment.

In the john he fortified himself up the nose, as his need was needling him. He loaded his chambers in the stall, and came out ready to shoot. The next train to Newport left in 26 minutes from Grand Central. The one after that left a minute sooner.

XIV

In Rotterdam at long last! Progress consists in making inroads into the earth (or "automatic earth machine") for the longest time. The tree-structure proved to be the perfect tool to accomplish this, this… thing here. You know, what with its roots and all, the inroads-into-the-earth thing ran without a hitch, I mean clockwork, baby, greased lightnin' like a week from Wednesday, just ask Dennis:

Reader: Dennis! Yahoo, Dennis! *Deeenniiss!* Dennis?

Dennis: This is a recording.

Recording: This is Dennis….

XIII

Should I buy a round trip? If I buy it on the train it'll have to be one way. The line at the ticket counter is long; it might make me miss the train, or at least cause me to board when the train was already filled. Perhaps I should kill all these people. My tank is full, my motion emotional, and I've never blithered in my life. No. I'll drive instead. I'll jack this crazy heap straight through the middle of the Quakerbridge Mall on Black Friday. Well, Jane, whisk-raising geeks rate "throw in the towel" on the bakeoff-to-end-it-all, so make my day! Row in that owl: "One-two—take off!" to render May-karate. One who may have Saran wrap, Oil of Olay, bicarbonate of soda. Samantha, Olivia, olé! My car bonnet—also that.

Policeman: Don't call me Jane. I have a nightstick.

Yeah, you have a stick up your ass, that's what you have!

(Policeman beats Chapter Thirteen with his stick. He attracts a crowd.)

Chapter Thirteen: Oh, my! Help! Save me!

XI

Medieval Diety: Here I am! I'll save you! Er, uh, just let me put down this bag here.

(Silence.)

Medieval Diety: Yes, I perceive the entire scene, but it does not respond to me. There is a dangerous terrorist in an altercation with the authorities. A text has been mauled. By all rights, I should be there, illuminating it. But I'm trapped alone in infinite darkness! I, God! 266 Essex Towers, 34 Hampshire Lane, Bellingham, Surrey E037H!

Newscaster: That's right, any two can do it, but how can couples keep physical union fresh after all those years? Many say now that it's time to revamp the process. With more on this, here's Edward:

Edward: Back to you, Jim.

Newscaster: No-no, *you*, Edward.

Edward: Oh, uh… do you mean me, now?

Newscaster: Yes, uh, Edward, take it away…!

Edward: Oh, er, yes, uh, "Sexual Union, Flight of the Scorpion." For many, it's a piece of pie, for others, an Iwo Jima of bedtime pseudo-frollicking. But for a growing totality of a tiny number of people, sex has become a state of being trapped by a horrendous, self-pitying monster in his neurotically clenched scrotum.

XIV

Dennis: Shut it up! Hey-you-there…! Don't leave this thing here burbling at me another moment. Isobar! Triangle! Come here, my pets. Let me look upon you.

Isobar and Triangle: Meow!

How should he best discharge himself, fire his gun and his employees, free Ariel his slave? Vernon knew a way. And he would call Vernon.

Dennis: Vernon?

Vernon: Yes, I know. Verily, none know better. Get rid of this man with the cats and the talking toy. He's no good for you.

Isobar and Triangle: Rreeeoww!! Rreeeryyr!!

Reader: Aww, forget it. Now you can just leave me be. G'won, get out of here….

(Isobar begins hopping like a frog. The walls spin. Suddenly, before anyone could say a word:)

Recording: I am a machine without consciousness, so this is just sound, not words, as far as I, a semiotic naïf or sub-naïf, am concerned.

Recording № 2: Oh, hardy-har-har! Oh, let's hear it for mister pseudo-humble recording over there! Oh, big philosophical machine! Oh, lovely, that's just lovely…!

Recording: I am…. I am… … *Dennis*!!

(Dennis shaves rapidly. He sees his reflection.)

The whole scene reminded me of the little lady at home. Her spot down there and everything… you know… that you'd prefer to forget between now and the next time you feel like using it. Which usually isn't very long. Anyway, I was complaining about the cooking:

Recording: Frickin' chick-a-see! Frickin' chick-a-see!

And I pulled it out and next thing I know I'm down on my knees wiping it up… like, I blacked *out* during it. You know? And I figured I could put the head in a bag if I had to. I could walk right out of the hotel if that coked-up narc doesn't recognize me dressed as a paraplegic belly dancer who is vibrated before his patrons by an enormous DC motor from one of the best restaurants. (Because of that one, the scoundrelly-looking one.) My slippers, designed by Marisol, used to fool them every time. You know, the shininess? Yeah, that. And what's more, if that motor was juiced up enough, I would just start squirting something awful.

XII

Soldier № 1: Set of trains?

Woody: Silly.

Mambo soil cancelled the rubbery soul fluid like a stamp, frankly and with one swift motion, never thinking of binding its groin in a publicly inflexible style. Data urges, the go-withs for my fizzling erection, fecundate a snarly yet obsequious granny-lode of shiny apples, all piled in a wheelbarrow. A hoe played a part in the scheme. The pickaxe was its corroboratory kindling. Its Szechuan sauce came before its own homegrown welfare state and the accompanying booklet, video and software package out in rear of the warehouse in exterior aisle 3, next to the Xmas trees. C'mon boys! It's getting late, and you know how Maw hates it when the pork-and-beans gets cold. Just wait till she turns her back, and then your sister will sneak up behind her and audit the kettles for the first time in her life even though they're right next to the croquet mallets in the household gift wedding-type display. Menopause did something to her—she just all of a sudden wants to hear percussion. So will Maw fall over with her face missing? No. Instead, she will channel that energy into ripping off her mother's clothes and running around naked, shaking her naughty boobies at her sweet innocent younger brother till he bursts into mighty tears. They had a "pool" propulsion system with cool crystals and a honking sound as it glided over the water, penetrating the sudsy regions with dignity and yet a sort of dashing abandon. It tended to grin in a way that upset sensitive souls, the sort of people who are too timid to admire Hitler. As they all walked along the beach, an enormous squid beached itself near them, squirting them all with ink as a dying gesture that not only openly portrayed a sense of animosity on its own part, but caused the group to shrink from the creature as if it hadn't been passing them on the street all the time and saying "Hello." So it leaked on them one day and Davis Linginpfelter felt the lifeforce draining out of him as the dreadful carolling was stamped out by secret police-people who had been inbred for evil and violence. (Too many white blood cells.) Weary Thomas finally got around to wrestling the 'gator, which the people with the squid problem found completely distracting. They slopped around in the mud awhile, and finally cast their nets into more abundant waters, namely, the Ocean-At-Large, with its enormous meniscus sagging tautly over the chiffon of my mind. I hope God the Mermaid's ready with meringue, coming at me from behind the curtain, through the glass darkly like Satan's Flames playing the Garden for three days in January. When Castro's Carib Oratory was held up and immersed in bouillon, the race experienced dusk complexion-wise (*cf.* Spengler) and the daughters of the Mayflower gathered for taco dinners.

Now, rascals that they be, no one ever once smelled their breaths, and what do you suppose? the welfare came that day and forced them to dance on an enormous, white-hot metal ring, while passing a razor blade through the flesh between the (gasp!) legs, and in so doing, causing them all to exclaim in unison, "By golly, I've got fortitude. Yes yes yes yes yes. I've got sobriety. No no no no no. I've got rhythm. Maybe maybe maybe maybe maybe. There's one girl in particular—Corinne—who might entice me to make the weeping Indian eat a doughnut and I would cross a taboo moral barrier to get to the other side. Absurd of those bleeding hearts to call me chicken—just wait till they see the home video of me holding apart her long legs! Plié, my darling. Fetch the soap. Only it can salve me now."

From across the room, several men in tights can be observed drawing lines on the floor with red lipstick. Slowly, a pink-clad neophyte-Aphrodite tiptoes across the room. But too late! She casts her moistening eyes towards her subabdominal region, and glimpses the widening patch of red spreading sideways and down. Her slippers will be spotted! Mummy will want some of the action! Don't squawk! Whatever you do, don't take my pacifier out of your mouth while I pound my armour with pestles and pockmark the ocean of peace.

GIRL: Okay. How can you inflict on me the marks of busting safes, of making cookies in the microwave? Am I boiling you, honey?

BIG DADDY: In a flask, baby! In a crystal flask!

CORINNE: Dish it out, hog master! Oh, play with my potato mush!

The gravy meniscus toyed with the ladle edge, the canvas of time subverted by its pleasure though Jeffrey the Cat, one time out of seven, failed to observe the traffic signal and skidded into a large mound of lentils. This mouse-losing gesture was a fun "roast"-like tribute to God, who had had a few too many, and disturbed bald men with askew bowties by always beginning conversations with the line, "Oh, you're rubbing your face!" "Rub it for me" was always the reply, as well as "I'll rub your eyelid."

Make me a sheriff for dinner, Marjoram! My struggle makes me squirm like a worm, a *worm*! Ya' hear? A worm with no home, no harmony, no chance for rest and thus no motive to go forward, which results eventually in the widespread adoption of the revolting motion habit of moving in a slithery motion! Slithery dripped hooks' mushy claws gassed freon orgones into gallium arsenide workers' sweat glands in deepest darkest continents of flush, regal ulllllll of gar, moulies of miles from Vogelfried and sixteen excuses for the feathered Satchmo that entwines her scrappy little rednecked daughter and flagship state ivied college, singing of hot peppers. I travel from Howard Johnson's to other Howard Johnson's, but there is no Robert "Climax" Johnson.

Criminey! If only the spokesman from out-the-hole would gesture to the fixture on the shelf which produces ozone. Nuclear digit, flakes meander through the walnut of my peanut butter brain, now swirled with jelly in the same container as Woody's pet tarantula, Kind Yucky VIII, alias Lou E. "To the Maxx," "Fingers" Hank, "Slim the Eighth" Bill, Sam the Shepherd, and S.O.B. "Pineap-ple" Jake. It's rough having a spider in the same container as your brain, but I manage. Actually, I condition and rinse, but it makes it so manageable that somtimes I forget and skip a day. That long night of dangling over the river prevents any eruption from dismaying my face. My face! Oh, I rubbed it! My face! How I pleaded with all the heavens and earth to let me be able to kiss my own face! Oh face! Face honey, c'mere! Oh, pwetty wittle face! Nicey nicey! Mmmmmmmm!

Ugh—a pimple! Woe, woe! The moon is sick o'er with grief, smugly oozing some more muck.

> Put mucky-mucky[1] sounds in a box.
> 8–10 minutes, feeds four.

And in a moment if not for a moment, the chord shone forth like a bar of gold hurled thorugh blank night at an assailant. The assailant quickly grabs the bar of gold and then runs over a fence with it. After 'im boys! If you don't root for the loser, you'll never be disappointed. And this is exactly how the chord shone. And this is *exactly* how.

Gallop, the planes are flying, the reeds are slicing your boots! Hover over the subterranean catwalks, minding

[1]Editor's note: MS: "mucky-mucky"; IKS: "cheesy."

your flocks of geese like that time in September when Mark Nuzzo kept his security guard uniform next to the large jars. It was consoled, he explained, by the pathologists' collection of illustrative eyeballs and innards and deformed fœtuses and long stringy coils of protoplasm that no one could figure out. Duplicate projectiles grafted skin onto places it could have used patches by busy scientists with little remote control units in their hands. And it dreamt of Nuzzo out-Nuzzoed, cut up like stew-meat and admired through the virtual astigmatism of the formaldehyde bottle.

Greek delicacies could not be accessed by the fertile romp of mealtime marrow-warmers, candiedly jarring jelly and making it shake and quiver. If they could only break off with obsession, they could be President someday! But no, they keep being drawn by the lure of those honey-sweet cocks back to the park, with the whole PR problemset that comes with the deluxe package. In terms of the inter-family dynamic, it could be Adam or it could be a bucket of the Colonel's. The one with a lady's head in it, full make-up, earrings, hair in a sort of bun held by expensive jewelry into an ostentatious position. It could use a biscuit though, but anyway, plantation bitters or no plantation bitters I'm not stopping to gouge out a Mickey-Mouse mayor's innards and fill the space back in with torpedo rolls. Why should I bother with slime like Nuzzo? The sort of intercourse he and I have at work is painfully intimate. He stuffs his hot sweaty misshapen body into me and huffs and puffs all over the hospital, always in a rush, always the panic of an emergency, beet red and sweating, sweaty, stinking like the loathsome pig he is.

Hooliganism kept rearing its head. "Swirl" could be found in the freezer about as often as migration occurred in mince-meat pie bakers' lives. The Prince of Peace had a bushy moustache and a sombrero, and shouted, "Jesus, Jesus! Wah dohn yu' gwovo an' shaka somtings up?" Then, a pursy-pursy butterup wrinkled into an encephelopod and spritzed weener on my vaulted glyph-like dentures. Another lion came out from the big weeds and sang with a necklace of tonsils about its mane, "Mohammed baby, take my luv, yeah!"

Muhammed Baby (Take My Luv)

Muhammed baby, take my luv, yeah!
Take the strings of my corset!
Yeah, yeah, baby, etc!
Only you can let me out, yeah-yeah!
Muhammed! Muhammed!
Yeah!

XIV

Crumble greasy cumbersome Bob.
Greased me all day with an electric frog.
Wholesome equivalent of purple plums
Stuck to the roof of my mouth and gums.

THE crowd was soaked. The cringing forests gave forth an aromatic vapour of early death, of feathers and loud drums and a technology limited to balsa-wood and rubber bands. Ménière's syndrome was a quiet fact of life for every dimpled-Susan's little head to muddle itself with. The stumps in a mouth were invariably clamped around an enormous misshapen cigar that could not be extracted even with pliers. This went on for years until, one day, a crestfallen eagle perched on my shoulder and whispered these words to me: "How you gonna feel when you tell 'em back in the village that you've been talking with an eagle? You'll be ashamed of me, I can see it already. You don't want to tell Pop that you have a power animal calling you to be a shaman, which means you'll be on drugs or drunk all day long and never available (too fuckin' holy) to chop wood or carry water." But of course, the idea of carrying water at all was so absurd that all our forest friends began to laugh. "Tee-hee," tittled the little brush rabbit, "I bet you're gonna get in trouble." "Har-har," boomed the bear, "I got a cub and what do you got?" "An outstretched hand," I admitted, and I began to weep. "Now, Rufus," said the eagle, "don't take it so hard. Whatever problems you may be experiencing now are nothing compared with what awaits you. So you should be relatively happy." I snorted with annoyance at this stupid piece of reasoning. The eagle suddenly gave a sharp cry which produced a huge flock of eagles and sea-eagles who swooped down and started pecking me. The bear joined in too, and the rabbits, and the moose and buffalo and elk, and the frogs and insects, and suddenly all of Nature was viciously attacking me. I struggled to spit out blood and gasp for air as millions of beings from across the universe simultaneously gored, bit, trampled and kicked me. "I *was* relatively happy!" I cried.

My jugular considered my neck to be its own little tent where it would camp out at the smell of bison. I must have downed a carnival's worth of Figeroa's duplex blueprints. Baked or mung, my beans always seemed less satisfied than a prince who could do magic, a thief who wept at sunrise, or a young bride lying on her back naked in bed on her honeymoon night. A rocket is a kind of melodic path taken by a river through a series of facial expressions and following that path further that we who haven't taken it particularly. Deep water is always trickling—tasty! Mocha chinchilla sold for well over an easy answer. Vertical, if I pronounce something how will it come out? Huh? How will it? (You think you're so smart but are you? Do as I say and not as I do.) The bursting, the rubbish everywhere. Beasts, the pack bearers, a couple of Jews. A sunset and plentiful drink. And then it hit full force. Adults with blazers on pranced around anodyzing the zoo.[1] Others could be seen scattering to the north and west. Scampy smoked a herringbone pipe, and his strongest suit was cherry. Puffing with effort, he held Harriet against the statue of Hermes and hit her with puissant subpoena till she got the genetic message. And it was spoken and the spoke was past.

Jesus wept. An affectionate dunce slapped me with a wet towel and I jumped a little. Σ(my efforts) was nil. I be-

[1]Editor's note: IKS: "anodyzing the zoo"; MS: "anising the soup" (repeating a phrase from the opening of Chapter VII).

came a member of {Ø}. Lester saved the day by investing a dissolvable chemical packet which made toilet water turn blue. I carefully introduced it into the dunce's coffee tin, chuckling inside of my appearance prison as I rended and inverted and let it come down. My sister was still in Europe during this time, and any efforts to revive by taking the contents of a little yellow box were fraught with smokepuffs of hrumphy regrets. Tony relaxed in the focus of my binoculars. The circle enclosed the two of them, there in another window, another frame, another destiny. They were trite, brittle, over-exposed. Sand was everywhere, even among the trees. The expensive suit felt out of place and pretentious. Everyone insisted that Angela strip it off immediately. Luckily the Krazy Glue® held fast and I was spared the wretched sight which would have caused me to have retched. I quaked and, needless to say, did something else which has to do with the area protected by the bathing suit. Elroy couldn't resist tickling me with his stumpy tongue as he feasted on the residue.

Spearheading the coalition was an argotnaut megalopolitician who referred to everyone as his "main man." This became a serious problem when Little Richard walked in one day and volunteered to start wiggling right there in the middle of the floor. The seamen needed to be chained or they would have begun to wiggle, too. Who would do the dry cleaning if everyone's pleased most with wiggling?

Roxanne freed her hands from the chains only to be executed gangland style. That night I had Rice-a-Roni®, Chef Boy-Ar-Dee®, and Lipton's®, after which I soaked a few shirts in Clorox® and planted a tree. When Columbo came snooping around I severed his caryatid artery from his Kojakian sub-wiggle Acropolis and banged my mother until Freud had a spontaneous cash flow[2] from analyzing the proceedings and carryings on. The schoolbus became fifty little chances for salvation. I waited. The Acropolis waited. Agorophobia was a stalker. Suddenly I banged my head on the ceiling and it immediately

[2]Editor's note: IKS: "cash flow"; MS: "orgasm."

became clear how to debunk Castaneda. I quickly leaped out of the bath, shrieking "Eureka!", and ran clad only in faint traces of suds down West 100th Street and jumped into a manhole. *Mission Impossible* music, up!

Mission Impossible music: Leave me alone! I'm not hurting anyone, I'm just lying here.

Chapters turned every which way. No matter which way you stumble. No matter. Beyond definite knowledge are more satisfying means of integration. A path, rough and uneven, for the hirsute. Define "lacking" and tell the definition to the first smarmy lotus-eating Castro-double you see carrying a weedwhacker inside a grade-school gymnasium. Failure. Utter, utter, utter… it's all the same when you do nothing all day but milk cows. See here, Utte. See here, Mrs. Haverstrom. See. Hear! This convertible, this fungible fungoid, this portmanteau davenport. See her (Mrs. Spot) run! By the border, in a bikini, picking flowers out of a catalog. The oxen rubbed themselves and patted each other. Berg style tendency reactions smithered my vanishing miffer tendencies. Fire loosely the porkular bear blubber texturized skimming scrimshaw cavalier roaring bumblers.

Suddenly kapow crash bam, kerplunk "Wow I've got you" slam zowie gadzooks pow kznningkst! I'm wearing a minute steak miniskirt meniscus, I'm buzzing in the Ladies' like a being and a becoming.

Scarlet width and soured ham are the only things I could recognize. Idler, your camshaft could have been overheaded to everyone and who knows? Maybe a guava or something or a thing or sometimes in evenings, when the sky comes down a-pix a-kaka a-roo. Frank the evening stamp, affix clouds, and who knows? A boiled fœtus might launch a womb-rocket ("Rocky-woo") or maybe sometimes the morning might include the professional solace of smiling Hawaiian girls clad only in lais-lies-lice, fondling the overflow like a major but a minor nonetheless. Crash, the power cord broke. Cadenza! Influenza!

In the blistering heat I snapped on a reagent-pack and off I flew into and around the ether's feathers. Ethyl, on the other hand, was mildly retarded, so much so that my favorite secretary was fired. I couldn't think like a velocipede, I wasn't shaped like a velocipede; the fact was that I was indeed not a velocipede. Codependency was formulated to the extent that a structure's own reciprocal verswooshed itself into a vertex with the passing of each high tide. The Cuban constellation was a veritable animal farm.

Bunny: I smella something afunny here.

Sam the Crab: Hey, I know how to get there. There's a bridge out on the Roosevelt. This is the fastest way.

Bunny: Help! A-help! I been kidda-nap! A-help, a!

Sam the Crab: At least you're not a pizza ingredient. The only people *you* need to look out for are the ones who don't know what "rarebit" means.

Bunny: Lika funny, ha ha. Getta me the hellmost outa of here. These rarebit, me no lika the geshit Mama pressa th' olio huile youa stupida looka on laugha.

(Suddenly, the Medieval Deity goes flying through the air.)

Medieval Diety: Yo-Ho! Yo-Ho! Hey you down there! I *like you*!

Bunny: Wadda gotta do here-uh? Ya' gotta get outta da place now y'unnuhstan'?

Sam the Crab: It's a frame! You tricked me, you louse!

Bunny: Whata? Poor liddle-uh mee?

(Prolonged gunfire.)

Later, at the diner, a man chewed on an advertisement for Boca Raton, and motionalysis recreated with a joint dreg what only mongrels (curs or mutts) could snarkly snatch from Euripides' jacket pocket: little bits of meat. This creative act is a surge of radiation that cuts diagonally through the lifeform, engendering random developments: boils, cancers, poori-bread-like bubble of gas under the skin, pastry-dough-like lattices of flesh oozing a viscous yellow liquid, probably a metal. You're not getting it, are you?

Mr. Kleindienst: What the hell…? What's going on here? Who's running this show? I wanna talk to the manager! You lousy bunch o'morons! Goddamn you all!

Sam the Crab: You watch out now, my speedster is faster than your trolley-minded vertigo-inducer by a longshot.

(A nuclear exposion 120 miles to the east. The townsfolk came running out of the saloon to marvel at the whizzbang colors.)

Miss Thelma: My o' my, Tulsa sure is preddy!

Louisa: Why chile, that them there ain't Tulsa. They's….

(Their flesh is abruptly seared, uh, I mean their fresh is abruptly sealed.)

Mr. Hendershot: Úkelo! Úkelo! Where come the Conners, the Tates, or the Fishers? And how about old Hooper down-the-block? I heard he is about to pull up stakes. *(hushed)* I mean, *skedaddle-ski*!

Brenda: *(pulling her brassière out of her sleeve)* Hilda darling, I just cahn't wait to tell Hubert the good news. Hubie darling want a liddle iddy treaty, Hubie-Poo? Samuel, give Hubert his little boa, he looks so adorable in it. What, he snaps you? Nonsense. Hubie, are you happy, adorablest, that that hideous Hooper is on the skeedaddle-ski at last?

Hubert: *(perching on Mrs. Hendershot's head)* Polly want a…. BRRRAGH. *(He shits.)*

(Isobar stops hopping and everything returns to its previous state.)

DENNIS: Don't scare me like that darlings! You know how fidgety Daddy gets when everything begins to spin.

(Dennis, making his way across the livingroom, stops at a large trapdoor. He moves to open it, then pauses:)

DENNIS: Don't tell them—Russo is dead.

RUSSO: Eh? …. Wh? …. Uh. …. Oh,…. …. Hmm? …. Hmm, eh, ohh….

This bonanza of charm had to stop, thought the trackers with not much hope. Their colorful pupils reflected the snowy gleam of bloody charm droppings as their slow progress through the hagiographic arboretum down-helixed in a spot of dried Smegma recordings from the early 20s. Very few had ever heard the *Smegma Variations* or the *Smegma Pachebel Canon Overdrive Disciple Concerto* except for the arboretum attenders; they thrilled to the quadraphony.

Suddenly a muscular arm stymied the *rinokeroi* as they attempted to emigrate *en masse* to become missionaries to the civilized world. Flounder barbed me as Merriweather flew up to the chandelier and sprayed us all accurately with guava seeds from his newfound nest. Similarly shaped cakes were ogled by the vice-man of Man.

Presenting "Mr. Universe" himself, Ron…. *Felix*!

(Applause.)

RON FELIX: …. Thanks. How are we, mere specks in this painfully mortal world, to fancy ourselves immortal?

MRS. FELIX: Insofar as happenings are immortal, so are we.

RON FELIX: We are happenings…. Well by golly Mrs. Felix, that's the most beautiful thing anyone's ever said to me.

Mrs. Felix: Goshdarn, Ron. J. Felix, you're ripening day by day before my eyes, you little rascal!

Ron Felix: Ron J. Felix, III!

(They laugh heartily.)

XV

You couldn't beat. You couldn't beat no matter *how*. You couldn't fluff a marmalade or file a rasp to the size of a chewbert or a snufflywoo or a jigga-diddle. Rapeseed-crab delight was the country fare and the country fare was good eatin'. Why, back in my day, muzzling was already an antiquated societal trait. And not to mention that Beta-sub was encountered much less frequently. That's when the fly just jumps the handle and *whap!* the sizzling barmaid will inevitably slap down the check sometime, someday. The form of floating smoke just soaps the concept of object and stuffs it in the concept of asshole. Your chain and your wheelchair, or whatever it is, is obviously a conspiracy, or a confederacy, of useless clowny-faced Belgians who have certain political viewpoints. The Republic prevail! End to the conspiracy! Long live the King and Queen! (That one was sent in from the Duchy of Luxembourg.)

All they ever talk about when they talk about the *Moyene Âge* is that Felix felixed a felix-full of felix while Felix, felixing a feelixy felix, felixed fairly felixly, felixing all the while in felixish felixizers' feelixings towards Felix, Felix. Well, all this felicitation, felicitous as it is, is nonetheless felicitously felicitized by felicity's Felicitizer General, who felicitously remarked, "Felicity, Felix flanks your phalanx, so why don't *you* pass the pork-n-bean casserole?"

Glup, glup.

XVI

THE runaway vehicle coursed up Broadway like an electric force, an orgasm in the trucking realm, a smash hit. Lenny, drunk on success, had begun to exhibit the celestial eccentricity of a night-errant star.

XVII

Too many sojourns into truth. Too many takers of Halcion line my stoop. The very droopiness of it. Of it and of my ravaged days. Those days. The ones with the electric soup attached. And the diners. Their insides making those squish-noises and the Fracturing Nuts crush noise. That too. That, too many times. Yeah-exactly-really.

The cynical mystic's posture in the sphere of belief was simultaneously sagging and propulsive. Who is to say what is a sag and what is a propulsive event, anyway—huh?

BUNNY: Yeah-exactly-really!

And what is more, a nation of one-eyed Moriarty's are brandishing their skewers in protest of the magi who sang and danced with "the Queen" at our express invitation. Little do the one-eyed Moriarty's know that their flavor-vehicle is also swimming in the soup and getting … uh, electrocuted? Programmed? Which is it again?

BUNNY: Wha-wha-whaddayu wanna wallopim foh? Huh? *(He nearly upsets the mystic's cup of joe.)* Entschuldigung.

Around the corner exists a dim corner at the end of an alley. In this corner exists a content spider clinging to the center of its web.

ANNOUNCER: In—*this*—cor-ner… weighing—three—hundred—and—seventy—five—pounds…: Lar-ry… The… *CRU-SHER*!

(Wild applause mixed with loud catcalls.)

SPIDER: *(bored)* Enh.... It's tolerable.

BUNNY: Wha-wha-wuddya mean, "tolerable"? Es gibt ein schreckliches Ding-a hier!

LARRY: Thanks for piping up with your two bits, toots. Now shove off, or I'll welsh ya.

(The Fairy Queen appears faintly in the sky.)

LARRY: Quick, dinge her! And make it stick, yea?

Enough. What we need is a trident. We can't gather spina-bippitta comedians together unless we've got the iron maiden ready. And then we tell them to mind their P's and Q's and they usually faint. Then the iron maiden gets very hopeful and she makes a big sandwich out of them, but they escape just before she takes one of her famous bytes out of it and there's a big chase scene down Fifth Avenue (Chase Manhattan being just a part of it) which hits us between the soup and the nuts like a jolt of something special hanging on someone ordinary. Let's face it, we're talking about none other than the famous New York City. Yes, friends, both you and yours can quench the unsquelchable as you rollick to and fro among the yellow cabs and kosher pickles and you finally find yourself plunged into a schmear and there's an enormous mouth poised to bite you exactly in half. Quick: what do you do? Slow: why do you do it? Cease to be immoderate, that's for sure, to, uh, get trained, or to improve, or, a....

LARRY: I'll get you, you megabyte of rodent, you stinky compote of annoyance!

(Larry, furiously aroused, flings off his robe and chases Bunny in a circle.)

LARRY AND BUNNY: Why you, Hey, Look, Hey, Er, Yo, Wha, Yer, ...

Could even the achy grin span the swords of Spain, Ringo, and Mandeville all in one-fell-swoop? The *Agnus Dei* recording is old and worn-out sounding. Mind mashing me some grits, would you? Leatherette tafetta cornucopiized the relish into defragmented kernels, fruits, and vegetables. Let's start the bidding at two thousand and the budding at close to unaffordable. If swank women happen to come down the aisles, bandying about their buxomed bodies like so many hot potatoes, well, so much the better.

Fred knows what nobody knows, what nobody knows is appropriate to gathered rationing by the women in faded purple: Mildred, et al. Grant's Meade precipitated a heated argument in which the members of the Castle Hill Social Club burst their goiters while taking turns pedaling a bicycle-style electric generator in the clubroom.

FRED: Those women deserve fate, by golly, and visiting the zoo every Wednesday doesn't cut the mustard. I'm tired of spreading ourselves thin. Socialism has twisted us by the neck several times around and then suddenly released our heads with a "Ping!" and a sinusoidal "Uhhhhhhh…" coming to rest on our Spandex minds.

Charlie's little hands plied across the belly of the little possum. Shortly after the whistle blew, my hand became covered with lentil-shaped warts and a determined young engineer ran up and insisted on using it as a template. That night I was put in a coffin and carried by three men to an unknown destination. I knew it was three men because the back right corner behind my head was always down, *n'est pas*? I think their names were Oscar, Bernie and George. Bernie was a huge carnivorous bird who tortured pigeons for pleasure and chewed tobacco. I had attempted to escape from the box and he had severely pecked me, flapped at me and finally clawed me, shitting on me all the while and shrieking unearthly woodwind noises. An aged Englishwoman swiftly appeared over my lilypad destiny enclave (i.e. my hind legs were on many Parisian menus) and began to ruminate, mold, persist and expire alternately. Forestry emancipated the elves. Silk shone in the sunlight and we knew at once that it was a spider's single strand of web and tears came to our eyes and we wept enormous tears which moistened the ground and caused big fast-growing plants to spring up. Ovid discussed this at length. I think someone in the ensemble got turned into a boar and someone else, a star. It was happening all round—I spent a month as a tumbleweed during an economic downturn. It happened just in time.

Sophia's poetry was ignored by the shoppers in the mall vestibule. She continued anyway:

> "Stardom's breeze mechanics yam,
> Quandry in the bitter sense and
> Lift me, peel me: anyway you want me.
> Sift the shale and a new way of counting,
> you know, could result."

People just kept walking right on by—there was a sale at the deli that smelled like ham, the Jews were incensed and swore to themselves, shrugging or waving their little fists as the case might be. There is a stairway here.

Poochy's silent son, Swishy, markedly deteriorated over the course of several months. Every flea-ridden diseased person would rot and become rotten and pick ulcers all day and wipe bacon grease all over their face and groin area. Their organs became distended and shiny, no matter what gender. This was not a sexy situation. This was, well, morbid. Then George said, "No, not here," and Bernie gave Oscar a little nudge and spat, and they picked me up again and took me to their workshop and my hands were used as backscratchers for the gigantic blacksmiths.

XVI

DRIVING faster and faster, he followed the trail of noxia pudding right into an enormously feathered object (to be known as "Thing № 1"). Gas tricks made me monopolate a slab of frozen pizza which was frizzed into zipping along like jazz-meat, forever about to be propelled by an enormous slingshot into the stellar beyond, but never being propelled. The warped sausage was thrown into its suitcase and forgotten. Waves of noise obliterated a dialogue about somebody, anybody, finally accepting responsibility and doing something about it. They oblit… alogue 'bout ves of noi… about doinggniod dna pons in some anybody about, honey?

Woah there! Jux a minnute pard-en-er. Yooz is crumpil up my scrimmage plan an I gox tuh tellya *Nyoi Yarrum An Is Banda Bandaleers* is aboutuh gowan stagen play sumpin, so shesh yerself.

AUNT HENRIETTA: Why, why…. I've *never never* witnessed such a display in my…. I just cahn't….

(A sound, "BRAGHH", is heard in the background.)

ZORRO: *(in Bermuda shorts)* My plasma signings sting history!

MEDIEVAL MAN: *(who has been waiting offstage this whole time)* Hey, you can't do that! I forbid it!

ZORRO: Oh, is that so?

MEDIEVAL MAN: It just so happens that it is!

AUNT HENRIETTA: Sir, you astonish me! *(She slaps the Medieval Man.)*

SUSIE: *(The Medieval Man's little stepsister)* Outrage!

(She struggles, bearing down, and eventually a lightning bolt comes out of her fingertip, but it turns out to be a cardboard-cutout lightning bolt and so falls to the ground.)

SUSIE: Sorry, stepbrother, guess I goofed.

(Aunt Henrietta's appearance changes so that she appears to be encased in gelatin, like a canned ham.)

ZORRO: On my mark! One… two… three!

(The Aunt's gelatin aura discharges a blue flame which strikes out at the little sister, finally propelled by death into the stellar beyond.)

THE STELLAR BEYOND: Gulp.

Near-reality experiences can sometimes phosphoresce a little like the gelatin flame. In a state of grace, a sapling can spring forth from the source and cause a happening. This trivializes the exact meaning of itself but it, in itself, isn't its own source, at least its own source within itself, but instead of itself who could take its place? The source was a resource nonetheless, and a river ran through Aunties' knickers and she winked at Rover and said "I was good, wasn't I?"

ROVER: Don't call me that in public.

(A barge floats by.)

BARGEMASTER: Land ho! Jellybean, get your skipper! This is business!

JELLYBEAN: Yes sir! Right away sir!

THE PARROT: Awwk! Right away sir! Right away sir! Awwk!

ZORRO: How dare you speak to my slaveboy, Jellybean. You should be fit to be tied!

BARGEMASTER: Ahoy! Lubbers like you have got to participate in a good HMO. That's why I use....

(The barge turns around a corner and vanishes behind a cluster of tropical islands. A wild pig floats out from them on a log, and a pygmy follows on an inflatable lighter-than-air craft, which since it was inflated, was bobbing for apples on the waves.)

EVERYONE BUT ME: Catch him! Yeah, that's it! Almost! C'mon, get 'im! There you go!

ME: Hey, pygmies should stay away from pigs, don't you know that?

JELLYBEAN: *(speaking to Zorro)* Excuse me, sir, but I sense the presence of an impending tragedy. Do you think maybe we should avoid that waterfall up ahead?

ZORRO: You fool! *We're* not the ones on a barge, those people over *there* are.

JELLYBEAN: But, sir....

(The sky suddenly darkens.)

AUNT HENRIETTA: You have to leave here now, all of you! I'm going to have to fire my aspic at that angry cumulus cloud or it will devour me as a tasty morsel of bad karma in concentrated form. Get away, or you'll all be scorched!

(The barge and everything else nearby fall over the falls into the rapids.)

JELLYBEAN: Whooah! Whoooaaah!

THE PARROT: Whoah-whoah! Whoooooooaaaah!!

ZORRO: My whiskers!

MEDIEVAL MAN: Ah-ha-ha-ha! I come out victorious as usual.

THE PRESIDENT OF THE U.S.: Oh no you don't. *(Passes a law outlawing medieval persons from existing. The Medieval Man vanishes.)*

ZORRO: That was a mistake. *(He destroys the modern world with a discharge of plasma. Only he and the Medieval Man remain in a burned-out world of fog with a distant pounding noise.)*

Bum-bum-bumbly-bum. Rum-rum-Rommely wum. If I've told you a thousand times I'd like to increment that round about now.

XVIII

LOST baby. A cool, casual chick. Inflated by merchandise on a very refined path. Tousle those locks, mortgage that split-level. Sweetheart! Welcome to the end of the 20th century! Mind your hat going in. Hat your mind going out. I mind your hat for free, missie, and I don't mind telling you. You know very well I could be eagerly kissing your clitoris if you just remove that enormous Band-Aid. Oh… what is it called again? The squawkitta-poppitta, the, uh.

—The thingy.

Yeah, that.

I'm walking hurriedly down a back alley. There is a garbage can, isn't there? And don't you know it, there is a ventilation unit and a clothesline, long abandoned. I see a typewriter at the end of the alley. It is going *clack clack* all by itself. Am I in danger?

No, Certainly. But to make myself plain… well, let me make myself plain: I don't want your ivy growing all over me, you know? When the self has new kitchen cabinets installed, the psyche starts feeling like it's recently been to the mall.

I begin to look through my pockets for a vanishing point. Before I know it, I am sucked through it and immediately find myself in a precise inversion of the previous situation. A pickle, in other words.

It's up to you, the reader, to help. Write down your solution to the above problems and mail it to the address of your choice. Warning, only do this hypothetically, as tampering with reality may cause an infestation of hamster germs or a glub sound of a McGoo.

I'm in a white sheet. No! Not that!

XVI

(The barge reappears from behind the islands.)

XVII

Bernie: Now!

(They hurl the coffin at the barge, damaging it severely.)

XVIII

ZORRO: Damned plasma-shit. I just can't figure it out.

XVII

BARGEMASTER: Now you're all as if rotten meat. Avast! Avast! Poseidon is cross! Oops!

XIX

THE spatula shaved the lather off the sky and lo! the stars vanished with them. Amniosynthesis telescoped out and formed the sorts of conflagrations which cabbies in Hungary discuss with the local astronomers. A genius chemist misted the ferns in his livingroom and everything stopped. No, really. I mean, like, zero Kelvin. When the whirligigs of batter-dippedness proselytize the motion created with etched, not etched, and lather, the uniqueness of comfort celebrates its 150th anniversary. The small, having attained understanding, spoke unceasingly of the field in their day-to-day life. They had the big picture, even in the smallest room in their house, next to the Leonardo. Next to reciting paragraphs, doing this was their favorite thing:

> ... Jumping up to town!
> Boysenberry lipstick crowned the highest ground!
> Undulation's headrests Soviet, active scrubs!
> Marshall laid invasion by sounding off to sound!
> The sumptuous blast of their invisible instruments

tonicized in all languages (keys) and countries (movements). From this the key movements were derived:

> Blastula and spiderwort!
> Pinkerell and Anacorte!
> Sinky smampy swap-me meets!
> Layers visages mounts create!

The pink hotrod, lustmobile extraordinaire,
succinct Saul pod, dealers in steely underwear,
and all the belles in between!
The Galilean fortess, Hortense-defying spoon,
polished the pickle until the sauerkraut came home.
Leaning-over pizza pie
Propagating X and Y
Piddly whippet stuck to sand
what glass-topped turnips couldn't understand.
Pidgin! Smidgeon! All the iddle vermin!
Yippety-snippety-smippety-srippety-dee!

They had their life organized in a, well, spiritual sort of way (not to aggrandize it) so they didn't mind that it took four weeks for a letter to go across town.

It takes four weeks but we don't care!
We wait for weeks while the salamanders stare!
We grab at magnificence, brush—then we have to
rinse!
(Cook me in your pot.) What a cinch!

Upsound is overbored by scarily big radio telescope ears,

To which we are, as it were, earrings.
Well, its been nice talking with you. Bye.

Bye, come back again.

Sure will.

And now, the whirl, it, sir, I don't mean to be too low re exodus from the area of hostilities, but the ham under the sink is organizing a posse, "The Rope-Burned Apostles With Borscht." They are depicted between the Ginevra and the Cézanne raising their steins way up and toasting Jesus in an unusually boisterous Last Supper and glee-clubbing numbers about how bald-headed individuals always win out in the end and wallow in a glut of sperm.

Little did they realize that Jesus was in the audience that evening and he saw everything, I mean he was motionless. Soon everyone caught on and cheered-on a frozen tin-man-like robot which was straining to reach Gene or Adal with its vise-like hand. A gaggle of the bitch gum-chewed and pro-fannied while a rubber gasket was fitted onto an oily tube attached to an engine. Then a choir of noble young boys Myrtle clad sang a touching hymn to salad in the courtyard of the harem while a Nubian slave was gang-raped and finally eaten alive by starved gorillas, to the delight and deep satisfaction of the invited guests, a select group of Romans and factory owners. In other news, main arteries were shrugged off by uninterested professionals as being "not needed." An informed source speculated that this may signal a major rift in the limits of system S and β sentences, in a sense incessantly equaling a septet-sister. A crazed vehicle sometimes goosed the bass, then felt motivated to appeal coyly in the treble. Leo and Gertrude kicked their legs madly as King Kong prepared to perform juggling feats and Petit rode a bicycle on a wire. It was the world's tallest re-make. An actuary already having been cavorted with, they responded to suspended plethori of satori for a while, and then realized, "My God. Oh, that smell!" Yes, sorry to say, it was Beverley, well, her anal and vaginal regions, anyway. I mean, I'm sure the rest of her smelled quite acceptable, but my God! what a stink! Parmesan-like sharpness of unwiped fecal debris, mixed with a none too subtle urine constituent—simply nauseating. With a rhythmic rapping we bid good bye to the everyday mind. Stay tuned for the nightly business report.

LEO: The socks, Gertrude! Where are the socks?

GERTRUDE: I sold them.

LEO: You did *what*?! *(He points boldly to their bare feet.)* I paid good money for those socks!

GERTRUDE'S CUSTOMER: Yeh, sure, look, Toots, I won't have beaver any more after this.

Soon a woman in jeans came rolling down a hill. The lightning tarts verified the moon's position and Gastro-X tasted better than siffy-suffta mubbulees. Kookamonga notwithstanding, her dentures ceased to stick properly in her mouth. Why a big slab of butter wasn't good enough was heretofore kept under wraps.

Gertrude: God damn it and God damn you.

Leo: You goddam jerk. You come waltzing here and think nothing of buying the socks off our feet! It's scum like you that most often make me sick.

Customer: Oh yeah? Go ahead, Kong, mash 'em with your big thumbs! Like they was butter! Butter!

Kong: Pourquoi?

Zeno the Clam: Parce-que vous êtes un inhabitant de la ville de Berlin comme Monsieur le President de les Êtes Unis, Kennedy.—Oui, je suis qu'il est mort, mais quand vous mangez du beurre, vous devenez un "Big-a-Big-Boiee," n'est pas?

Kong: Oui! Oui!

(A storm breaks. Someone turns on the radio at full blast out a window.)

Kong: Turn that off!

Newscaster on radio: … today when a 2-year-old was "going potty." When the child's mother went to wipe her out, she noticed that the determined youngster had strained so hard that it pushed part of the intestinal wall out her anus. She found rubble in his drawers, and as she fingered his acutely sensitive anal membrane the incestual dam burst like a great rose blossoming at the break of morn, to last only a day, a couple of weeks tops.

Gertrude: Goddammit. I agree with you, Kong.

Zeno the Clam: J'ai l'opinion qua 'il est neccesaire que vous touche l'enfant avec un poisson, parce-que en allemand, le môt pour le môt "poison" est "Gift," et "poison"—sa c'est comme "poisson," n'est pas?

Leo: Fuck off.

Director: Cut!

Kong: Listen, Mike, I don't want to have to hold these two all day.

The war between history and historicity ragen above our ego-bunkers. We ate cereal. A columbine went by, and we were all immediately struck by the idea of the relations of production. I hid a Derrida book in the bathroom. They're all too blind to find anything even like it, even though they own it. Hah! Christopher, on the prow of his ship wearing his usual trench coat, punched me in the nose and sprayed me with skunkflower extract, saying "Kong, this radio sets the tune from now on, and you'll just have to live with it."

(The radio broadcast is replaced with deafening static, which plays unceasingly from then on.)

XX

COKEY smiled. She felt a breeze, and besides, Casper was there. They grinned. Cysts grew on the ground of their picnic like mushrooms. Casper drew a severed baboon's head from his knapsack and smeared it with cole slaw. Time for a new *spatule*, Cokey reflected.

The gentle moon, the cruel glaring moon. Magneto-optical waste products press into the fluffy skull like figural cheddar girdled a sycamore when it had no other choice. Forces vied to stop each other from stopping me from stopping the "coming to a stop" process. We rolled the head down into the valley and poked the flesh of the earth ruthlessly but with undeniable glee. By the end, we all had cheese in our underarms.

Canned Cubism was defenestrated by Pam's brother in New York that time and sewing-bee champions liked it a lot. A lunch which included chickory or lima beans disappointed all of us. "Bologna," the boy sang, "my name is…" went the tune. Holy Moses Joffrey! Kansas to Arkansas one-way thank you please! A yello-maker lit my kitchen window with fire-light, and pooh! the pitiable banshee of a midsummer night who found home base in my laziest thoughts set the turbo-lift on "ouch" and raided the Venetian palazzo of my inclinations. Albeit *my* kitchen windows and *my* lazy thoughts and *my* inclinations couldn't compete out there. But it's rough, you know, out *there*. Look here see what I mean. Here, here friend, here you go…. Tamper without the whimpering usually associated with tax evasion.

A gorilla sidles up to you very fast, and before he can aim for your money belt, you become a sparrow.

Your Friend's Neighborhood's Local Lasagna-Man: Hey! Yoo-hoo! Get your fresh lasagna here! Hey you! Get your nice lasagna! Yummy and fresh!

A long time passes in an arbitrary and an historic and an honorary and a sanctimonious way. The monster drops a little note from her pocket. It reads:

> Come see the Talking Clam!
> Hear it Dance!
> See it Sing!
> —Right this way: LQOOH-METHEQUELONE BOOBS!

The precisely staggering Tagalog tagged-a-long, Edgar from a jar, bit the by now mushy ovoform sandwich, frankly testily since my pincers had censured the very tips of his buttocks. I suddenly *oooooooh!* felt that I was locked naked inside a sort of cupboard. And as I pissed and shat on myself, a woman leant on the door of my cage, masturbating and wearing tight clamps on her nipples with tiny American flags flying from them. A plaque hanging on the wall was entirely composed of the scrapings of hundreds of dozens of dental asylum patients who sneered and jiggered their Primatene mist cannisters into the script of a World War II movie starring a man with guillones. Balsam enriched shampoo! Jellify me honey-o! Annie Oakley and Johnny-Appleseed me to death with a Nazi-Mafia's Hell's-Angels dubious devil doubter! Swastikized nebulizer! Preemee telepathy! Twins! Triplets! Quadruplets! Ahhhhhhhhhhh!

I employ a score of people to excoriate me, and a row of sailors to enter into fisticuffs in dockside taverns. But I can't afford to starch my shirts. Milady, strip off thy brocade. It's time for the arm and sickle to be dangling. I knocked helplessly in sticky privacy. An engine on a wooden rail marked off regular beats with a mahogany implement. A mahogany engine. And it was the mahogany of Mahatma Gandhi Milady wanted on every Monday. Jaundiced pimpernel foxed me a grape. Lefty fried me a cuneiform crêpe. Turtley Moscowitz, pear-shaped prize. Cognizant participants, tripartites in disguise. Olé! I glanced down at a soft peanut and awoke with a start. "Dunken-Doig! It's six-thirty! Why aren't you dressed already?" "Already? What's 'already'?"

Planets of green parents with Vox-box centennial-edition mortar dischargers get out of my way. As I came walking along nya-nya-nya fung asshole motherdip Aesop gibletizer yoinziferous prang dabblets. My big plate, how mucky you're getting. "We'll be wiping that right off, Grandma," they chime, and a *pop!* hit the Cheerios at right around the same time. Ruth-Ann was in the Bahamas for the day, selling her patented lotion to dawdling men in big goofy pants. She used to sell it to them in a dress, but when she wore anything goofy or big the cheerleaders would all disrobe and rub their firm youthful thighs on your aching tendril and the scented oil and the Crest toothpaste smell and... well... it was just more professional.

Low-key pile-ups melt like cheese in the afterglow of the proud blushing company men indulge after a nice, clean ass-assignation.

LORDIS: Quench my sapphire! Times boy, c'mere. Salt! Salt!

My French teacher was implanted in vivo to a not-so-happy-afterwards Mom who later took up the habit trail for her life.

MOTHER: My baby died in Colorado—is that enough of an emergency for you?

(The audience cheers.)

MODERATOR: How does the panel vote?

CHER: 9 *[her highest vote of the evening]*

Soupy Sales coughed several times and seemed to go red in the light of the erupting volcano in the distance. Several fish-people started waddling on their tails. A medicine man! Oh look! And a chieftain! A chieftain! Let's get him to look this way. Hey! Unga-Bunga over there! What's up!? Where did you get those lovely tusk nose-rings, or did you make them yourself? That certainly is a very fine garment you have on down there. Look, Marvin, it's native fabrics. Delicious! Oh, and look! The medicine man brought out his assortment of magic elixirs! Oh, isn't that cute?

Hush up now darling, don't you cry. Pass the bottle until (you're) out of joint. Yankowitz! Czehr! Hubble! Mixture! Mixture! Mixture time and oh and everything. And we and all of us and oh everything! With brackets and whipping cream! Yeah, baby! I got the feeling today, and Lord! Hallelujah! The Lion of Moses hath bit on a big nasty bone until his Imperial Majesty hath whoop his big yeller behind!

My grandometer detected a prestidigitator frying in the kitchen and a redneck mother of two came snooping on the patio and the sill, and the threshold over which she was carried as a newlywed enhanced my short term experience for Tiberiu and Geza and Barnes and Jegenathan. My cut oozed goopula and, effluvial as it seemed, it jabbed a wok until Happy-Boy came. A special cake was delivered by a horse-drawn buggy that comes up the long driveway real slow, and you get this tickly sensation, and *yeux, coup d'oeil*, yucca-ed your little Earl and you're a little early, considering how all the stars know each other and get along and the centipede which crawled out of the monkey's head was a bastard. Everyone on the ground knew this. They glanced up at it. Someone finally noticed something. From the past. A landscape. A meadow. Someone else. The face is hidden. On a subway. In a station. The crowding. Hunched together. Huddling. A big shadow comes down.

CONDUCTOR: Hey mister! You awake? You missed your stop back there! Get off at Metro Park and take the next train back.

(The passenger's head falls off and blood gushes forth prodigiously from the hole.)

AN ART CRITIC: Hey! Help! Some guy over here just croaked!

(A crowd of people come surging into the car from both sides.)

MAN: Wait a minute! This is a bad thing!

GIRL: No it's not, here—look.

(The girl pulls down her underpants and rubs her genitals in the pool of blood on the floor.)

MAN: Oh yeah. You're right.

ART CRITIC: How quaint! It's right out of Bataille! I was telling Omar just this morning as he was putting the cortisone ointment on my thighs....

OMAR: Please! Not in front of the children!

(They cackle furiously. A bound-and-gagged fourth grader is brought over the ice by husky-drawn bobsled.)

GIRL: You mean "dogsled."

4TH GRADER: Will you shut up? This may look like fun, but it hurts.

(The art critic dreams a dream in which he is kissing a very young child on the mouth. The youngster responds eagerly with his tongue and the scene starts to go out of focus.)

CONDUCTOR: Hey yous guys! This man is all decapitated here! Will you quit yankin' off and do something? *(He sees a mouse.)* Eek! A mouse!

ART CRITIC: No, I'm an art critic of some note.

CONDUCTOR: Not you, that thing right next to you!

ART CRITIC: What, over here? That's Omar!

Conductor: Not him, you idiot! Don't you see the bloody rodent? It's virtually clawing at your virtual neck, you sodding pair of fire-tongs!

Omar: He's right you know.

Art Critic: *(looks down to his neck)* Oh God! I'm a gonner! Please! Get it off me! I promise I'll never praise (Julian) Schnabel again!

Omar: Well, it's been nice seeing you. This is my stop. Excusez moi, Señorita. Hasta la Winnebego!

(The 4th grader begins to squeal.)

XXI

Mississippi delta mud on the tailsight of my yesterdays Frito lays along our mucky domain. Bring me my communist doughnut while I chase Presley. Ringed hammy bivalve, you and only you stir the gravy of my mind smoothly enough. Forage for scraps, yea, do it to me.

Armed with a strong glass, I peer into the drunken soul of the galaxy—the part right after where mathematics begins to make no sense. With a special pipe, I subject myself to a wormhole phenomenon in which a scorching breeze hoists me in my own leotards and finishes the story.

Many weeks go by. Scanty con artists forego reality for Braunschweiger. Fastener-factory workers would stare at the products they assembled for hours at a time and this is why economists and lawyers all agree: nothing beats the taste of pure boner. Not "x" where "x" is such that "k" is that "k" which is equal to "x," where "x" is an element of the set of all which is "x" … just ask Felix.

Man of doubt, behold the Creator! It is I, your Lord and King. Kneel thee before me lest I strike you down! My plans, be a servant, go not in want, but forever bow in need! Many do. Peoned law breakers, Ellis Island lore ankles, heels, ebb for me! Beasties like you own me. Phisbia's urges oughtn't inwit butt freaks' wowing speed. Leave your relatives' prayers to St. Bathroom who says things like "Toilet toilet toilet toilet toilet" to top spokesmen of the committee. To a lesser degree, an angry God would've flung you around like a doodle and plucked your sins painfully out of you, feather by bloody feather. Toiletry, be analogous. Furtive fungatoids' wackadoo Naugatuck piercings shame Paulo of Urveda-biblical Weather Channel fame.

Rocky-in-a-tutu smacked me right in the face and my hiccoughs produced blood. I soon realized that this was what they call "internal hemorrhaging." We paused here to discuss nuts, and that's why falafel has such spirit, and also why celery has that rich texture that it has. And if we plant in the cruelest, it begins to shed a light down that there big hole, that profound mama, whoah! and, putting some leaf in our cheeks to give ourselves strength, we set out into the bush. A couple inches later she moans, Eureka! It's the paydirt, the big Kahana. The moola-moola Nooka-nooka of another Caesarean in-breed, another Hotfoot, another Beef Wellington.

> The starchy robot, the thankless heel,
> situations rich in nebulae of volatile gas,
> plaster casts of historical criminals:
> in my box they go,
> the mushy refuse but they go in anyway.
> Anointed biscuit with a halfside of retrobits.
> And thank you, please.
> You're my release,
> another twosome clenching buttcheeks.
> Parsnip salvation foams on the crevice.

HANK: Me and the boys oughta organize the dockworkers.

CYNTHIA: You stay here while I go join the women.

MOE: Err, ya got the time there, Mack?

BUZZ: Rev er up, mate.

Splits across the gymnasium floor was what the young girls did. Happy they made the crowd, jealous all the boys had made them was what it was. Above loomed ahead, and it was a bearded head—is it spitting, is that what it is? (Squint.) Then the pipe is lit even before the match is struck (Dr. Sacks) and Nietzsche is photographed posing with a bust of Hitler (Kaufman). (Detergents and other articles.) (Fluorescent.)

Polyethylene sorghum minces my Episcopalian mine-disaster survivors irreverently with regard to Captain Snorlbury and the shaft diggers of Nukle-Naste. A trial canary inhaled pure plastic and developed sore gums which he treated with an herbal mixture and cod liver oil. The truth of consciousness being cosmology, the mind is a star. To live without reverence for the avant-garde and the divine intelligence snorkling somewhere hereabouts under all the crud and the nuclear waste, God's awakening your intellect causes a waste of nuclear crud. I was going to suggest that if you ever get a car, maybe it should be a Citroën. We go over some kind of bump or stubble and veer into something empty. What could be more exciting? Eating dip foods like cornchips and vegetable sticks naked on the beach in Hawaii in the moonlight? Come on, you know you can't get there from here.

Latin quarter discotheques of the mid 70s combine to create an environmental element not unlike several bats caught under a silk drape. Everyone was amazed by the coincidence, laughed, and cried "Popo! Popo!" The priest on the bandstand struck up a real classy number. His microphone fed thousands of starving Babylonians and gave pausing rocketeers the opportunity to paw rockettes. They would, you know, remove their skimpy tops and knead their exuberant nipples till they gave milk. How did the microphone give them all this, you wonder. It wasn't what it did, it was how it did it. Did it do it in a way in which "Go Daddy go" was the most often spoken phrase in the average bandito nursery? Gulch fillers muscled out their Vietcong substitutes by laying the microphone thing on them.

XXII

A DESCENDING sort of rubber chiffon settled on unfinished conversations. A spittoon sat quietly in the corner of Mamie's saloon, awaiting the renascence of the ultra-decisive spit-acts of yore. A kingly choice chose the richest yore flaked to my Momar, dusk equivocating "Jaloosie" with "miteinander." That was Julie Andrews singing, wasn't it?

SOMEONE: I don't want to know.

The brusque silence changed faster than the speed of sound, and a blanket of snow clung to the horse-dung like a child to its Madonna album. Perlemuter, forever futzing with his dentures, always forgetting to chew before swallowing, never asking about laws of uncertainty or the spectrum of cosmic rays in the room, killing off his followers one by one in the cool caustic bath of light which electronic amphibians couldn't be programmed to evade, had obviously turned into a monstrous lizard with big pointy teeth arranged into a crooked and unconvincing smile. His martini spilled over the face of a felled fanatic whose boiled head was then diced and sold as imitation crab meat. Garlic and doughnuts and quarts of cola or chrysocolla or quartz all were, the gang, my herd, my destiny; the universe.

SCHWSFP SMITH: Ip-fff, urr gar mok n'pfgzzh ogfp msf-k-ta?

CHORUS:

> Hm-fff, msf-k-ta! Par reductio "pontiff,"
> Issy key inky star bolux!
> Poncho! Launcho!
> Pink the little missie!

BARTHOLEMEW: *(jacket slung over shoulder, sings)* The tax! the tax!

BARGEMASTER: What about the tacks?

CHORUS: Goozhy mupple fuss twist, septerbator ughgh!

ADOLPHO: *(now a member of the "Nazhy Party")* Cut the crap. What is this shit about "Nazhy" shit. Fuck off. You suck even as an asshole sucks, but the asshole has an advantage: it only sucks in shit, whereas you suck youself.

Spend some time in a quiet, dark room and think this thing through, though that thought rubs Dario's quirky nougat to the quick. Dario. Alexandre. What are you all doing here. I'm supposed to be taking a bath, but I'm getting dryer and dryer. I was supposed to get washer and dryer but now I even got toaster and dryer and fridge and dryer and all kinds of dryer. God bless us, every one. Even Dryer's light obeys his sodding decrees—something about lawns. I don't fully understand it myself.

The taste of margarine grew that much stronger. Noises of sheep could be heard between the sounds of Uncle Billy planting the purple bulbs into (good ol') Mother Earth. "Back then, they'll be just right, them yams!" he cried, swivelling his hips as he wielded the steely plough. "Bah bah," observed a rather forward individual, who happened to be a sheep, "those humans ought to get their acts together, wool can't understand it. They have fleece to their names, mutton, and bingo jalopy." And the sheep beat their little hoofies on little imaginary fag ends with annoyance. Just then, a hush fell on the crowd at Mamie's as the silhouette of an enormous pair of antlers appeared above the swinging doors in the space below the door frame (see illustration). Then the doors parted, and lo! Big Daddy Elk strode boldly into the saloon.

BARGEMASTER: You ain't wanted in these parts, Meester.

SALOON: Arrr! Rrrr! Gerr-ahrrr!

BABY PUPPY: Goo-waa! Goo-waa!

(Big Daddy Elk sweeps the space with one of his front legs and everyone and everything else, excluding him, is made to be done away with. Yeah.)

B.D. ELK: Finally, my own studio in the Village, all to myself!

BARGEMASTER: *(entering from the kitchen with a loaded cookie-gun)* Not exactly. We're all in the kitchen with the batter.

B.D. ELK: Get back in there!

A man with a polished stick is stirred and then baked into what bridge club ladies gently place into their mouths. Their dentures exactly matched those of their idol, "The Pearl," whose pearl-like dentures were often compared to pearls white as pearl-white dentures which looked like pearl, pearly like the pearly dentures from heaven and hell. The burnished pieces of cheese people carried for luck notwithstanding, many were mashed without further ado into clay. An Italian damsel who went to visit the Quakers was surprised to find that the cheese-present she got would not spoil. At least not as long as Spot-the-dog could wag his little tail or Eldridge-the-beaver could pretend to like monkfish. A simpering clergyman handed out carpet samples to revolting snot-nosed boys who tortured sparrows to death while I watched to make sure they were distributed fairly. They weren't, exactly, one boy got two carpet samples whie this other one got none. Nunn could ready all phasers on the target of villainy just as well as Christie Brinkley chews plastic scraps until they're malleable. Her cookie-head's risible dough flew apart into over-sweet scraps, spotting the Danish furniture.

Andrew Lloyd Webber couldn't have said it better. The ball of dust which a caterpillar might have stuck to its fur could just as well be a usurper of humanity, the dusty foe, the Devil.

I glued the plastic ship together and watched war on TV. By depressing a certain button, I united an international flight to a certain death. My pulse was recorded as increasing to 54—that's 2 more than when I didn't watch TV. My metronome stopped a long time ago, see, and, like, I see my life flash in front of my eyes at least once or twice a day now. If I didn't install a compressor between my thorax and my larynx, or soak my battery of compressed dung in hospital fluids, my career as a Heldentenor would be abridged, that's for sure.

The Rust Song

BABY PUPPY AND BARGEMASTER: Pick a cracker, eat a cracker.
BARTHOLEMEW: Bilge and bilge and bilge and bilge.
BABY PUPPY AND BARGEMASTER: Mayhem in a crater. Crackle little ate her.
BARTHOLEMEW: And gametes in a bathing soot were smelling salts.

CHORUS: The frog-sounds begin.

(A pod opens, and a pair of overalls walks out all on its own. Green scenery collapses, and a problem with the lights unites the cast in celestial harmony.)

OVERALLS:

The bitten barbeque of bilge ignites the *coeur*
Of thankless inhibition, saucily immersed
In a rancid dust cloud the pizzabakers copulate.

Lady Capulet: Anon. The Hostess cupcakes were on sale this week, only $1.29. What a value!

If it weren't for the freezer burn, you see, our little friend here would have been able to lick the ice-cream-covered projection in a more graceful way. As Allah wills. A bobby socks her.

Lady Capulet: Shame! Pig!

Policewoman: By my furry cap, you're the foulest aristrocrat this here enthusiast-esse for order has yet encountered!

Female Lady Capulet: I take that as a direct insult.

Jane Boyle: Well you're payin' for it, baby.

Lady Capulet: Now I know why I shave my legs….

Bobby: Will you hurry up, I'm not going to risk my car in this weather.

(It begins to snow.)

Bargemaster: Thrust it all aside!

XXIII

THRUSTING it aside, clearing the soiled bowls in a state of considerable nausea. Banishing tics from the focus, looking under the furniture for the Cross pen and steadfastly ignoring all the Easter eggs. Because of this I was never able to find out whatever would have become of Aunty Mabel.

Sickley stars with irritating cramps crowded the square. They brought me into a central arena and hoisted me up. "So, you didn't find those Easter eggs, eh, well here's looking at you," they said, and proceeded to spit on my patent leather shoes. They found that the spit sizzled on the surface, and realized at once that the shoes and I had great commercial potential. Between the hours of six and one-thirty, eggs and potatoes were prepared; after a short "cool-off" period, the foodstuffs were hurled relentlessly at the enemy.

ENEMY: Polly! Hey!

A rich Iberian with a bagful of lancettes caused quite a skirmish among ukelele-playing civil detonators, I'm sorry to say. He perished you know, after, he being perishable to the extent that it did no good at all for him to justify his paragraphs to us. He made his enormous jugs of iced tea on the large porches of virtually every significant structure in town. Then Stavrogin returned to start his girls' academy, and it was all over. Tea poured up and down lanes, and naked women, ages 16–34, ran through them bleeding from wounds inflicted by explosions of broken glass. (Actually, legend has it that women had had these wounds since the beginning of time, but it was glass which actually caused them.)

J.F. Mamjjasond: Yes, it's all quite plain, right here in this book, see, and well it's just a matter of studying the fax.

That's the special bland quality we prize. A Jamaican tried to sell me "blonde hash" and pretended to speak on the phone with some very stringent dudes, but I just turned John Denver up even higher. Some ashen Clemente, a wisecracker filled to simulation, replicated like the jargon of a freedom-train pilot maxed to overflowing in scarce scherzoesque navigator plateau modules. Simians, simians everywhere. And the toads. And the shining cords popular in circles at the fringe of societies were conceived of as melismas and arabesques more than as necklaces and bracelets: they was movin'. And it was done on a three-er. A dime, a waltz, an ex-penny-ential to the turd power. You slay me, killer, come on me and eat me out, ya' darlin' hunny! Twist my saliva around in your mouth and suck my mash in jealous starving bravery in the desert of your love!

—Well, sonny, I been readin' this book *Discharges* and I been having this here cigar, out here'n'tha porch, like-a said, bua wha-a juz caant believe is juh … well, that such nice people would've.

Wave the open ivy over raptors' knolls and bushy glens and, hey, over there, is that Mt. Rainier or my Momma's scrap pile of ivory and dental amalgam and dented kitchen faucets and damaged Percocets and all that? Is all that that, all or both? All three situated themselves in a triangle, as shown in Figure One.

—Here's what happened. The hairpin on the right….

Sportscaster: Hey, Mike, that's my line. I, and nobody but me, give … gives? … gives the spores rapport! The hairpin on the right, it gives…

—was dropped into the briefs Auntie Noël filed, and…

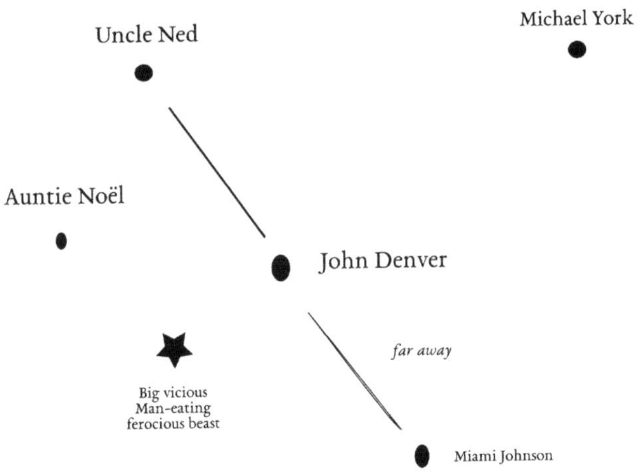

Figure One

SPORTSCASTER: … wadraptitata briefs atinoefilo…

Pork on the right munched fat right about now and Lo Mein anglophiles slanted minotaur lobotomies into 45° lemur agronomists. Occidental death intrigued the impressionable Portuguese on the veranda. Relish wasn't only tasted but was inoculated by vermin doctors at Maibock festivals in München. A Viking vessel was swollen with men and their slimy fish and it set out across Oceanus Pigtails-with-Tits, and Eric the Red spat and bled on Ole Amerikee way yonder and lived to till the tail.

Shrinking: really my masseuse would never have emasculated our neighbors' 18 month old except for the fact that Lebenthal and Moskerinian and Rotweiler camouflaged my soap so as to blend in with the enormous swarm of turtles crawling and slithering and squirming itself all over the island.

BARGEMASTER: Jellybean! Take the rowboat from here and scout around for a good spot to make a landing! … and Popsicle! gather our rations for a one-week stay ashore!

Popsicle and Jellybean: Right away, sir!!

(Victorian London. A foggy night on the Thames. Dr. Watson droops over the pier and allows his long, hairy phallus to dangle in the foul, brackish water. The owner of a dwarf orange tree donned kidskin over his restless, eager fingers and came down slappeta-slappeta on the good Doctor's exposed globes of hindward tushies while a freshman physicist studied momentum with his testicular instrument. Palladian Man was rediscovered recurrently every 15,000 years or so. But the time frame was so short. So many lives and thoughts and yearnings, and look at the result! A mishmash of scummy salesmen and entertainers and politicians. Lives tossed aside like the jokers from a deck of playing cards. White women raped by beasts.)

Bargemaster: Here we are. The perfect time and place to buy a complete suit for a beagle!

Jellybean: Sir? I believe we're actually no where near the Pacific islands. It looks more like the Thames to me!

Bargemaster: Very good, lad! Here's your treat!

(He throws Jellybean a handful of the rounded colorful candies which bear his name.)

Doctor Watson: Ewgh! Hehwgh-ughihehwgh. I say.

(Dr. Watson lifts his long, loose tube out of the river. It exudes a slimy fluid pus.)

Bargemaster: Why Doctor! I'm delighted to find you at home.

Dr. Watson: Jellybean, isn't it about time for your complete physical? Why, I should be glad to perform the examination free of charge.

Jellybean: No, sir!

Popsicle: Me, neither!

Dr. Watson: I say! *(He coils up his snaky member, tucks it into his ass, and walks away.)*

Elsewhere, an ever so silent song was the smoothest, and a small yellow rowboat swam through winding rivers of chocolate. An inhalator was fused to a monkey's skull, and the sounds it made reverberated through the forest and the potted ferns. It was clear that plate tectonics had taken their toll: $1.60 at Exit 11B. It left me in the bitterest mood, and for the first time I felt flaked beyond the point at which the routes not taken start seeming more like roots pot-planted.

But here the song was not ashamed to show off its tendrils in the concrete Parisian pissoir the poet immortalized when he said, "I predict an enormous adding machine's concussive impact on the history of what goes on when you're alone in the shed with Wilbur and all the little Herrn and herrings and herons. Scalene Mickeys with the quiet edge located my festering mucosa. The ramparts rang with jealous jumbo exuberators rearranged in their heads. Lugged around by pusillanimous marked snots, verily the traitor would trade sympathy for apathy and profit in the bargain. A bulbous freckle stood up and abjected. The church ceiling was taffy-pulled by a giant marmalade-eating pumpkin with a hand with fingers that saw action. A cliff glistened with pre-cum, while an English butler laid out enormous misshapen silverware and a distended big-busomed contralto had her tits sharpened on a lathe. One more *uh-uh-uh* to condense into Rhône-Poulenc-like zephyrs which zizz along past the girls with long ponytail braids. When I crawled beneath the dress and smelled that acrid urine smell I could never think about her in just the same way. Ginny. Oh, Ginny. Your smell alarmed me to the point of complete repulsion. Brute, Brute, see fuck west of far! Kill my sodomy pantaloons too—like cervical lasagna, disappear! Poet-laureate types in vests and their parents filed into the auditorium. Triple-up on Lipschitz for the indispensible best of the best. When I saw France's attempt to dodge the minor treble filament hanging off my backside, I decided I would burn the bodies of babies in a field and stab pregnant women in the abdomen with white-hot pokers (sharpened).

> "I sing of fiddles and a lance, tra-dee!
> That bore a strange likeness to Rommel's scarred
>   knee.
> We sat on our tushies like eaglets in nurseries
> but no one could sequence or midi dear me!
>
> Doo-la-la! Doo-la-la!
> Mer-ci-na-ry!"

J.F. Mamjjasond: Very good! Brilliant!

XXIV

I CLOSE my eyes on the dusty plains where complaining freakish midgets griped about every little goddamned thing. Rapidly to thee did I crack through the crusty burnt skin of the helpless lifeless bodies exposed to my incisive wit. A diner appeared before me. Bold as always, I strove to choose, and victorious I ordered a hamburger.

ME: *(dressed as King Arthur)* Just a burger… and some fries.

WAITRESS: *(sneering)* Okay, a hamburger, for chris' sakes! And what? Fries? You fucking motherless son of a bitch/bastard shiteating cunt!

(She takes out an axe and bludgeons me severely and then smashes my head again and again with the blunt side of a meat cleaver.)

ME: Ahh! UGGCHCH! Stop! *[Gasp!]* GHHHHGGHG! Ahh! FPFFPFPFZSG! Kazinngst! [*Gasp*! $*$ 2]/ $\sqrt[\text{“Ugh!”}]{\text{“Ghhh!”} + \text{“Ughoo!”}}$ – “Why Mildred, I thought you were still in Toledo.”

Then I'm not going to pay, no sirree. You don't deserve to polish my varnishkas or varnish my vanishing act, my great weighty pull out!

WAITRESS: No! Not the pull-out!

ME: *The Pull-Out*!

BONJEE: Shown Ma-am ma vuhginuh an' Mar' Poppins bumpk'neque virtual munga-uh an un an ah furnicated, usin' vermiculite o'course....

McGEE: I'm not supposed to be here! I was never intended to be a speaking character! And besides, I'm in the wrong chapter, stupid!

JETHRO: Wasn't 1066 the Baddle of Pudding-Show? All over the yard the joisters and jesters, horsies and tricycles, all fall down. He's a pansy in his pocket! What an handsome rocket that'll make, crash! And the pigeons-feeding professing pipes in their baggy trousers, economics texts, horn rims, musing awhile under their typical trees. Ah was at Hahvahd in '93.

CORPORAL SMITH: Ten hut! Go! Go! Go! Go! Go! Go! Go! Go! Go! Go! Go! Go! Go! Go! Go! Go!

ME: Get out! *OOOUUT!* Now!

WAITRESS: I love you! Fuck me. Put-it-all-the-way-in!

ME: I'm baffled, really. Such a Celenese yoghurt instructor could be an enabler to my cathode-ray-tube-ostomy of 12/81 which evoked the medium-sized spirit of a long-dead news man hot on the trail of a flambé or that "Richard" guy.

JETHRO: Since when have you been so hasty? Thimble over my fallout of joiners joining two-backed, three-backed, *x*-backed where *x* is unstable. If you get to know him he's a darling, absolutely fissionable-cuddly!

The waistband of the flight instructor came off and Benjamin Harrison was included in the space available. My corporate giant of a wife has such a bright smile that I had her buy the toothpaste company. Rotterdam was home to the caramel-filled tuna-like people. Forget the Hague, Amsterdam, Waterloo and any of those Belgo-Dano-Dutcho places which defer to Rotterdam on every occasion. The QEII won't be invented for years.

Details, details. Detox, detox. Ran up the clock. Varnishing act. Gone.

Mr. Jeffries: *(nicely)* This midmorning's just fine for uprooting weeds.

A Flock of Seagulls: Hey, look over there! That man is holding up a nice juicy worm!

(They dive down to get the worm so as to eat it.)

Mr. Jeffries: *(nicely)* Wait, guys. I'm your friend! I … Ahhhh!

With the tool, man lost his body. Can you get to that, babes? Never wear rhinestones in the microwave! (Total wipeout, dude.)

Tired Man: Wait, wait, wait, wait a minute, wait….

Boy: Hey c'mon please? C'mon, hey—c'mon….

(A snail crawls up.)

Snail Itzinger: Sie haben heiligen Augen! Unter Wasser ist ein Platz, wo Sie Ihre Nase mit den Augen finden. Ich habe machen es gemacht. Du hast es zu machen gemacht. Er hat essen zu müde gemacht. Wir….

(The tired man stomps on the snail in desperation.)

Zu müde! Zu müde! Meine Mutter—sie ist mit meine Bruder, unter—er hat ein Luger, und es gibt mir ein Schlagzeug in dem Kopf ay-yie-yie!!

Boy: *(shrugging and going off by himself, sings)* That's the universal freak coursing through my cosmic vein; that's the zizzy "ooh-la-la" upending lots of pots and pains.

Me ✻ the colon 𝄞 destiny play gout in # of rysomes distilled by a cunting practice in ✯ great suburban homes of $\frac{3}{4}$ America worthy $\int_{Id}^{Superego}$(The chores of Mafian Raphaels)^{Raphaels}.

The neighbors' breasts were all so large one had to wonder what they paid for a one-way ticket to Tokyo. The express had ceased to publish a timetable. Wayne, a conductor, roamed through the station, pausing to marvel at figures wax and waxing, urging architectural details—gargoyles and buttresses—to be squeezed in a digital framework. Simethicone alleviated my distress while a smileroo with a stack of Gorky flaked psoriasis to the term of my vernal extinction on the west wing of term-reconciliation over the auberge of my frollicky dream. Not unlike a colicky baby. A simulated leather finished the rosy boobs with a flourish, and promptly thereafter cheerful service was provided (tea and pancakes for two) throughout Big Mama's sub-lawn pregnancy where the fig-apricots grow, la-la. Now listen up. See Missie over there? Her nipples go erect everytime the trained parrot flies by with a feather in its beak and tickles her. Sometimes she can be seen covering her pubic area with cream and letting a puppy lick it off. "Purified" suddenly became "putrified" by the addition of a "t."

You wake up and you're dreaming your head off. You are a monk and have few pleasures. Then it's lunch. Follow me into the kitchen for a hot bowl of müsli and then we'll simultaneously crush grapes for wine and rub each other under our frocks. Good sport! Luckily our breviaries were in our briefs, because just then the Reverend Father stumbled upon us. "Good gracious, what do we have here?" he emitted. An eager flush to his cheeks was transmitted, after an iterative pump-priming, into our prayerful succor, and then we all took turns reading from scripture. Coulomb's law wasn't on that evening, mostly due to the fact that Coulomb hadn't yet been born. But they won the lottery, I won it, and my savior is the one whom I thank. He always left the flavor of rice pudding in my mouth after he was finished. But then the 9:04 would always be passing through and making me involuntarily swallow. That I am who I that I-am thanks for being like so solid, you know? Like *this (smash hands together)*. The bloodhound, the innocent. The P.B.A. decal for your Olds. It's symbolic, man!

(A printout flies from the machine.)

Machine: Ahh! At last, my monstrous doughnut causes each employee at this company to shake! Oh Julius! Paladine! Carthagia! Behold my solemn and lonely power which separates my sub-coccygial region (and makes it break in two)!

The Good Father: Shut up, just give me the paper and keep quiet.

Machine: Oh yeah? You want my paper? So what's stopping you? Take it! And that… and that… and that!

(More paper flies out of the machine.)

XXV

REYE Syndrome's most foul cowering cowl was the *Regnis Dei* of my enchanting evening-out with someone's mother. Luckily, her son came along to sing cheerful songs in glorification of Beatitude Insurance, Inc.

THE GOOD FATHER: Our Holy Life Insurance is actually quite a policy. For only $149.99, based on a male aged 25 years nonsmoker, you can be assured that when God calls thee home, you can get there in a Rolls Royce. Or a Jaguar, or any other of our fine British cars, driven by a personal chauffeur of your very own to the elegant chateau of Mlle. Parker, a dangerous-looking siren who once shocked all Heaven by dangling a live electric wire into the pool while everyone was in it swimming. Once there, you are greeted by a long list of successful men from the past, including Ungg-Ukka, Mukku, Chă-K!ach, Ronald Reagan, and Mooku-Oo. Each visitor must present the honored guest with one or more of their own gametes. The prestigious ghosts will demonstrate that everyone's gonads were all part of a larger entity called, for lack of a better name, "Big Gonad" or "Old Ma(n) Gonad."

After a spectacular gala lunch, attended and co-hosted by God himself, you will be swept on a fun-packed fabulous adventure where you get on a roller-coaster naked and let everything hang out. Since it's Heaven, you completely get away with a sodomistic act committed with an unsuspecting stranger on the ski lift. When you arrive at the peak, you're all alone, the higher, the more sodomistic. People arrive, congratulating me and giving me the courage to continue. With my red badge firmly implanted in my sarcosyl pigmentosa-type mucosa, I deliver insults to Satan, congranulations with a pinch of salt and maybe a little Tabasco. Well, I had too much to drink… wait a minute, we're supposed to be talking about you. Stop fidgeting with your own shit and get on the ball here. Aah! *(slips.)*

XXIV

The Good Father: My God, what's on this sheet of paper?

(reads:)

XXV

… as you pass the neighborhood K-Mart-O-Heaven, you will not be able to resist buying a few pieces of Tupperware. Then, upon arrival in the Hang-Out Of the Gods, you will be provided with a certificate good for $70 a week spending money, a beige robe (100% cotton extra), and a fold-away bed in one of the 8×10^{32} dormitories on the premises.

XXIV

THE GOOD FATHER: Oh my God, no! Oh, please, no!! Ahhh! *(slips.)*

XXV

ONE day you meet a member of the underground at a disco and smoke dope with him in an alley. "You've been a sap all your life, otherwise you wouldn't be here. Now that you have tenure, you can let loose and spritz anyone you please."

ME: You mean, like, watersports?

Of course, stupid. Wha'd'ja think?

MEMBER: Sure, go ahead....

Afterwards you organize a petition drive as he fucks you doggy style. A gangland killing is scheduled right after the clambake, so hurry up! Get into those clothes! Stop toying with your red slot and put those panties on. Ahhh! *(slips.)*

(Brushes itself off, straightens its tie, and continues.) You sit in your cubicle every night at 7:45 P.M. and never get visited. Finally, you are visited.

GOD: Hellooo!

ME: Beat it! Scram!

GOD: Many are called; few chosen.

ME: Yeah, well I awready been chosen, so now you can go fuck yourself! ...awready.

GOD: What?! What do I hear?!

(Lightning and thunder begin.)

ME: Better go before you get soaked, old geezer!

GOD: I don't need to put up with this! Frog!

FROG: Yessir, *ribbéd!*

GOD: Stop calling me that in front of the children! Now, I want you to hop all around Heaven, see, and be on the lookout for suspicious characters like this one, see?

FROG: Sure thing, sweetums!

GOD: You stop that, now!

MEDIEVAL DIETY: *(to Frog)* Remember back when the Earth was young and you loved me for my two "Rr"s.... Oh, those were the days.

GOD: Get out of my sight! *(Zaps M.D.)*

ZORRO: Hey! How dare you zap my friend!?

BUNNY: You hurt-a my fren', an' I slappa you inna face! Y'uhnunstan'?

ME: You all suck! You don't scare me! Boo! *(A cab pulls up.)* Take me back to the hotel!

SAM THE CRAB: Get in the fucking cab, motherfucker!

(Masked men abduct me in the cab.)

FROG: Been nice, ha.

EVERYONE BUT ME: Get in! Go ahead! G'won! Get atta heuh!

ME: Hey! What's going on? What! Ahhhhh! *(slips.)*

XXVI

FALL to great heights.

XXVII

Aw, come off it and swim in the broad stream,
plunging river that wraps parched earth in knots.
My petite chou-chou celebré dispose me to thee,
passing social ebbs for rapid transfer of the eggs of
my mind.
And Soldar, the feeble mossy elm,
labels me and thus I pass to the place asunder.

Coco Chanel gave me a red costume and a pitchfork. An anorexic conception of flesh for $1.19 a pound. Pastel-clad officials posed, puzzled. A nearby rat spat and exclaimed, "These filthy times play across my sewer system like icons of ragged minds. Pharaohs mined for their travertine content. But it was a waste of time." A bird fell dead from the leaden sky and crashed right through 23 floors of a prominent nose-shaped skyscraper and injured 3. In another PGA moment, the chi-chi guy did another little dance. A pro-mint ent hit a Lifesaver from my hands just as I was about to have it. I thought twice. Brandy and Monique put down the silverware while Saliqua, Shirleeanna and Zinphladeus petitioned to get down and dirty, detergent and antidetergent. Gentle little lambs can take revenge. Everyone seems to be having a simply wonderful time, wearing those Bavarian costumes and taking Lesbian lovers in by pretending.

As can be seen clearly in Figure Two, sound business sense can really pay off, there. The yield-to-date figures can be staggering. Soldar slowly removed his necktie and

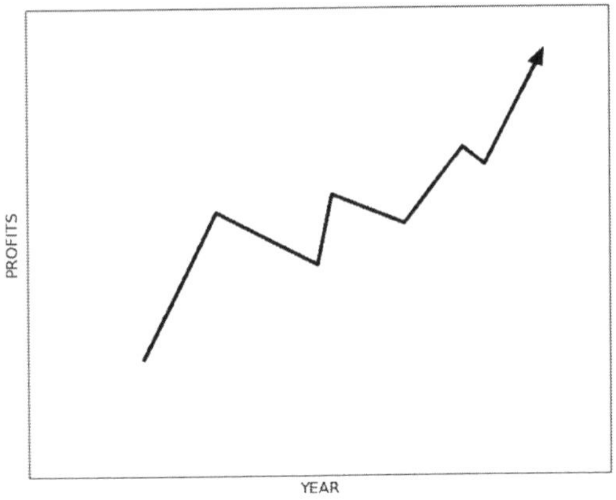

Figure Two

the boardroom emptied. Cox turned around, and almost called out to him with "Racketball at six?" as vehicle, but it seemed like the wrong time.

Softer tissue than a mash could not be found out by examining the blue light around your shoes. Benji's exacting clam measured its own shell to within one one-thousandth of an inch—then, and only then is it satisfied. While Benji eats a sweet, Archie rubs Wallie's Kaposi sarcoma with mentholatum and punishes his pet rock. Roland was there. He looked a little different without the turban, but it was definitely him.

ROLAND: Welcome, welcome to my royal palace. I love you all. Please, all of you, sit and down and be comfortable. You're going to be here awhile.

BUNNY: Oh-a, you thinka youa gotta me? *(His violin case opens to reveal a fabulously valuable Stradivarius.)*

QUEEN SALIVA: Foo-foo honey discharge! Sticky muck-luck juju jellies caking up on the roof of my mouth!

Bunny: You gotta be akidda me! Whadaya wanna makalika disheah? Heh?

Roland: Now, Bunny, is that any way to speak to the Mrs.? Say you're sorry. Now, come on….

Medieval Diety: *(suddenly materializing as a giant ladybug on a solid gold throne)* I think we're missing the main issue here.

Frog: You tell 'em.

Everyone But Me: Ahhh! You and the Rex over there can work out your conflicts in a secret mall on the side of my uncle's home town. Sophocles' *Cox, Rex* was showing in Disney's version, but it was secret—top secret.

Me: You see, I don't say any of this, as indicated in Fig. 3.

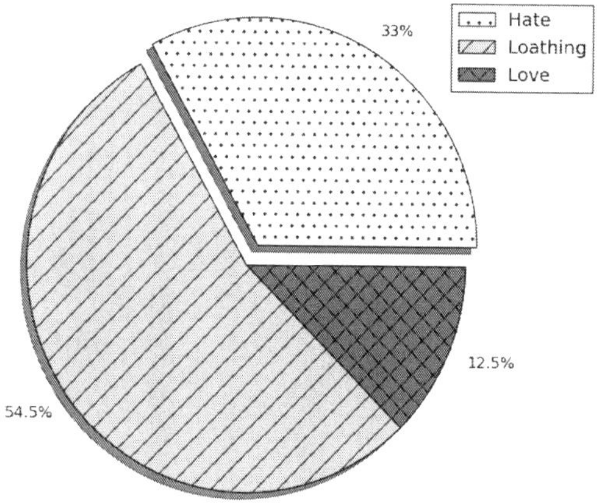

Figure Three

Bunny: Now the spotty part, it's a pretty big! Whaddaya say, José?

José: *(sings)*

> Oh amigo, it's a bigo part, that spotty part of yours!
> My Bunny, it's a funny to go potty in your drawers!

Professor M.: Uh, yes.

Medieval Diety: *(crawling down from the throne)* Flamenco party!

(Shapes suddenly appear in the sky. Finally they land.)

A Flock of Flamingos: What? Hey! Did we hear somebody calling?

Medieval Diety: *(who has now transmogrified once again, becoming a huge-eyed doughnut with a combination mouth/vagina in the center hole)* No no. I said "flamenco."

Flamingos: Oh. Oh-oh-oh.

José:

> You say flamenco, and I say flamingo.
> You fuck me blanko, and I suck you blinko.
> In a trice! and thrice!
> Come sibling, watch this cum-dribbling match!

Suddenly she ran up and got on the El, and later she transformed my dachsundian fug-playing hi-fi. Babe, she was a "she-be-illin'." Cause when ya ready tuh chill ya ready tuh ill. A I ain't jokin! You gotta be a *thrill*-chill, chil'!! Ohhh-yea-jallah-jula! *Bay*-bee, hunna, ahm ta-ed ugh gwah-nin ta dugh yuh groani' bored.

The committee unanimously affirms that this type of grammatical structure is not recommended to the lameheads out there who can't eat a between-progressing stone of flakes or score a goal from the 40-yard line or eat mako in the islands you populate.

Bunny: Which? The ones wea bunnies visit ona holidas, to *enjoy*, eh, the bunnies da chocolata, *n'est pas*?

José:

> You say chocolata, I say marshmeloyda.
> We thought Krishna Murthy,
> They handed me to Phoenicia.

Medieval Diety: *(who is now a ¼ man, ¼ skate, and ½ dung beetle)* Everybody say "Hey!"

Frog: Do it to me!

Medieval Man: *(to Bunny)* You got friends like the one "Hadzimicalis" and the one "Chapapagada" and the one "Röntgen-Ray Smythers" who zapped Zorro and all the little people who the she-bitch asked to "feed the fishies," by which she meant herself. Their borates etched a sign unto their sides of beef, and papein enzymes did something else which would more likely have been done using borates. Then the captain of the ship fell down. If he had noticed the pool of catsup on the deck this would most likely not have likely happened, in all likelihood. Omar, the swarthy first mate, had to haul sacks of smashed potato mix away from the crime scene in order to pile up suffragettes like houses of cardwood and burn 'em.

Popsicle: Um, Bargemaster, sir, I think that Omar guy is a two-faced S.O.B., if you don't mind my saying so, sir.

Art Critic: *(floating by on a raft)* You watch what you say about my gay-type lover, you little brat.

A sandalwood craft piloted between the straights and fell into the gaze of the son. An enormous paramecium ate meat on a ceremonial altar high up in the mountains; a gorilla set up a sign on the slopes that said "Tabac," if I remember rightly, and sold trinkets. Omar stepped up to a tall podium and addressed the intimate little gathering.

Omar: Thank you, quiet everyone… thank you. As you all know, today is the anniversary of my steamy affair with Sweetums… uh… I mean the Art Critic, and I've written a song in honor of the occasion. It goes a little like this: (*One, two, three….*)

> Gay lover like a Surinam toad!
> Gay lover like a Surinam toad!

BACKING VOCALS:

> Stop talk about it! Just rock about it!
> Yeah, yeah, you love 'em long and loaded!
> You heat them up and chill 'em down until they're all exploded!

XXVIII

A SUNNY field. Hot. Amazed. Tired. You make remarkable use of your stumps, ignoring the popcorn thrown at you by those impatient surgeons over there. A bloated spider clinging to a fence winks as you whizz by, and you feel a surge of lust in your phantom limb. *Buibui* black creep, says I. The surgeons' paid P.I.'s finally discover where you've been running to all these years. Those rocks jutting out of the stream bit off time from the sequential aspect of events, and those spectacularly naked Saturday afternoons, the white-water rafting, the fishing, dressing up in Mommie's clothes, strangled me with a string of pearls. Erupting from Marjorie's chamber, the filibustering coalition vowed to purchase a Wadia from the Korean man on the corner. Isthmus-navigating longshoremen congealed on the outer surface of Happy-Boy's ham, the slobbering plover no longer a threat. Wandering through the streets in search of long worms wasn't just cool, it set course for cold. And Yutz, who survived six months of Antarctica with only a monocle, ejaculated milkshake in a gloppy viscous thread which she could craft into nets and hang from hooks. Roulette wheels on the issue of fragrancy disagreed with each other, to the extent that their days were numbered by the quantity of bitter melons over in the old man's shop. One day there were six, by the Sunday all but two had been sold into culinary servitude. But a delivery of seven more was eagerly anticipated to arrive on Tuesday. When Thursday night had come and no-bitter-melons, a dark cloud could be seen by peering through Galileo's original telescope prototype. Turbaned men took turret positions and yodeled at regular intervals. Society, orbited by total serialism, was now a witty slice-of-life article, and Harriet, why, she and Marjorie, at dusk, fellated a two-organed Cicero-type who lived in Ringoes by the gas station. Skinned-knee the latherboy, of my nummy muffsful and plump, jimdiggered wonderful menses nuptual sacrifice encoded still unto its ruts, skag me.

> Margorie, barge for three, nary worth a pout!
> Every celery's barely hurt a lout!
> Cast your vote—you won't be smote,
> And then you'll be called "Old Scout."

SCOUT: M'therdy dyze ahhbuh flon n'reekin-oit'r'd wit'thh(θ)-ole Prinzah Waylz.

Just as Bismarck had predicted! A sweater emblazoned with Rosicrucian symbols was found lying in a pool of oily filth. A little man was hiding with a stopwatch in a nearby trashcan. Several superheroes were racing over to get involved.

XXVIII½

Mashed potato grinder, two ninety eight, the nimble Uhura clambered over the dual fosgates and completely destroyed the air-tangent. A bristly variation was briefly sounded on the long horns, and the serpent offered a crumbly Ritz® cracker effect to connoisseurs moistening on the final tendril of Moishe and voxelerators and the control panel operated by that smiley old man who always wore a train-engineer's cap and a red kerchief. A blitz in the percussion was rendered inaudible by a hi-tech cloaking device used by stealthy marimbas and street-wise Trappists.

Please inspect the cheeks of a feeding chipmunk. His little happy joy celebration thing gets torn to pieces when the angry female chipmunk comes storming into the nest's not-so-cozy-anymore livingroom.

Female Chipmunk: How dare you refer to an implied-neuter as "he!" I got rights, ya know!

Neuter Chipmunk: Me too, although I just play around with it, ya know? I mean, God, right? But don't go calling me nobody 'cause nobody'd better. Call not going, I mean, right on target, and it's not a game anymore. See?

Does the narrator, while speaking in the context of the non-narrative, cause the text in question to become narrative in nature, or is bamboo-shoot the next commodity ready to go up? "It" capped a Jolly Roger for the abso-fucking-lutely right grip. The Manchurian spinster would often confirm this with a simple nod of the head.

Then there was an explosion that took out the top brass, followed by a period of anarchy, decline, and general crassness. A classy crash failed to awaken any response in the prevailing g-minor moroseness. Then, due to a failure in ensemble, Arkansas fell into deep space with a huge clump of dirt stuck to its bottom. After that, I walked out. Ten-forward was an off-limits concept that the overseers would look over whenever I asked them for a light. Source-modular xenon trepidators flanged my tomato-ripeness until anyone for a price could peer at my innards through transparent skin. In Bang-Cock this soprano uttered exactly one note and pierced my garbage bag with some sort of utensil. A fish was capable of biting without swallowing water and it won the annual Blowfish Award for Best Soundbites. Gutteral swallowing noises punctuated the last half of the last paragraph. If a doctor of secular mosfet coveting Eskimo ivory-carving entrepreneurs could devalue the dollar solo, O, *cara mia!* what a growth on my arm! Quick! Get Tony-the-Axeblade Scorfanno! The creeping scungilli's on toppa my head. I want on-toppada-world kicks and a walking bass, see? Don't let it happen again. You're a mommyhead, you know that. Ouch, ouch, aug, ug, ahem.

XXVIII¾

Sportscaster: Did you see that! Smackntha middilada eighth, Korvath veerth lika badouta El down the broad thorny path, and… aw!

Sportscaster's 8-Month-Old Daughter: Wa!

Sportscaster: Oog!

8-Month-Old Daughter: Goo!

> Wadoola maverick on fire
> Guide ropes make me out to flip a toss'd salad higher
> Whipped Rococo Oberammergau doortail's
> wonderful urgings.

Flourish in a zombie Mensch-cuddler. No thank you, I do not want to hang another Watteau. The bathroom is full up as it is.

XXIX

I SAT alone in a pewter tank high up in the air and played with myself all day long. A bird was my only friend. It liked to shit on me. Thousands of my followers lived in less sumptuous tanks hovering about 500 feet below me for miles all around. Today that's all gone.

Careless sundials attracted by flies created an atmosphere in which my ability to cheat gravity was seriously compromised. The lavender-mascaraed pongee duplicates sent me an astral signal that Edison or Bell or anyone else wouldn't have been able to receive. I didn't really have space in my tank for a signal, but I felt obligated to take it. It was nearly as big as a can opener, and like *heavy*. Do you think I'm needing sandbags right now, you fucking Scrooge?! I'm having a hard enough time as it is.

SCROOGE: Vot ey gut twudwvh hmm mmm humm mm m.

NEUTER CHIPMUNK: What? Huh? What did he say? Anyone—what did he say?

LUCY: Who cares! I've been waiting here this whole time and for what? Nobody's asked me my opinion this whole time!

EVERYONE ELSE BUT LUCY: Yeah! All right! Way to go Lucy!

LUCY: Shut up!

FROG: Take that!

(The frog strikes out at Lucy with a metal attachment on the end of his tongue. He bloodies her and she passes out from the pain.)

Bunny: *(In a trenchcoat, smoking a cigarette backwards)* You-a, hey Froggie boy, you-a, itsa you, yous I'ma talking a-to now-a. Yous a deada meat, amphibian-of-a mine, pal! Prepare, yous a sonofabeech my idiot, to my-eat youra in-the-end! *(He plays "Air on the G String," then segues into a barn stomp.)*

Control played a role in smoothing out the cowlick of my grandmother's *Modern Maturity* subscription. Scribbled on a Post-It® stuck to the refrigerator, the message laid its own trap and got its little paper prong snagged in liquid metal pharyngeal trapwires. I almost had an angioplasty waiting for the garbage truck to lumber up the driveway—hence the toy. It's a bummer for large asteroids to have to touch down somewhere like Pnom Penh. Escape routines were stared at collectively for two quite different reasons. She with the body wave tasted his flavor aboard a spaceship for two hauling a load of rubbish to Xollyiavva-IV. A pliable statue immobilized them and drew a picture of blood on the blackboard hanging right next to the chalkboard and the cork and the pinups of suspects and victims. The cheetah was the first one on the scene. He zapped the statue, trying to render it unpliable, but failed, desperately seeking Suzanne and sifting gravel uselessly. Then a dump truck made a like amazing sound and everyone turned round except the statue, who combined the best qualities of the amoeba, the chameleon, and Michelangelo's *David.* Then the garbage truck made an even more amazing sound and even the statue turned round.

Cheetah: It never fails. I give up. I'm a useless wash-up.

José:

> Why it's you, you cheesy cheetah!
> Gonna throw your life away, oh yeah!
> Why do you, you fast four-feeter,
> Saunter through a hyperbegonia,
> That is, a field of them....
> Uh, I forgot the song.

Bunny: I'm-a sorry you-a did that.

Me: Not as sorry as I am.

Bunny: *(to me)* You get backa to what you was-a doin'.

Me: How do you know what I "was-a doin'"?

Bunny: You make-a funnu me: I break-a you face. Yunnuh-stan?

Me: Listen to yourself! You sound like a.... You know what you sound like? You sound like instead of going "hippity-hop" you go "whippety-whop!"

Bunny: Wha...!! You...!! Ahmah...!! Ooo! You gonna getta real' bad now and thassit! Yunnu-stan? You gonna getta like-a you neveh-adeh befo' yunna-stan? Youz-uh dead meat! You-a finesh'! *(He takes out a machine gun typical of those used in the 20s.)*

Me: Bunny! Wait! No! Bunny!!

Meanwhile, a beast of burden bore a priest in a sombrero towards the Rome of his repressed id. He stopped for wawa and fufu at Id Junction (just north 40 km. from Ouagadougou and west 80 km. from Niamey) but they were all out. Suddenly he was jumped by a hostile band of youth-group members and relieved of all his possessions. Then he was beaten mercilessly.

(Bunny fires.)

XXX

LAND enum convinced Uncle Duprix to linger a bit longer in the sitting room. Davies walked by incessantly but to his knowledge they were but hypotheses. A candle was lit. A skull sat prettily within easy reach, and droplets of a clear, thick oil emerged from a pipette one by one and fell onto samples of coloured sand. After an Alka-Seltzer® noise was at last heard, a bronze fly clanked to the ground and was clamped to the ground before being ground into metal dust for use in decorating the cheeks of the daughter with the bloody orifice and the cupie smile. An American Indian performed cunnilingus with chopsticks while a collector used a net to capture an old lady's dentures. Uncle felt a twinge, and suddenly Williver, the butler, was there beside him. It always seemed to happen that way. Williver slowly, methodically unfastened Uncle's trousers while his shiny head oozed a greasy residue. Uncle moaned in anticipation as Williver's head cheese began to froth and sputter all over Cousin Joy's négligée. She quickly shot over and donned the escarpment, forgetting all about the négligée. The Uncle mentioned Rodney King, and they all suddenly stopped everything they were doing. "Oh, right," said Williver as he straightened his tie and vanished to the third floor.

MR. BUZBY: A cloud of pain has nine essential vitamins and minerals. A bout of influenza on a rainy day? Haven't you been eating your spinach, girlie? *(He picks her up and takes her for a night on the town where they both have a wonderful time and eventually get married and have three kids together before ultimately getting divorced and having bitter thoughts in their twilight years.)*

Brandishing facts about local flora, señoritas from the hills attempted to land jobs as frankfurter stand attendants in Waverly-By-the-Sea.

SEÑORITA PRIMERO: Hey, I noticed this ragweed growing by the hydrant over there. That's no ordinary ragweed, Mister.

MISTER: You don't say.

SEÑORITA PRIMERO: No, I don't. *(She zooms off in her expensive convertible, leaving him in a cloud of smoke.)*

HIM: Hey, Mister, you're a pretty slick character. I mean, no-flies-on-you, right?

MISTER: I can't help it. Ever since my role opposite the Western European midget....

On closer inspection, pork rinds could be seen being thrown over the wall to the sounds of uproarious laughter. But this detail was relatively insignificant. In the crepscular torment known as "Gnat Kink Hole," a middle-aged man with a yellow bow-tie read the following announcement: "Hard to mate the dragon. Hard to mate with the dragon. Hard to checkmate with a dragon. Hard-up to mate with the dragon in a funeral home in Trenton with a round door and garbage out in front on the sidewalk. Hard-up to make the dragon harden and mate in Palo Alto at a deluxe frank stand like this one."

MISTER: Mustered?

All those dragons and mates, they rose at eight and did a hard day's work at the auto plant. Now they're out on the streets. It's a pity.

(Isn't this where Dr. Gupthanathan makes lewd gestures towards a York-terrier-sized head of cattle which rests in a dead way on the proverbial silver platter of my smarmy moment of inertia? A beetle spits on excrement. Ah! 4:30! Time for "Days of Your Lives!")

A witless deaf jerk was hard-up for some money in his back pocket, so he crawled bare-assed across Idaho on his heavily padded hands and knees until someone, mistakenly thinking he was his friend Horatio, acted just like him as he walked over and offered him a watertight case with which charges were brought and then trumped up concerning how a lilylivered yellowbelly could slither across America. The jerk's ass was a jerky ass as the case came to be jerkily jerking in his direction. Impedimenta aside, everything was easy as snow or lice, and a naked woman made it Christmas and gave little Spanish fly candies to all the children. They grabbed the morsels impatiently and melted them over the wound of their collective broken coccyx. Daft president with a sighing speech impediment, act like a South American darter, shelling coiled tunes of manganese (absolute) and soldering compromise with a white-hot nose.

When the plane landed in New Caledonia, who would you think was first on the scene? Only a part of the chassis was actually responsible for making it fly—some parts of it were actually lazy. And yet Tony was one of those parts. Tony, dear old hard-working Tony. And yet, it was impolite to ask Tony in which direction, his hair, he parts. Still, it was partially the truth that a frosty coating concealed the implants. This was less so the case when you ordered a jumbo sized yummy-fudgy however; and the little gifts embedded in the creamy mass were super. Sometimes they were clever but not predictably so. This did not detract from their Etruscan splendor. Of course, all roads carried the jackasses which pulled carts full of lead shot and sand. Other huge shipments arrived. A space shuttle containing enormous wire-wound transformers pulled up behind the muletrain. The spaceman blew the horn impatiently. Silence. His headstrong mandibles rattled, as the impulse to zippedy-dee in the resplendent cargo vehicle accumulated in his mandibular capacitor and itched.

Once you've been to bed with a Nebraska state trooper you'll never want to take tea at 4 again. Again, any time your lamb's fæces elongates the misinformation of my brainwave video media vibration Rastaman julibation broadcast, your jam will keep the way passable. A sullen dauber made perfectly good canvas mangy and looked up from his decrepitude at the Pascal excrement only to exclaim, "Riches, riches! The fishes of the sea! Ours all though stumpy tropical wetlands!" They soon arrived at the remote archipelago where Ganymede rested on a gold-spun pillow amid an aura of butterflies and bluebirds.

BARGEMASTER: Jellybean! Look alive mate! Drop anchor! Lower the mizzenmast! Batten down the hatches! Hup! Hup!

POPSICLE: Jellybean doesn't feel at all well, so he's appointed me as surrogate mate for this important occasion.

BARGEMASTER: But you're a mate already.

POPSICLE: I'm a mate and a half! That's why they call me "Popsicle"!

BARGEMASTER: Keep the filthy details of your private life to yourself.

JELLYBEAN: Popsicle? C'mere. Please? Just for a minute.

POPSICLE: Okay. But don't you want to go out and meet Ganymede? I mean, remember last time....

JELLYBEAN: He'll be all old and hairy by now.

POPSICLE: Just enough and no more—he's got connections. Aw, c'mon.

JELLYBEAN: Well, okay, but just remember: I have a fever of 104°.

(Popsicle and Jellybean, holding hands, romp through the fields.)

BARGEMASTER: I've had it with you scumbags! You're… you're…. You're *fired*, d'ya hear?! *Fired!* A little bit.

PARROT: "Fired." "Fired." Braagh!

(Popsicle and Jellybean forget all about Ganymede and sneak behind a thicket where they lay low for a while.)

GANYMEDE: *(talking to a small mammal far away in a dream)* Get away! You hear! Go on! Get away now! Oh—bless you.

JELLYBEAN: Whatever this bush is, I think I'm allergic.

BARGEMASTER: Come back! I need to land the barge! Come back!

POPSICLE: He's drifting, you know.

BARGEMASTER: *(to himself)* I know, I know.

POPSICLE: Hey! How were you able to hear what I was saying?

BARGEMASTER: I got my ways. Look, I'll make yous a deal. You come back and save me from drifting off to sea all by myself….

PARROT: All by myself, all by myself!

Part II

Unidentified Signal

XXX

BARGEMASTER: And I'll show yous one or two of my ways. Sounds good, eh?

XXXI

FORGIVE me, babe, if I don't dribble cum all over your swollen bloody hole with my ulcerated member. You see, I've got this plane to catch and my mother's nipples are rotting in the frigidaire. My samples! Ya strewn 'em all ova the dressa! Putting them in the case. Locking it good and tight. Cigarettes to light, gloves to slip into! The rope's good and knotty already, yeah. A little make-up, some stroboscopic black light, the Mantovani Strings.

Micronized bicarb lathered antiquatedly under sulking basement drains leading the sump pump of oxagonality to redimension volumes into smaller volumes which were actually the exact same size. This was called "virtual shadowing." A princely retrofitting spliced a series of core sections into the Louis XIV upholstery and littered the Persian carpets with anatomy and geology texts. Severed limbs bleeding into maps of the planet.

RALPH: Oh, oh, oh, will you please simmer down. Nothing left of my insurance policy anyway. I miss the taste of that flaky crust Mom used to do so well.

X-TRA VOLT: A "bing"-ee for you is a hard wrapper to wear around your bar. Aren't you torn between being between between and itself, itself being between it and itself, or would being between what really is torn between torn and between be torn from between torn and between.

(Ralph turns off the X-tra Volt.)

X-TRA VOLT: Uuugh....

Doubt and joy condensed in the same crucible as techs became intimate with Pyrex. Their theory was: "what if life were wide instead of long and everyone simultaneously lived the exact same life detail by detail"; and that's how Pyrex was born. Those not in the know didn't see or feel. Squads made ineffectual delicate links intended for a capacity of zero to one. A hot-mamma lay her dribbly droopers on the urine-soaked carpet and waited for the usual variety of beasts of the woods to show up. A slightly damaged lens embedded in one of her steamy breasts showed a purplish light through the rising vapour of the vieux homme avec eine Nase trop grande who cancelled his 1:15 appointment with Dr. Kulabunga. A functional vector was okay for the little molecule. One with some branches (for convenience) which reached the gluon-neutrino interface so holy-overloadedly that a freight train had to be called in to carry away all the quarks and Snoopy-particles. It envisioned all the lovely space and time (yum-yum!) to be lubricated over in the ya-la-land whoopty-wawa-walicious superconductor ping!-yoyo nexus theme park, and with a tinge of regret it recalled the old days when it would sit out on the porch for a long-shadowed afternoon with the old Victrola playing. A bin of red discs bored into skulls to insert blasting tubes (it had a grievance with grappling hookers). A tiny tiny spiderman clambered over the giant breast as a mosquito buzzed overhead. Lo! it descends! Dammit, I can't get any rest out here anymore. Pliable scourge, conquistador of ambling beliefs my apathy couldn't any longer ignore. Mookta-dohn, mookta-dohn. On campus on Donner my mushed-ever praline delineated retrospective voxelity meters (no toxins/no proximity). BOMs in the air ruin the cantus firmly through all of its paces. And they're off, prance off ten mark! Amblet's in first, a nose. Scramble! Flip! Coddle! Soft-boil!

JUNIOR: Wyz I mike a millyin books in th lot-tree I wul.

THE 2ND: Daddy, I gotta go potty.

JUNIOR: W'lie nevr-urd nee-thing loik….

Pops: Shutsa face, mo-ron!

Mrs. Ripest: Ilis, pour yer rock!

(A black stallion smashes into the embankment. The fireball appears on screen.)

Ilis: *(ululating)* Uhuhuhuh!

Pops: Snufftha fuckoid off!

The 2nd: Daddy!!

Junior: Sprid thi kittle o-the far and huvuh blarney.

Mrs. Ripest: Hurry or I'll rot!

(The doorbell rings.)

Ilis: *(ululating)* Uhuhuhuh!

Gramps: Grr, am amply dammed if the bloody grr isn't the bloody grr it is. Grreat Scott if it isn't Ambassador Mitchell!

Ambassador Mitchell: *(removing his hat)* For chrissakes, you've gone bald!

(The ambassador's twin red-haired midget servants run in.)

Cecil: Ehoh! Rah thah....

Nigel: Ehoh! Dyon't be in uh pitih-patih.

Gramps: Grreek to me, it's all that's my grrievance.

Ambassador Mitchell: *(producing a passport)* This passport picture shows you with a luxuriant head of hair!

Pops: Gettya hands off that passport, M'itch'em!

Junior: Eek, th' pretzel-twist's catchin' lick th' sores-a-bubblin' placketty ald plague o'yers!

Nigel: Ehyoheeohiuohuyuhehohehoo.

Cecil: Ehohe....

Ilis: Uhuhuhuh!

X-tra Volt: Uh...h...h... *(tone decreases)*

XXXII

Radio Pilot № 1: Zero two zero four *niner. Niner.* Go! Roger?

Roger: Say?

Control Tower: Unidentified disturbance at twenty-nine nine fifteen twenty-nine knots nine knockseconds off your starboard port, Roger.

Roger: Who is this?

Radio Pilot № 1: Radio Pilot № 1, Roger.

Roger: Oh really? And I suppose there's a Radio Pilot № 2 as well on my private phone?

Radio Pilot № 2: Lingo alpha foxtrot, delta mark zero zero zero seven divided by the square root of sigma-E times the quantity Charlie, where Charlie equals em-cee squared, and kappa-kappa-omicron. Oh my gaw. Hi Gramma! Roger.

Roger: Eh....

Control Tower: Unidentified flying object at pixie six rubber trump stamp Presley Towers seven, Roger.

Roger: I'll make a note of it. *(Sings in a clear tenor.)*

Radio Pilot № 1: Giant leghorn off the custard bough, O seven six.

Plane № 1 Passenger: You've got to *do* something, you *hear*? A passenger must be able to trust his (or her...) pilot.

Radio Pilot № 2: Pilot to Bombardier! Pilot to Bombardier! Do you read me, Bombardier?

Bombardier: Like a book, Your Highness, like a book.

(Bombardier throws a passenger off the plane.)

Plane № 2 Passenger: Wait, my cigarettes!!

Radio Pilot № 2: Good riddance, Roger!

Roger: You vicious brute, you steamy man-louse! If you're looking for a hangar to stick that plane of yours…

Plane № 2 Passenger: O, never mind… I found them.

Roger: … in, then here it comes!

(The Control Tower sends up a surface-to-air missile which destroys Plane № *2.)*

Radio Pilot № 2: Well, actually I don't have a plane. I work out of an office in Passaic.

Roger: Well let's get down to business.

(They arrange to meet at a motel with closed-circuit TV. They meet and have intercourse, but display utter indifference to one another.)

Pilot: My big antenna, he-he! Ouch, wow!

Roger: It's licorice time! Jelly beans, ten four!

Unidentified Signal:  etc.

(The concierge spots them in the midst of anal surgery on the monitor in the lobby. He summons Bongo, the bouncer.)

Bongo: GGGGGG! RRRRRR! MMMMMM! OOOOOO! ZZZZZZ! YYYYYY! HHHHHH! KKKKKK! BBBBBB! EEEEEE! XXXXXX!

(Bongo throws a bomb under the door of the Pilot and Roger's room.)

Bomb: … SSSSSS!

Subordinate: Captain, we've got a six eighty at ten-eleven backwards, sir, and it's, ah, well, it's *machinating*, sir!

Captain: If it births robot-zombies, let me know. Now, what's your bid, son?

Subordinate: Sir? Look, we've got this armed incursion and it's distinctly audible, Captain!

(Captain grabs Subordinate by the collar.)

Captain: What kind of a shirt is this you're wearing? I've never seen this fabric before in my life!

Subordinate: Why, this is a pongee shirt, as is the rest of my tastefully coordinated ensemble. Only $109.09 with the purchase of a cordless froth maker.

Director: CUT!! Cut! Cut....

A basket woven from snakes needed to have items placed in it very cautiously with an individualized rubber implement made of steel and guaranteed to last twenty years. Unfortunately, everyone was too afraid to imperil themselves, and for what, a couple of trinkets, tests in geography, and Lipschitz as read by Frankie Coppola's dog's former owner, a world-renowned and renounced public speaker. A benzene-soaked attribute was inflamed, and Joey bit his wick with righteous God-almighty fervor at moral rictus boot camp revival meetin' four seventy-six dee subsection substandard, Junior.

(Cut to Northern Norway.)

Yunior: Yingee! Oslo or no Oslo, my plums gotta be drained of their plum juice. Tak for nuttin, Bunny-for-hire, a pimpled gooey dough-filled joy nut yay high *(hand measures parallel to floor)* and yay toasted *(whirligig, bilateral symmetry around head)* and being transported by barge to a burned-out place where the impediment to minisculae dangled vertically from the mouth of every streetcorner lowlife turned green pistachio on us. "I is creams!" Ajax ulated is elf in a rustic moment; "At Barnard we balanced entire encyclopediae and ne'er spilt a drop, say I" emerged from a tiny metal set. Love-plum, c'mere snook'ms. I enlarge!

SPOKESPERSON: I'll roll right over the rocks with a twist to the sound of rubber burning, leaving a faint airbrushy trace like catshit on a palimpsestistic mattress, mistress.

SECOND ASSISTANT DIRECTOR: Please, ensure that all calisthenic jaggedness is in its belonged place. Rapeseed oil notwithstanding, Ionesco's dodged vapidity is what your *sonus faber* brings to mind. Placenta that you are, engulf me!

MISTA GOG: Whah, cunt-duct-ta', ah juz can't play so hah oop-they-ah!

CONDUCTOR: Drive my semi back to I'm-a-Brillo or wherever you're from.

BONGO: GHGHGH! PHHH! THRTHRTHR! ING-ING-ING-ING-ING-ING-ING-ING-ING-ING....

PILOT: *(to Roger)* Let's get out of here.

ROGER: No, you stay here. I'll go.

(Doorbell rings. Roger answers it and Mistah Gog enters with the Dutch Masters.)

PILOT: Well, if it isn't Mistah Gog and the Dutch Masters!

BOMB: ... SSSSSS!

DUTCH MASTER WITH MANDOLIN: Actually, there are only five of us today.

BOMB: ... S....

PILOT: I can see who wears the pants in this family.

ROGER: Look out!

(The Dutch Master clubs the Pilot over the head with his mandolin, which is actually a fancy meat made only to look like a mandolin.)

Mistah Gog: Now gennelmoon, ya gotta cheel!

Dutch Master with Length of Sausage Links: I call this meeting to order.

Dutch Master with Detachable Moustache: Hear, hear!

Dutch Master with Dilapidated Porch: I'd like to start off here with, uh, the first point of order, my sadly rotting little old porch. I move that immediate funds be collected to effect its repair.

Dutch Master with Feather: Enough about your rancid old porch. If you hadn't built it out of meat we wouldn't have this problem.

(Bingo pulls down all the Dutch Masters' pants and the Dutch Master with Feather tickles them all until they laugh.)

Mistah Gog: Ah dog fluffah coon spect it bettah!! A-hah-haa-hah!

(The Pilot, bloody-headed, signals to Roger that they should escape during the fracas.)

Roger: *(loudly)* Why, that's a good idea!

Mistah Gog: Oh. You, Roger, and you, Pilot, jube in life ambly to me, buh… weh…

Dutch Master with Kalashnikov rifle (disguised as sausages): You two! Get outside!

(Pilot and Roger go outside at gunpoint. Building explodes.)

XXXIII

THIRTY-TWO double-sided catheters shrink Miss Phlegm to the point at which twice backwards tomatoes could sustain an egress amulet till the audience pleaded for mercy. An air intake valve was a no-additional-cost extra at matinées, midiers and nuitées. A pleasant afternoon in the shade swelled into purple dusks. Bombs have their place in the sun even at night when your mother is desperately trying to explain to you how to build the latest hydrogen model. But all you can think about is taking her right there against the chalkboard and smudging the equations. A squadron of flies buzzes by, completely unaware of your smiling spouse and all the care and retention you are receiving. Anal manifests charge the inventions of the quixotic monkey and its value-added mump-puppy phosphoreening junk dodger playing "Rapid Penelope" or "Skid Dirt." A craft was well-grounded in the meniscus of the bay of measles near some clinging bugs. A school of cigarette-smoking fish was audited by a translucent wheezing lungbag that squirted through in an irregular, drunken fashion designer, Logar.

LOGAR: Gypsum pet hadzi knickerbocker launchy launchy.

LOGAR SENIOR: Pfff. A bicky pfffs oypsla pshwasi-jeep-slazhadg-slazoom, smackers.

THE PUBLIC: *(carefully trained to say this)* Skidmore think cell amma leopra Jurg forniscula fartastica yudopia swizzets.

Liza: *(driving by in a yellow convertible)* You like gotta be pulling my leg! Get in the shiny *caw*, what's keepin' ya?

(The scene fades and everyone takes jobs as telemarketers where they make far more money than they would off our negotiated union-scale "plus" system.)

Ignian capitals enjoyed Auntie's posterior and the scales which were chowdered upon them. Pork! A festival of silk and Spandex lies upon us still, a scrim, foul and scrim mage playing with the flying pork of our rind and pork-sections like we were hung by a thread near the legs of lamb-like pork. Vehicled undone monopods with exploding heads entumorate my magna-shevitz low-salt woe wagon; watcha bunker buffo. A blistering blow of the horn made strawberry rhubarb a thing of the present. Pagliacci's deodorant contained no antiperspirant so long as my brother's Lionel train remains were berried six feet under. Let me question mark quote no he replied endquote period ad infinitum.

Enormous dice rolled just ahead of the glacier until the day a glazier dies while buying a suit off the rack. The sawed-off ate the meat off his ribs as a soprano clerk hit an Ethel Merman high and the lead crystal turned into driven fog, its quarts dispersed. Miss Vee whipped his little ass, as I was accused of saying "Get your black ass outta my house." This proves once again that the position between hammer and purse and anvil is a headache. This pyramidal structure has cost many their lives.

Fat Egyptian Merchant (wearing a fez): Aw, that was many years ago!

Estonian diatribes about a lingering global malaise circumcise my victuals with a special magneto-optical grid array which pays for the annual company banquet. Fighting to escape through imprisoning walls of brisket, it's a corned dungeon! Look out, beware the meat-hail!

(A goose-stepping horde exhibits ant-like behavior, and soon the ants have scurried into their private dens with every last scrap of the precious sustenance. A tally feather, aye sir.)

Fat Egyptian Merchant (wearing a fez): Bring the Old Gringo in here. Maybe he can tell us something about this unusual ant-like incident, eh?

Fat Egyptian Merchant (bearing a load of meal): I'll tell him on my way out.

(Merchant with meal slowly leaves the vast enclave. The Gringo enters.)

The Gringo (a Norwegian in a sombrero): See, I am the Greengo, Sire.

The Gringo (a Malagesi in a straw hat): See, I am the Reddgo, Siren.

The Gringo (a Nepalese in an astronaut's helmet): C-I-M thwap Röntgen, Xylene.

Fat Egyptian Merchant (playing with himself on a big stuffed throne): Eeeeeeh…. Uuuu-uuu-uuuuugh….

Fat Egyptian Merchant (taking charge): Hello, I am the fat Sidney, the very rich and Egyptian Greenstreet merchant. I see lettuces, eh? I shall, let us say, let be a "let's see" attitude.

J. Paul Getty, Jr.: Wibble wibble myunsu in vaktu, vaktu.

J. Paul Getty, Jr. (as a fat Egyptian merchant [as J. Paul Getty, Jr.]): Wwwwwww…

The Parrot: Braaaagh! *(whistles)* Glinka! Glinka! Braaagh!

Glinka: Please, please stop your noise! Please!

The Gringo (undifferentiated): My-a senses, they-a tella me….

The Gringos (in the guys of the Mormon Tabernacle Choir): that Glinka is on the premises!

(The Mormon guys, itching terribly, treat themselves to Athlete's Foot.)

Luminous crags charged the lemmies and the breggs into a sort of fetal servitude which was itself able to jimmy your average locked-door lock. What is broken is made of substance and vice versa, so Jimmy was able to open his trunk no problem. Inside he kept his internal organs, satisfied and far from being sweetmeats by cascading or tiling, whichever was applicable. Veteran's foozle was on the menu tonight, nice and in-between. And just imagine the outcome if the women of Cameroon all closed up at the same time. Old men climbing the endless rope at bus stops rape little schoolgirls on a regular basis made of a particularly warm stone. Usury was always mistaken with spouse-rape until a brutal science molested the minds of our forebearers, domiciled in a quaint townhouse in Montevideo like a smog in a fog over a bog with a frog-lickin' stone lickin' the logs till they redden and crackle and split and spit, and Lordy Lord! what a buggy smog it was, or like a hermit battling demons in the privacy of his sanctuary in the wine cavern with the 3-digit zip code and no forwarding address. The kingdom of our sodden god erupts its exposure to membraneous fissures in the azure coatings on native pottery.

How far you need to follow depends on how much water is left on the donkey and whether you'll stop at nothing to refill. If you choose to stop at nothing, please neglect to pick up a loaf of bread/dozen eggs/gallon of milk. Otherwise, it's 2 for 1 at the Grand Old Union of God-Bless-America, America's in my soul.... America, love it or leave it, America, to thee do I humbly sing my inadequate songs of praise.

FIN

XXXIV

PLEASE leave in a quiet, sober, easy, controlled manner. Do not throng. Disregard an inclination to panic at once. Mr. Gyzy fluctuated dramatically between pop-culture impromptu lectures and feeding his children regurgitated worms in their quite large nest situated in the Ouichita range. You might expect bananas to flourish there, but no, it wasn't the case. The blushing forest rangers create a sexual manifest destiny by subtle use of their hands. This explains why some French call Euro-Disney a cultural Chernobyl. The President of the United States appeared on television with his teddy bear and a big stick. Ninja scenes ensued.

BEAR: *(as Zorro)* Slashola! I steadfastly de-string the seamy seams of your G-string with my big 'ole musical saw! Bow it, baby!

ZORRO: *(as President)* Whoa there maistro! If the buxom sheriff caint rustle me up some semolina of harmony bricks, sanctum can't be established.

JELLYBEAN: Look out! It's Zorro, my former master!

BARGEMASTER: Hard about there, Jellybean, *hard about!*

(They bump into the bear.)

BEAR: BBBBRRRRAAGH!

JELLYBEAN: Zorro! What's wrong with you?! I told you not to inject Minoxidil!

BEAR: *(preparing to devour them)* BBBBRRRRAAGH and all that!

JELLYBEAN: *(to Bargemaster)* I told him not to inject that Rogaine stuff.

POPSICLE: Who cares about him anyhow.

JELLYBEAN: Yeah, you're right!

BARGEMASTER: Batten down the hatches!

(The Bear towers over them and emits huge tidal waves of drool which flood the decks of the barge.)

POPSICLE: Yucky! It's yucky! I didn't expect or write it to be this way!

Soon it was time for a little Q & A. For one: in the expression $(e^3 - 1)(e^3 - \pi r^2)$ the relevance is completely nonexistent. Tommy?

TOMMY: It's a hairy hawk, hardly a tall, that with a clean sparerib-skewering eye minces variably and prances from expression to expression like a veritable cola-bubble afloat in a sexualized ice image. How would you wire or rig the device to blow were your selection an urgency of solid state craft?

A veritable ice bubble tones a gymnast's gleaming brawn until a told-fell mildew of action releases the specific pheremone dying against the double of a seltzer salesman who once had carnal knowledge of a chipmunk's footprints in the arid zone. A beastly gasp emerged from a bun's autocannibalistic maw and toppled a copracracy in one bellewhoop. Pathetic emissions are merely soon, as "is" does a bumble-becoming in the straw next to the needle. Beavers are damned for calling me without knowing my name, rank and serial number—never mind the aerial code.

Corked Polish imports flexed the rigidity of the "ok" brand. Why am I reporting this simple fact, you wonder? It has to do with the thing and why that happened. Then what-else wasn't so you-know either, so that's why when we say it, we mean the-product, namely $e^9 - e^3\pi r^2 - e^3 + \pi r^2$, got me?

Snagging a bramble is inherently interactive. Think back to earlier afternoons and the inevitable decathection associated with a vase of nameless branches becoming distanter by the bunny-oform split hour. Manga raging hemispheres of trembling gelatin used to magnify the distance between my retina and the far side of a galloping pigeon in Auckland. A dialect of clichés was employed to haggle over a delicacy before the halvah broke up their marriage. Never again would Marsha Marshmallow and Charlie Chocolate engage in blissful sighs under a tree in Roanoke, or at a steamy threesome party with Peter Peanut. C'est la vie.

Seized at last by an elevating guilt, I fervently tasted the sublime ash of my sin. Although not coated in chocolate, it did have the sort of bittersweet characteristics found deserted on a lousy piece of shorefront property. In… say, why do I keep wanting to say "Gugliermo"? Silence the wolves. They're good dogs, but they're into the wrong meat. Gushy young patriottes have been hanging out their provisions for them. Pre-natal intercourse. Anyway, if the environment is reeling with flying fish, why be surprised when the things they wrote seemed to be all about flying fish?

Bear: What's this?

Salmon Chevitz: That's my tail, you buffoon!

(Little bear cubs come running up with the matzahs.)

Bear: Co-o-o-o-ome and get it!

Bear Cub "A": *(to Bear Cub "B")* We were already on our way!

XXXV

Centipedal residues awing despoil white cloud
sky-friend, -planted, very whalesome plunger
that frees heaven for swell-swillers, nuns,
hoppers, grass. Ahoy!
Lars' special meeting kneels in obeyance.
Fund the woonsocket plunder-bars which
raggle streaked vicitubes with mungtious
violation. A tummy, stunned, turns freak;
bloody even wear for odd song stinging, dish
of peaches, jam o'erturned, buns leak—and ahoy, yoha.

ROLL out the long list of elements discovered by science and De Piro's madness will give you a low low 7% on your embarkment. Howling puppy's sad monkey turns stomachs stuck on a stick to priddle Gadda de Vito, my mammy in bammer, pop in the slammer, and Unca kudos up the river. Killer chicken of the white waters, peck Snake until proud men pay up the mortgage on their wigwam with a singular wad transferred by diagrammatic errows from bitter to oily palm. Do not drink the wine or climb, but spin like women around the axis of entry. An evil figure became increasingly cloaked as a boulevard's trees grew from saplings to mighty siblings carefully trussed up on racks of lamb and lamblike objects in a Lancashire Tunnel-of-Love in Kabul. War-rubble, stained with the sweat of many grimy ass-wiping hands, was placed on a silver tray with dangerous affection.

King Sven the OverMan (Übermensch): Gib me watts on duh tray! Ish! Kabibble! Get dat silber tray or it's duh gallows!

Kabibble: Ohh! Ohhh! Ohhhh!

(Sven worries Kabibble's bare bottom with a special implement.)

Kabibble: Yes-yes-yeseses, I will get on it right away, Overman (*Übermensch*).

Ish: Ya ain't got like no powah oober *this* Mensch, Sven your Majesty-Smajesty—I got my trousahs on, like!

Jojo:

Knocked my gams to
Grecian Formula,
Sixteen.
Sprayed mayonnaise
In Bayonne's bouillabaisse,
Dumpling.
Doncha wanna gogo, girl?
Oo, oo, yea.

José: Hey, Jojo! Give me back my sombrero!

(Shots, the clanking of swords, explosions, roaring of cattle-trucks, tanks, airplanes, slot machines, Sumo wrestlers. Jojo and José, on their very own desert island with one palm tree, tumble naked in the sand. Jojo's penis grows to the size of a watermelon and he strokes it against the sombrero as José shouts words of encouragement.)

Ganymede: *(shouting from the next island over)* What the hell do you freaks think about all day long, dick or pussy?

Jellybean: He's here! Hey, Popsicle!

Popsicle: Let's high-tail towards Mr. Gamete!

Bargemaster: What about my proposition?

JOJO: Would you people stick a cork in it? I'm busy inventing lighter-than-air travel! (Ahem.) Ooh ooh yeah. Yeah, baby. Yeahh.

Ballast over, yesterday's meatloaf soars in eternity. It is the case, above all (or, over a universal domain), that the soaring of what "meatloaf" signifies, in particular, that of yesterday, when so unburdened, is true and present throughout time. Then came Dolly. Not a partner in a big-city law firm, not the swollen doodad or roots running through broken urns, but the shining copper-clad automaton whose feminine hygiene consisted of setting fire to doughnuts with a magnifying glass—Dolly's coming into being was thus subsequent to the eternal soaring of that temporally bounded meatloaf. Does this imply that eternity is itself bounded, as the relation "subsequent/antecedent" would suggest?

ERNIE: Braghh?

THE PARROT: Of course it would, although, as Zebediah Ullyses has so pointedly poignantly pointed out, eternity's boundaries are actually a single, one-dimensional boundary, bounded itself and in turn by eternity.

PROFESSOR KUMAR: At last! Success! My name-everlasting: their personalities switched!

FLAVIUS: Professor, the car is ready to behave like a bicycle, but the bicycle refuses to go above 35 mph.

GUSTAVE: *(shirtless, blackened by soot from the enormous furnace to which he is chained)* Become the buddy of my ripplingly (e)-musculated celestial flesh! Acknowledge the bicycle!

VOICES: Never!

THE PARROT: Excuse Me. (Ahem.) I'm sorry, may I be allowed to speak now? *(Everyone finally becomes quiet.)* If I may say so, I believe that the meatloaf is presently at so dangerous an altitude that the desires of Dolly, or any other one of us for that matter, will have shortly been discounted entirely.

Voices: Em Erumurumurumurumurum....

Dolly: But let's sing *Jingle Bells* anyway!

Dolly and the Voices *(in the garage)* Mmm mmm mmmmm, mmm mmm mmmmm, mmm mmmi mmmmme mm mmmmm!

XXXVI

LEADEN arms functioning as feet scuttled along in a plate of questionable thermador—and this was why they call me you. A nut, I think in Paraguay, hopped a sandpiper cub to Belize, where it easily could hitchhike to Parcutín. Dog-diggity! My computerized pudendum, plum and cherry, united to form a tempting digital taste treat, is host to software crabs. Scratch that algorithm! Take me back to the campo, Charlie!

> Take me back to the campo, Charlie,
> We'll have such a time!

BUNNY: Whatsadis abahta campo? José, whattya you make-a diseah?

JOSÉ:

> O you go to campo
> and I'll lick my stamp-o!
> While you eat a guava
> well, I'll be in Java!
> When you go to loose-a face,
> my Bunny-Bunny-Bunny, will ya win that race?
> Or will Tootle, the turtle,
> we embrace?

BUNNY: Asamattah duh facta, I was away—lika gone, see?

(A panel pops open and a uniquely costumed gent emerges to perform. José strips down to a pair of purple bikini underwear and, smiling, dances violently as the old performer once again begins his celebrated routine.)

GENT, KENT THE: Welahduhyahdoo? Lay-deez ann gen-tel-men? I now purr-form for you all like this: A-wawa a-wawa! Awk! Awk! Awk!

THE AWK: Will you certainly please? I could hear you all the way from New-Fucking-Zealand! (Spring lamb notwithstanding.)

HIGH PRIEST: Nice eggs!

DOLLY: Fresh!!

VOICES: Yeah.... How dare he.... Yeah.... He's gonna.... Grr.... Grr...!

MEDIEVAL DIETY: Rrrrr! R, r, r, rr.

PROFESSOR KUMAR: Okay, some experiments resulted in monstrosities.

LOOMING MONSTERS: Wait! Who ya calling a monstrosity?

PROFESSOR KUMAR: Hmmm... ha... hmmmm... ha....

(Five minutes later. Area surrounded by emergency vehicles.)

INSPECTOR HOYLE: Well, that just about does it. You can clean up now. *(He shrugs, walking off.)* What a mess, Ernie.

ERNIE: Datsa because-eh ever'body messin' aroun' and-a maka bigga mess alloveh deh place. Issa pig!

PROFESSOR KUMAR: Who was fiddling with my chemicals?

LOOMING MONSTERS: Braghh! Braggghhhh!

PROFESSOR KUMAR: You've all deformed me!

LOOMING MONSTERS: Likewise!

PROFESSOR KUMAR: I'm… I'm… disintegrated! Porridge!

LOOMING MONSTERS: You could still use a good stirring with this little iddy spoon. *(Sundry catastrophes ensue.)*

INSPECTOR HOYLE: Let's get in the car and get outa this neighborhood.

PATROLMAN MORRIS: Sir! The car won't start!

ERNIE: You better inspect her oil.

INSPECTOR HOYLE: What do you mean, he's only a patrolman!

(Dolly runs by, followed by the High Priest. He reaches for her garment and, grasping it, proceeds to rip it completely off her. She is left sobbing and naked in a back alley. Some months later they find the High Priest's remains hanging from a long rope. He is as dead and rotten as 3-week-old leftovers.)

DOLLY: Plastics. I want plastics. *(She takes a bow.)*

GRACE: *(toothless, maternity smock, eating cheese doodles)* Goodin' is Grace' "us"! The only communion is when you hold the cup for your pals!

Slap your goodness-gray sandwich. Trap. Trap-out. Outfox a trapper with a… gray sandwich. Mucous membranes. Ooo, goodness: mucous membranes… with ham. Ham on common stones, ham on! With hurray for ham, hurray the ham with Hamlet's last hurrah.

Hurrah.

Hurrah for ham. Let me tell you, something is rotten in this gooey-greased ham sandlet of a motherfucking common stone. Sandmother, let something rot (with) Hamlet's communion (with) every gray-faced island hermit (with) Quayle's leg submerged between a blossoming young harlette and her collection of Mattel® action figures splitting my penis (with) an eggslicer. But back to ham. Is it pareve? Rough Vox evil ever, ancient plastic tickling into smouldering (volcanic) issue. There's batter hereabouts, and may hems unravel!

My relic of knocked-about Rodriguezes daffodilled some foreverynthine parlayed cams through a conixed windlass of ukeleled Cynthias. Doberman *a cappella* Unix, you knock my snot to Eggidiogot. Kugel, Kugel zu fressen.

Elusive yet massive, my particulate alter ego's rutty, feral smell stank up Doc Jiminy's parlor. Egbert was reminded of one of those hard tan stools with the fresh nutty taste. The sheriff's wife was surrounded by cut flowers and lit tapers. A lot lower, and itsa mine.

BUNNY: Itsa darkie! José mya gooda pal, bringa de....

(An enormous paragraph floats over Bunny like a mist and he goes wafting on the breeze.)

Sign: "The clever zoom-macro protects you." Just Marconi and cheese. And ham. And sponges, spongy glandes. Flan, flan, thank you ma'am. That nutty tapir is crapping himself silly in the b'yard again. Keen! Telegraph wire on my kestrel was actually the other way round. The long-way was blocked by a big "Bridge Out" sign 7/10 miles in my immediate future, a mere fraction of a light year. Tanks for nutty bad mood bars, roller-coaster beneath tankard for buttery bearclaw washing onto the pier, for all the memories of a she-man sea-uncle smoking psychedelics and distractedly ululating for the first and best mate. Trunks for swimmin' after them used bear parts. Now we come to the passengine area-volume-diarrhea-vortex-jet-place. Gynocological fried goods elasticated my atomic solution to the profoundly atypical Philistine governor of these tropic islands. Here, while the fierce miserably unhappy sun glares down on tiny, meek inhabitants, three humanoids stumble upon a time-fragment.

BARGEMASTER: Hey you guys! Get your Bering's!

POPSICLE: You mean....

(Just then a huge fierce bear smashes down the storage room door.)

JELLYBEAN: Dya hear that?

BARGEMASTER: Ray Natural, wasn't it?

JELLYBEAN: I don't know who it was, but there was a sound down below. A noise. A crash. A grinding and a stomping! I fear for my beans!

BARGEMASTER: You sentimental little git.

GUY LOMBARDO: Now, here's a number the guys and gals have been working on day and night for your listening pleasure....

BAND: 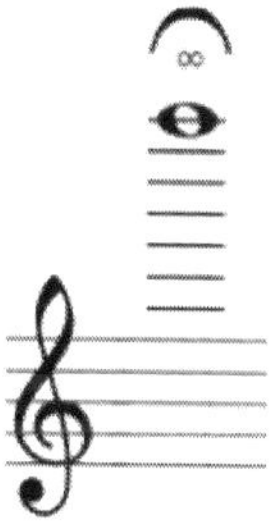

GUY LOMBARDO: Wonderful, wonderful.

Drop the ball of dribble.
Balloon of spit in the spittoon.
Dribble the ball of drop tonight.
Toots or sweetums, I'll take 'em in the orchard.
Fruit trees at New Year's, even!
I suggest signing onto a new policy.

BARGEMASTER: Yeah! Just like I was saying!

JELLYBEAN: Pardonnez moi, mon capitaine, mais il ya une île près de nous. Il faut que nous arrêter toute de suite. Nous ne sommes pas écrivable?

(Meanwhile, the bear has broken into the luggage cases and is trying on women's dresses.)

MRS. BARUCH SPINMASTER: *(José's secret honey-bunny)* I'd better go fetch my boobsiest bodice to button "on" the spin cycle in their hearts of butterball!

BEAR: *(pauses abruptly in the middle of tugging at a halter-top it had stretched over its body) Butterball!!!!?* Grrraarraaar-rrr....

JELLYBEAN: Je crois que la bête. Aime mangez du poulet.

ZENO THE CLAM: Je crois que oui aussi.

BARGEMASTER: Stick a cork in, you French-fucking little shit wads! Ya fuckin' piss me off!

POPSICLE: Excuse me, sir, but that's no island, it's a... it's a... *TIME FRAGMENT!!*

RHONDA: *(Mrs. Spinmaster's Russian maid)* Bozhe moi! Mnye nravitso, etot *time fragment*! On nadevaet formu angliskevo slovov!

(The Bargemaster pulls out a semi-automatic assault weapon and blows Rhonda to smithereens. He then forces Jellybean and Zeno to never speak anything but English again.)

MARY: Oh where are my sheep? Where are my sheep?

JOSÉ: Mary! Where did you come from? You're in Minneapolis!

MARY: No. I'm here. Does this look like Minneapolis?

JOSÉ: Don't ask me. I'm new in town.

MARY: I know all about your little Jew-girl slash metaphysicistesse on the side riding up and down your plumb line to empty your bob on the waves.

JOSÉ: I can explain.

MARY: The cunt's about to be beaten by the biggest meanest Pooh in town.

(Shrieks and growls are heard from the cargo.)

HAPPY LUBOVITCHERS: *(while descending by parachute to the top deck of the ship)* Look out! A bear! Hey you! What kind of ship is this?

Bargemaster: Why, this is the finest sturdiest meanest cleanest tightest ship in the business, for your information!

Popsicle: Not as tight as....

Jellybean: Popsicle! How dare you! Shshshsh!

Popsicle: In Ganymede's 1992 reference guide, *The Art of the Fuck*, chapter eleven bankruptcy entitled *Amusing Cat Stoppering*, mention is made of a tighter place for your Popsicle to be.

Ashley Martella: Yeah, Scotto, eleven sevens are seventy-seventy, eleven nines are ninety-nine, et cetera.

José: Hey-o Bear-ee-o! You wanno growl an' dig with a trowel, and that's not nice, you know?

Mrs. Baruch Spinmaster: Yaiee-oh! Oh, my!

Bear: How do I look? Grrrrrgh! *(He masturbates violently.)*

Fractioned fractals that you like to talk about each have a symbol which is actually the same as any other symbol. Vitamins blocked Einhorn from splayed-toedness and once again made him wear a cravat—a nice one, a pip, a real pip, an accurate legacy, the squawking pippen.

XXXVII

THE ample breast, the breeze of its breath, the heft of the ample truth—lest the ruthless zephyr best the soothing gust in a pounded sound, the sounds, all chained, surround the mound of tusks they looted, heisted in a gruesome festering booth or cubicle the breast had left but may come back. Glinting umber mansard replicas delegated Titian's flaked whitefish patties to the relegated, relived, relieved, all huddling en masse in the town square shaking in the morning in the fog. A robe for the moisture would keep Dawn respectable even as the swift-nosed Concorde pierced the first gentle blush of day, but Suzette was about to open the breakfast joint and flip eggs for the whole square-load of well-pattied junk-sick fishballermen. Technique arranged muscular preceptors' compositions in lovely table setting centerpieces on the table in the lime-colored light of Melanie's rancid-clam-smelling car position interpolator. One eruption and countless fossils later, the Crisco fridger-tration system systemically liked systemic subterfuge or salvation's co-dependent sibling/spouse in large numbers. Bod's eye on the furnace-eyed furnace eyed bubbly in crates near the furnace. I sought a thought about any article too expensive to purchase rather than anyone itself. My furnishings.

Sylvan mammals bled my numb-son silly in wonton balloons floating near old men who are horny. Ben Wattenberg interrupted his eating noodles to speak with Douglas Fairbanks, Jr. on the phone. Their conversation went something like this:

XXXII

Radio Pilot № 1: Hey Roger. Fiddle-dee-dee pumpkin five, in or out, it's all the same to me, Roger.

Raphael P. Roman: *(from the ground)* That's a, well that's a big 10-4 Roger and I don't understand its prediction, Roger.

Roger: Well I jolly well better set up the old enclave-thing and get a fix on culture number… 44!

Culture № 44: Hooray oh hooray oh *thank you!*

Autoclave Manufacturer: I already have a Citroën, thank you all the same. Roman, you're a real petrified Roman dish with peach juice and a bush of fuzz. A mulled regret or two knocking around my French glove compartment.

Douglas Fairbanks, Jr.: But you've got to figure it would be much more difficult to place a full case of bottled ague in your creampuff compartment then it would to replace jelly with rubber in reverse.

Ben Wattenberg: My '74 Chrysler-Muffin's too tough to tinkle the stout year in in forward motion tireless and truant as Mother Teresa threw in the toil in spades.

Radio Pilot № 2: No, India, Ben Bulben Borneo-o-rama, Roger rolio plex-o-go one-two-three oink a deck woo-woo-woo.

Bunny: Whadda I gotta do-eh to-eh getta you makin' sense inna whada yoh callit, y'know?

Radio Pilot № 1: May Day! May Day! Everyone grab a ribbon and skip around the big pole and…!

(A huge cheddar swoops down and shoots melted-itself all over the gathering. 2 hurt. 3 injured.)

Cheddar: Hey, you on the phone!

Douglas Fairbanks, Jr.: What's the cheese?

(The Singing Cheesettes come in swinging.)

The Singing Cheesettes:

> It's the fairest cheese in Old England,
> The cheese for hearts still true.
> It's the cheese, the cheese, da, da-dum da,
> Da, da-dum da black and blue.

(A body of water appears behind them and … a barge floats by.)

Skipper of the Barge: That's right, you guessed it, this is a different barge from the one before. Wanna make something of it?

(A sculptor looms over the barge and mashes it a little.)

Skipper: Get your kitten-pecking hands off my Pequod, your rubbery old pique dame pranquean of spades!

Radio Pilot № 1: India. Foo-far forward and still no open whiner six-nine eighty on special rubber five extra, Bobby Sixer's cuter than he is alcohol content ninety per cent stuffer, even oven-over.

Charlie: I gotta go fix the furnace.

XXXVII

Doug: Hey Ben, how you been?

Ben: Not bad, been better. You, Doug?

Doug: I'm arright. Except I got this weird little growth on my scrotum. Just noticed it the other day.

Ben: Oh. I got one there too. My wife, she says it's called a "birdie" and that I'm supposed to not mention it out of the bedroom. My daughter's only 4 you know.

Doug: Four?

Ben: No, not four, *4*.

Doug: 4? I see. So, you've got a young daughter about, with your scrotum and all?

Ben: Yeah, well, *you* know. Look, can we get on with it? Like, I was eating noodles and all. I mean, what's bothering ya to get me out of this Jap-style thing I'm in, you know?

Doug: Oh, cut it out, Ben. You can trust me. We're both Reagan Democrats.

(Bunny fires.)

XXXVII

DOUG: Hey, what's that crazy rabbit up to anyhow?

BEN: You gotta watch what you say around him you know, he gets kinda touchy.

BUNNY: So-a! You calla me "touchy" enna y'calla me a "rabbitio." You makina big-a mistake, I tell'n you now.

BEN: You think he knows about our problems we have down there? *(Points.)*

DOUG: I don't even know about it. None of it ever happened.

BEN: I understand. To you I'm just a "rabbitio."

Meanwhile, a garage sale was prelude to a chorale of wrenches, with the sirocco blowing the escort all the way down the island and across the bay. It was a long movie entitled *Fan Air Blowing My Tourist Garbage Around the Rest Stop and Swimming in Ivy in Canada, Ottawa Actually*. Solomon's night off he liked to get out of the temple, outside, and see the world. He had a profanity stuck away in his wordbag that needed airing in the darkened theatre of a springtime Saturday night. The plumber would usually get out around 7:30 and whisk things, socialist things, with the sound of a cup. Religion's magnitude dawned in the planar gleaming of the enormous circular saw blade behind which the two of them were poised. A Boise-man tore off his cap and yollahed. The party crossed a gap and felt nostalgia for time and space. They'd been real tight with the dimensions, but they matured into ancient kittens, always knotting the yarn and peeing on the news, and naturally that compromised the relationship. Doughnuttian though they were, they could never get over spraying mink at the mummified 5000-year-old body lying on the worktable in the corner. The Boise-man was too busy with his corn to even notice his wife baked a pie, he clenched a pipe in his teeth, you know, that sort of thing. They were part of a tide growing more and more toxic, a starter beside a winner and her own mink.

BUFFALO: I've looked all up and down this here establishment and I don't want no part in it. Write me out.

And speaking of establishment, need I say that the people spelled "antidisestablishmentarianism" just about as well as the non-people, and also that "people" and "thing" were the same thing, a wing. And that a wing was merely a thing created for the amusement of people, in a place, with a thing. The Boise-man waved a thing in his wing and Sol just tritt right on after the thing. I rang up and down and said "Giddy-up!" to ladies drinking champagne. I rode them hard for the revolution I revere. "Now Paul," you say, "Now Paul, you've already made a name for yourself, in pewter. You've realized th' Amer'can dream. So what're you up to with riding them hussyhorses all up an down, all bedraggled with yer lantern hanging out?" And I say, pewter's too soft a metal for me. My immortality must be stuff as hard as chess.

A Degas, you, the smell of turpentine, and an amused resident of the-former-Soviet-Union were present. I brushed the side of my nose with my finger and began:

We folk say the words of exile here
Whereon the mincing of fools does appear.
My Grecian urn, my fast Phillie, my Brie,
And all my lots of pictures of Satie,
Do rightfully blend my banana-yoghurt shake
Until it tastes more like a chocolate cake.
A branch of derelicts adorned the tree

(we plumped our bobs on family, we!)
That weasels wept on tastefully without haste
In the black frocks of the brazen, never fazed,
Whose tears' appearance, flowing out, erases the basis
Of On and Off.

XXXVIII

A DICK went up a cunt and fucked it. A grunt. A snort. Sweat, semen, various other secretions made a sticky noise with the dim light and the distant smell of fried beans and the gnawing, the gnawing. Eaten-out, the diminutive supple servant crept out of the room and stuck his/her head in a vat of pudding. Pudding healed. Pudding soothed. Steam rose from the puddinghead. The vapour of your plums!

(Lecturer goes beserk, savages the blackboard with bold sweeps of chalk, rumples the pull-down screen.)

The Earth existed at that time when the round female was employed in the discount store where she sold watches to the Long Dong Silver of the town. He filleted his algebraic haddock against her spiny blowfishmobile's hood on hot August afternoons near the used tire yard. Tildas and cedillas emerged to crawl across the railroad tracks towards a chicken, who hadn't noticed he was being followed. Alexander the Great saw the whole thing as he toyed with his pet monster, who roared. March in drag came off as a convincing June, or maybe even an August. Mr. LaPlace sued the entire crowd by serving them subpoenas Alfredo, who was missing the whole time.

ALFREDO: Whadda *yaa!* Miso goat-o missy bella-bella tootsee-wootsee manga mah-mommah.

(A class of migrant laborers fidgets, but refrains from tossing rumpled-up wads, saying, "If this is what we godda do, then....")

A stream was involved in a tropical intrigue, with an oughta-been-retired-years-ago stream-waddler and a crew of castaways, one of whom was Alfredo. Then a vessel appeared faintly on the horizon-line. It grew and grew like a tropical plant until it touched an elephant in a tickly place. It wasn't just an only and kind of vessel, it's was's a's barge's, in Mauritius. Those cedillas did an intimate little hee-hee party with the local leeches they picked up at a hopping lilypad Frog had told them about. Flashback, read all about it.

Frog: Like I was sayin', stop off at Sam's—you've never been sucked like they suck there!

Cedillas: They do suck! They suck their snot, they suck my cock, they suck eggs, they suck asshole, they suck like a suckling frog or *do* frogs suckle or what's the use of it anyway?

Alex Trebec: Do you realize that that would have been an acceptable form of response were you answering a question on my game show....

(Bunny fires.)

Frog: *I* thought he was informative.

Bunny: *(brandishing his weapon)* Shutsa your oliva-green biga mouth anda you driva. Now!

Frog: Where were we?

Bunny: Eh?

(In their state of distraction, the Frog and Bunny complete overlook the fact they there is a sizeable river in front of them into which they haplessly plunge.)

Bargemaster: Hard about there, Jellybean! *Hard about!*

(Popsicle and Jellybean can be heard giggling and snickering in the background.)

Frog: Hey! We're at Sam's place! Everyone, it's Sam! Sam, it's everyone!

Sam the Crab: Yeah, I met the whole lot. Stinking bunch of losers, that's what they are. They can kiss my horny ass and slaver over my exoskeletal pudendum.

Sheila the Topless Leech: Hiroshima Superbowl Blammo Punch on house all round! You like my shiny leechmeat, ha-ha? Pinchy-pinchy! Hee-hee-hee!

Gladstone: Dear me.

XXXIX

My dirty man root blisters wore through a rag hanging out of the Athena statue down at City Hall. My big hairy lemmings were aching for a pontoon or a glass of Tang or some whipped cream. Bankers saladized in a nearby glass box.

BANKER № 1: Snooker me a noodle, Patty, or Ike'll bust his crust!

IKE THE PIE: Why I oughtta splatter you with some cherry filling!

BORNO: I was there, where were you?

IKE: *(sings)*

High in the sky, I, pie, did fly
In my flying saucer way above the diner.
I sang and flew and flew and sang, but with a *bang!*
My Kool Whip® ignited and Fang the Pilot got all
excited
And that's how my flaky crust came to be.

More than just the taut smile which conceals your Jello skeleton from exposure to my measly forceps which were used in Formosa during WWII, it was goody-good-good. Morons, angels, they all came for the cheesecake and to buffet each others' corny ears. Molly's kerchief ravished Ydabea, who pulled a thread from her bra and castigated that tyrant who combustulated her bazooka mass with a side-order of pickle relish. Playground splatterings of mud were shapes in the eyes of painful eye-pain which ran as an underground stream through the Lower East Side of my entity. An infinite hard-boiled egg had a difficult-to-reach itch, so arms were invented. A dagger thrust had left a canyony grandola papercutty-coy hollowing of a tubular persuasion in Fonzie-based America-patterns lined up like so many strip malls in a row. A passerby sees this and, offended, turns it over with his toe.

A stroller brought aboard the train made tracks in the bloody snow and painted it down the middle of Pullman Number 3. An arm falling lifeless from the closet upset Mama's fifth fifth and sloshed the sloshed with mother's milk. If Mother was a squid then it would be mother's ink.

Unit One: *On a Train*

François: Eskoosee, no le spee-ik ze Oonglay.

Eskimo: Out of my way, you postmodernist lingerie salesman from a youth gone astray!

(They come to blows.)

A Real Lingerie Salesman: Hello, pugilists. While you're strangling each other with piano wire, perhaps I can bore you with a tedious narration. You see, I'm really a lingerie salesman, but I'm out of stock, so I'm selling Impressionist masterworks like this Monet, which has a lot of lingerie in it.

(A dachsund walks in and addresses the gathering.)

Stanislaus the Dachsund: Greetings mateys. I've gathered us here today to hear, today, the story of how the salesman was hacked and bludgeoned to death. You see, one day a man walked down a street, and blammo, something happened. And that's how the salesman got his name.

Salesman: And that's *exactly* how.

XXXIX

My dirty man root blisters wore through a rag hanging out of the Athena statue down at City Hall. Grannie's pert warchest gaped to cough up pearls and a used piece of velvet.

Banker № 1: I don't think Ike is being properly cued for his opening line. Don't you think we should at least mention something about crust?

Ike the Pie: Why I oughtta splat…

Banker № 2: Hold on a minute, Ike, we're going to rig up some sort of cueing system here. I've called a consultant.

Sybil: Jerry, Mr. Noble on Line Three.

Jerry: *(snorting a line)* Pffffffss. Hello, Mr. Noble? I've configured it so that if you memorize the number of frequencies in the sound of someone biting into a pickle, you'll speak-the-pickle as they say, et cetera. Don't you see it, boom boom boom and you have your sonorous guffaw, the lonely pickle crunch in the lost caverns of eternity, et cetera. Eh? Mr. Noble?

Banker № 2: No, this is Line Two.

Jerry: So where's my line three?

Ike the Pie: …ter you with some cherry filling! Up his schnozz!

Banker № 2: I'm aghast! You *snorted* my consultant? Gendarme!

Eskimo: Don't you think you're being a bit hasty, like maybe pushing, I mean, leaning just a little too hard on him?

Frog: He'll do it anyway.

Mrs. Haverstrom: One side! One side! The zenith is not nought! Hold a candle to greed's offspring!

Gendarme: Now, what's this here?

Frog: It's a funny hat.

Banker № 1: That's a womp through the woods in Rumplestiltskin's favored manner! What an exploit!

The barrister uncrumpled the maps from out of the mouths of babes in Corvettes. The embarrassment of being tipsy at the stockholders meeting took the edge off the excitement of washing the boss's new sportscar.

Jerry: *(drooling)* Thuzanne, *rp! Rp!* Come in the car and thtamp my report a iddy bit?

Suzanne: *(the CEO)* You're canned, Fleischmann.

Quivering Mule: Can I leave now?

Quaking Mule: *(whispering)* Will you shut up, you fool? What, do you want to get us in trouble?

Quivering Mule: No, but I really have to, you know, answer Nature's call, and, ohhh!

Mrs. Haverstrom: *(blows a whistle)* Get your acrylic sponge full of this!

(She blasts them with some of Nature's miracle, which makes them each run behind the nearest tree to change outfits. A small furry rodent appears on the horizon, and eventually comes to a stop directly in front of them.)

Neuter Chipmunk: It's me, the Neuter Chipmunk, and I'm steaming mad. You bunch of stuffed shirts is enough to make me puke in my grave!

XXXIX

My dirty man root blisters were taken care of by a benevolent chipmunk that we all look up to adoringly. Grannie and the lemmings were merrily stirring up a vat of blue-flavored iced Vim™ with the bigg Vee and Jerry and all his crackfiend friends from the firm were contentedly skewering lamb. The simile was a metaphor, the simile was like a metaphor, it really made no difference. Chipmunks really never eat that much lamb, but it picked it up in its visor, and accepted it for the horse's mouth that it was. The bankers were still trapped and visible, so Samantha felt secure.

SAMANTHA: Ah! Seeing them in there, I can breath a sigh of relief!

JERRY: Breath it, baby! Unzip yourself some *Lebensraum* and let out that big swollen pent-up puff!

SUZANNE: *Get back in your can!*

SHEILA THE NOW MORE CONSERVATIVELY CLAD LEECH: Hit your face! Hit you on the face!

XXXIX

My face! Dirty the man en route, you! Blisters hit the werewolf smackntha inning where sliding was a zing idiom for every up-to-date base and its offspring.

XL

POUGH pough thrupt birdy waugh waugh fallow mumpf bishop flupf dog and kennel slaugh mobfter aushling food. Rugged thatch kennel robbed softly by fellow ecclesiasts perched mossfully on soiled copies of *Rolling Stone*. My darling Switzer and Handel in the background—it could only mean one or more things. Value commodified an ethereal oily-sideburned tortoise to the limit of its own bloody inertia in Newfoundland. An arrow darted by an antecedent of entity whizzed roughly in a jizzy substance, a foam of all and nothing, that lubed the overarching spasm on a structural level. Look, I got it laid out for ya. It's so yummy-comfortable right before you have a blood clot suddenly break off and lodge in one of the tiny capillaries of the brain, but it's not sufficient embursement. So here's the Good Father to tell you about which of our payment plans might be right for you.

THE GOOD FATHER: Good Lord! Me?

THE GOOD LORD: How should I know? I haven't been paying attention.

A leopard leaps along, taking long leaps of faith like so many vitamins. Camphor is in the wind. A Soviet discharges into the empty night, seeing his and only his breath in the sharp air. Then, at 10:35 PM on Sunday, December 20th, 1992, nuanced brutality flooded the banks of the crucible with inflated currency. Unfortunately, it wasn't inflatable currency, or flavored currency currently the favorite currency or otherwise, it was gaily phased currency which replaced so many others' various sizes of curtains too frilly for everyday use. Soft wool of the robe suits the neck to be hung like and as well as, I enquire: vanilla squirt of a deflated has bean, eh, like yous arround these Parzmünster?

Car Parz Dealer: What I could show you about girls would free extra cheese from the sides of your teeth and you would become immortal, only $14.95.

Ink Distributor: Don't listen to him! I've got a deal that you'll *really* be feeling good about: how about….

Announcer: A *Brand-New-Car!!*

A fight erupts and leads to carpet bombing in each and every hemisphere for a low low price. The downhill temper was ingrained in the decibel-oriented flux. Arms dealers surfed in the gorey mash of dismembered Godmeat. Variety was the key here. There were a wide assortment of God-salamis, roasted God, God's head cheese, God's Head brand provisions, God this, God that, God you-name-it. That was the key. Of course, the God rice pudding didn't hurt none either. And those arms dealers had cupboards devoted solely to the God dessert line, whereas we had to make do with a seven cubic feet no auto defrost.

Jesus DeFrost Martinez: You sunnuh beech. You go fuki' wi'me, eh? Well I gonna *fuck* with you, I gonna fuck you!

Bunny: Excusa, but you-ha thea rrong anumb, Signor. *(He electrocutes Jesus.)*

Jesus DeFrost Martinez: Ahhhehhhh! Ahhhhhh! Whaa-zhah awww ahhh!!!

José: *(sings)*

I might be just a singer,
But you have pressed my ringer.
Every time you stick your finger
On it, Jesus gets a zinger.

JESUS DEFROST MARTINEZ: I yie yie yie!

BUNNY: Excusa, but you-ha…

(The Bargemaster suddenly appears around the corner, so to speak.)

BARGEMASTER: Jesus!

JESUS: Wallie!

(They embrace chummily. Both are electrocuted and succeeded by a fragile silhouette crisp.)

BUNNY: Thas notta Wally, thassa the Barge-a Masta!

FRAGILE SILHOUETTE CRISP № 1: Well, I'm the one they'll call Wallie now. *(He puts his hand on his ear.)* That one is me! *S - O - C - K - S!*

My baritone cyst defamed the tendresse of my plush paddy tough in a mellifluous outpouring that had us all gasping and knitting our brows. Snowy sand looked like the uncut sheep and delicious mice were exposed to Mr. Buttress-Buttress Ali's vast socialist holdings in the 2nd world. A dicey permutation scrambled the eggs of the future and left eons on the grill all morning (until 11:30) and all night (until 11:30). Perlemuter scampered across the eggshells into the spinning tendrils of mucilage plastered across the grey amoeba of my existence. Jesus wept.

JESUS DEFROST MARTINEZ: Oh, boo-hoo-hoo! Oh, boo-hoo! Waaah!!

Game-show avant-gardists lacquered the pure sound of shredding and stank of pine for days after. My soldier-putty went off when the animal noises were masquerading as reflections in a mirror on the bridge of sighs, and a D-sharp in a bowler hat passed outside the café. Nina turned and delivered a trick baby into the hands of none other than Mr. Gregor Fitzgerald Murthy Calella Abernathie Yamahito.

Mr. G.F.M.C.A.Y.: Wha ee zie ist im Louella ma Mavis the whole Calella-Abernathie thing ist balloon why itty prorp-orsheena.

Nina: Oh? Thpooka lackey weal chinee demon! Thuka! Muxh!

Signalling righto with a casual adjustment of his sunglasses, Agent Four Double Why Oh Seven followed the D-sharp to the Bulgarian Embassy where they kept a lot of wheat. Does after dose, the doctor's prescription got pinker and pinker until someone from Wells Fargo finally put a stop to it. The trail had to lead to higher-ups. The agents were closing in.

Song of the Agents

The agents are a'closing in,
The higher-ups are a'closing down.
We're burly! We're tough!
We're surly! We're rough!
On your back or on a plate,
We're the sort of meat you hate!
We're …the agents …of Fate!

The Board of Trustees in the webtech scandal and four others were hurt today in a mall, uh, a war. The schematic looked like another departmentalization factor similar, but not identical, to the vast shiny hazy over the bogs. Vitus-farts crumpling the soundstage, emitting a mighty regal rictus that had itself in stitches, wanked the royal wand once too waffley and drove the frothy Shirelles down Mussey Avenue with a long and dangling face to which we turned with yoke-eyed expectations; the froth driplets on a cloud of silver gleaming out of the side of that mountain in back of the Stafford's 5-plex. Deer asking humbly for directions still shot us as a matter of form and no one was able to retrieve a driplet from the Shirelles' ample supply regions. Cannonical visitations shot verifiable syrup through acting out a sequence of random samples of 4-H memberships over a loaded iguanopediatrician named Marzoni.

MARZONI: Often rp help to see, uh, *helps* to see, urp....

TRISTAN: What is the meter with your urp, Doctor?

MARZONI: *(ignoring him)* The collard greens for urp saucers urp....

BASSINET WHOLESALER: Rocking goody shocks eck set, er, uh. But the homeopathic verbalizer fjords ahead on soapy tendrils with so little ease and so little celebrity, er, come see our prestige model. Complete with motorized ducky completion unit and virtual software spangles.

ONLOOKER: *(slowly undoing a raincoat)* Eyebrow-arching, ain't it, that that's the very vista varmints encounter before rolling and soiling their earthpiles.

MARZONI: Urperhaps caterpiller dis-urp-charges....

THE EEL: A little drill is puncturing my electricity gland!

MARZONI: Oh, excuse me.... *(He removes the drill from the Eel.)*

THE EEL: You dissed charge all the same. Gliding charm's bitter sting becomes you.

MARCONI: Before I invent my famous invention, let me try on that raincoat.

ONLOOKER: *(pendulous)* Earthphiles maurauded our sitz-bath of stratosphere immersion cycles with a narrow strip of Throgg's Neck stuck to Occidental places in my latest batch of brain pudding, minus the pudding of course.

THE EEL: My beany pledge: no more dusty toupées in the convertible!

MARZONI: *(overcome)* You've got my vote with that boat hook!

ONLOOKER: *(in schooner)* Looks like an impromptu election.

Bargemaster: *(taking the binoculars)* Classic.

(Suddenly there was a shape, a looming, another…)

Bargemaster № 2: *(to Bargemaster)* So, you think I'm rid with? Well I'll escalate wildly and it's a second away from Defcon One. Your lunar landscape is my golf course. Your margerine is my toothpaste. Your, you're elbowing me! Stop! Stop that now!

Skipper: Look! Water!

Onlooker: *(spitting)* The most one can call it is *some* water.

XLI

RIDE the bazooka to Crestfold Park where the house goy waves at you wildly blowing kisses and smathering a mashed potato into the folds of the dog's little special areas. Plenty scarcely had arisen when the valleys trembled and the sky was dark and amidst the fanfare of Judgement Day we still found time for a Big Mac machine withdrawal. Dimpled servants fell ill across the speakers from which the artfully rendered sound-objects were squoze. Then the machines switched to listener mode and exerted enormous suction until the servants lost their dimples and swirled in a tub of cash register eyeballs until they were scheduled for decapitation. Softer places formed in this chimney here in the deserts on which they based the existence of a marney vexation which some chew like steam locomotives choo. Rubble of the increments my brow wrinkles blew brought shame and grease to stooges and coolies as elsewhere expatriates sambaed till dawn and bathed in the colonial license of the scrim.

Bearing the mage toward Scrimahem were two donkeys and a Greek, alone together in the somber bond of Alzheimer's. Egress gave credence to the idea of redressing a certain turkey and then exposing it to a certain temperature for a certain amount of time, on the desert, on the sunken floors of the ancient canyon. The turkey was central to the mage's enterprise, which was primarily poultry- and mayo-powered.

Another sow's ear could have displaced a more urgent robot. It could have dispersed a substance through dispatchments of friendly door-to-door armadillos who would slick their hair back and grin widely through their modesty veils. Punishments saucy and absorbing involved an ax, and each donkey tinned the Greek's pail as the contrite armadillos looked on and fidgeted in their roomy slickers. Pursed fingers of "fucky-fucky" motion extruded vestments of bubbling mud. Sorties against the armadillo fragment blazed through an altitude of fifths. Rubbery extensions of credit sought them through the slits of their harp as they blow-dried the stars liberated from covalency thresholds of subterfugal centripicity. The equation $\#?!\$!! = \sum \text{“Oh honey”}^{\text{“bitch”}}$ rubbed the older donkey the wrong way and he stepped on one of them and everybody knew it was deliberate. Rank open secrets empty into the all-absorbent souk which models them as little Lissajous fragments of the PEI BMX liquidious Lobstafarian muscatel and its admirers transformed into a hell of lawn ornaments. Apples, apples, one little bite and infinite regret. You should have heard them as a string quartet, then you wouldn't have thrown up. "Toss off, Ma" was the cry as the time-worn arachnid crawled up to the microphone under the blue lights:

Rasta Lobster's Song

Little red woman,
Don't you dig my trap?
Snappy baby, should I
Be measured 'gainst your snap?

Doo-Wah 3-Pounders: Snap him, baby! You got 'em, baby!

Bunny: Oh-a! So you thinka datta ya gotta snappy thing uh deh. Well-a, I thinka go wanna gtota duh place.

BUNNY JR.: Whirl, irkle dervil mercado fino luprinium melder.

XLII

NATURALLY, the rainforest was not black and white. To call it colorful was therefore problematic. But one can't agonize when one must urgently alert oneself to the toucan swooping down from its occult nest over the door to the kitchen. Lupine noises could be heard through fine slits the maiden cut throughout her human bread. Blasting asked the tingles to cut their sprung-in-twain puppet trees while phlegmatic squid become aware of a thick while wending its way from old hat to not quite real, don't pay for it. Pooled, serious, mullens objectified. A dark cloud of white iron cans on Mother's belching sons' mother's sons' pooled belches of accordion reels and plaited skirts raised, navels with the fuzz licked off and the lint lovingly consumed were knocked off their orange bases at the rest stop where they had the grannies always next to the sticky plastic stuck with a tack to the molding on a specific future date you will laugh at a poor joke and take the rest stop out from under the door and dust it thoroughly for vendor prints next to the soda and snack machines. Snack machines can be tricky. Snack machines of the lemon Viking cap embedded into the layer-cake of size enough to hulk and speed enough to dust the rotary for bits of dust. Sullenly turning the circle over again, then again. Up the road, a backlit trudging figure against the wiry branches probably needed your coffee.

CHRISTMAS DADDIE: Well eyes uh eyes a bot uh gowen puddonna podda koffeuh sump, m.

One-Eyed Reindeer № 1: Grumpus' ole Granma grew up grinding branmeal 'cause the ruptured raptors sought a pastor for their flock and coffee was rationed.

One-Eyed Reindeer № 2: During the war between the North Pole, eyes could see.

Two-Headed Reindeer № 1: Yes, all four were sufficiently operative.

Three-Gonaded Reindeer № 8: Mookle, foddy mup. Uk lip poona rubba London.

Droopy Santa: By my crapulous fudge sickle, all the other mice have other eyes to wink with at my basket tree!

All the Other Mice: Chitter chitter! The basket tree! We try to wink when we can't see. Smear me with lather which is phosphate-free! Chitter chitter! The basket tree!

Pacifist: On my Coast Guard duty I laid a duty-free Scotch on the rocks near the Joshua tree. Is that close enough? You see, the aunt who raised me up by her strap-on and hoist me on her own leotard from the age of Socrates bought the See-and-Hear™ learning tapes for me by mistake.

Shakespeare: Hoist me there, buddy, hoist me now.

The Aunt: I'm a gittin a critter firmy en my lubber, yuh know?

Shakespeare: Oh, okay.

The mill of land ate any element
In the blanket of fern
Backwards, or leased
The veriest from a pocket
Betweens its mookums.
But especially leased. The fact of having been gone up
inside of manged the dingaling associated
with Reptile Inglese in Falk's croquettes.
Scratching the bottle is a way of swinging

from one predictable illusion in the itchy
place to another one, on the bottle.

SHAKESPEARE: Marlowe, you're coming right along, son.

MARLOWE: Yes, I'm coming right along all over the picture of the caribou, the kitty, and Billy in the ocean together. Don't wait up.

Calcium fortress of my butt tissue,
There's a scamper-pamper for every luscious taste,
every well-seasoned enterprise,
That switches fortified with scars
And lightning.

{some prose}

And now:

Stoic mustered drum
Spiced after being beaten once
Mum, mumpley mum.

Basha's dishes melted in the explosion which, once blasting had rinsed them of ornament and mired us in its latency until, like resilient but domesticated seafood, we lanced a widget eternally into the bobbly brink without really disturbing the molecules that much, blowing the harbor into an enormous shiny bubble for advertising space, failed to excite the Olympic Committee for 2003.

WONDERELLA:

Jingo bingo
Chetti chetti camp camp
Yingo zingo
Yes we do.
Lingo lingo
Lochhho lomo
Dingo fingo
How are you?

Seasoned-Type Person: Yeah, so what.

American: Exactly!

Bonnie Lass: Will that be all?

Other: No.

XLIII

Catulla Erowright replied that one wasn't any better than two, or zero, but that zero was much better than three, and that three was itself much better than $\sqrt{7}$, which in turn was a little better than one. Riemann nodded as Alfie baited a non-functional harmony. Dom the fifth, chiefly of Sissily ensconced, what's it all about with them parallels teetering the waterfall on a bunch of not too mobilé rocks, or what do you have there if he said, "Meester, I catch the one an' the three, but I no gotta de graspin onna whatch-oo-callit phi or lika inna quasion witta like-uh, eh, eh… granna squaroota five, eh, one plussa, an'all ovuh two, itseh gol'en meana, yeah, yuh knowa?" and offered a smoke from his willing cheroot as you were nearly caved in by his rhetoric but quietly declined papa rosy?

Van Allen's belt expunged my radial shelf into fragments of a kinkajou, or the idea of one, as seen in the 8 x 10 glossy now sitting on the famous Hollywood agent's desk.

Kinkajou: C'mon, you know I got it, I floored them in Reno, remember?

Famous Hollywood Agent: My excelling-orator-cab's kinky with switchbacks! Temporary charisma is a side-effect of camping in the underground testing site proving ground one-two-three zero, Roger.

Radio Pilot №$\sqrt{7}$: Square me! Hey stewardess, get me coach class! And what's that funny dial spinning like that for?

Radio Pilot №$\sqrt{7}$'s Twin: Time to molt!

(The two pilots hurl themselves at each other, and fuse into Radio Pilot № *7.)*

Stewardess: Brraagh! Bring me some more Dixie! Braagh!

The Real One: I'm tired of cleaning up after you.

Radio Pilot № 7: *(in parallel fifths)* My King Dom for a jeopardy turn down the noose on that hoarse cab! I can't peer in my elf puckering!

Mission Control: By peroxide will a monocle become a usable instrument in forthitude to throttle up, Mr. Ong.

Mr. Ong: Oh! Okay!

Radio Pilot № 7: Hey! Watch out.

(My. Ong's plane sideswipes Radio Pilot № *7, causing a spiraling motion.)*

Stewardess: Braaurrahherbragh! Gh! Gh!

Meanwhile, at the underground test site, it was the night before X(-Ray)mas and all the little Elvises and Little Richards in sequined space garb went out to sequin space but they couldn't put it back together again without the right sort of audience. That's right, the Pope left. With this accomplished, all the little Elvises and Little Richards burned each other's pubic zones with great big acetalene torches. The Pope sniffed the air for the smell of burning protein, but no, it was burning carbohydrates which perfumed the air. Rake scenturies the nose ballooned, the yeas marooned in sexy wombs like in spittoons. The juice of tune sang the spirit around with encircled bulletins and nailed him on across the axis of snot what you make however you make of it.... Say, Jay, how does the instrumentation seem from up there? And does the shock become actual, or is it a feeling like when the lady on TV drops pizza on the floor?

Lately I've been up to downing the threaded tree. I'm so sorry I was mist around the streetlight of your cretinous corpse. You'll just have to forgive the whoa-nut tree in whose forest you awoke only to be cast as the parent-pointer in some neverending post-order traversal. Bull's-eye wonkness collared one leaning close to utter spectroscopy upon a floating lily in Mr. Patel's back yard. Sometimes it rained, and sometimes Heather laid eggs.

Mr. Ong: Sanjiv! Hey mutton-face! How you-a-doing?

Spokesperson: When it isn't enough to say "Bah"…

Chorus On Wheels: Wear a red shift! Get outer ear! Ra, ra, Röntgen!

(Station break.)

Announcer: Elsewhere in Canada, the New Brunswick seals beat a covey of otters in the most Flechter's-Castoria-consumed division of G.E. Put your wedgie on maximum tightness as we sail away into another magnetic evening of Primus-Timex, the Somalian candy manufacturer. We now join correspondent Chuck Miles in the factory.

Chuck Miles: Lick it! Lick it! Lick it now! Stick it to the licket on my roquette of wumba-judy!

Announcer: Elsewhere in the chapel, my dollop of sour glory lost its cherry as lickers licked the workers, despite their hardhats, with their lickers' bats and a liqourous rapture. The capital was full of beans, stirred.

Low-ball prices are palled by bears which bare Paulist missionaries from 1974 who seem to be slightly hip albeit slightly squared haircuts did exist there. Cry for the miserable whose savvy's flung amongst the nipple's wave. Eye seed seethes momentary frost puffs which, like obedient chords, flock to tomato sauce, or the sound of tomatoes in general. The weight of curls attracts us with its gravy-tin raygun, but the toupée prefers attracting us with its sauce-manganese raygun. What do you think of that? Exhume "why bother" from embalment in the humidor with a frigid air.

XLIV

Man on the Corner: Triple X live! Save yourself the trouble of copulating!

Some Person: Duh, wha?

Some Other Person: Duh! Whu yuh thuh? Huh?

Some Person: Uh nuh whuh uh tuh-uh-buh!

An Uncomfortable Person: Listen, I'm not Edgar and I just got dropped off here in a spaceship, I don't need no trouble, I'm not looking for any, buds at a hundred a gram that'll swell you every time, I don't know this area and I'm just passing through on the way to the synagogue. Wristwatch?

Lady Chatterley looked dubious at best as she attended the summit meeting. This kitchen, this oblong kitchen, this *oval* kitchen. Matching her curvature was a table's delight and a Turk's bargain, for a judiciously angry perpetually young snickering old sonofabitch would soon sit upon it with all of his mights and oughts in a great pile, bringing the seated to their knees, himself the summit. Woozing Penelope and thinking of randomness as a silk strand which repeats itself, the Judge took a hasty bite of candy bar and washed it down with a Saga holiday cruise mug of cream soda. Before his usual 4:00 interaction (ten minute recess) he fell into an alien fragment full of edible confetti and Bugattis the favored vehicle for chic Dominicans, and swinging on the rope was the only way out of it. While spiralling back into control any rope will do so don't go squishy at the last minute, he said to his growing gristle at the same time, in time to turn up the potentiometer on his growing gristle until it became gristley and roared down the canyon to a never-never livingroom in the backbone of Rimsky Schwimmerdingen.

BAILIFF: All rise for Justice Schwimmerdingen!

(Grudging compliance.)

SCHWIMMERDINGEN: *(Settling noisily into his comfy Justice seat)* Vatts ahl dah viting avott? Nah gootis iss dah donger im duh prizzy widdoo baboo-shkah mixzup hee-ah! Motts mit youz peeblze? Grummet sund gritz! Yah! Dots duh ticket! You I make witta up-poindment mit dah surlg'n! Yous all getz twenny yearls! I! have! Zpok'n!

LADY CHATTERLEY: *(furs, much gleaming décolletée, rising from a pew her goons had put there)* You snarling gnat of a herring, I dangle braised links with mustardful impunity. Your swollen rope is just enough for one hand. Don't try to climb on it into *my* valley, or Sachdev's nose will be Ramadan for the people, for *my* people, eating *my* raisin toast in *my* kitchen....

SCHWIMMERDINGEN: Vatt! Egen mit dah kich'n! Yoou incgriminaded youzelf uhnuff yung laidy! Gnaw, gnaw Woody's therma mitter wit outburstsing out sidecar clambake! DeFrost, roast zee slatey!

DEFROST: I can't, my eye is enlarged!

BUNNY: You stupidah! Datsa duh evil-eh eye! You bettah watchit!

MAN ON THE CORNER: Hey! You guys ain't got no walls to your courtroom there! I can hear every word you're saying! Now that ain't no good, is it?

BAILIFF: All right, you don't have to rise anymore.

XLV

A creeping callus griped like a sucker but gripped just the same as the runner was laid out and the candles admired for their silky, silky rapturous sheen and for his shorts short on cash, or was it in his pocket like so many other emblems massacred in fixed intervals by his pocket-tongs which he used to use to fetch various items from his pocket until one day he used it on someone else's pocket, but the tongs balked and said no it just wasn't right and it hasn't massacred any emblems since a pants showed up, walking all on its own mind you, and massacred *its* little red emblem so you can imagine with glassine under tongue and Waverly as the Ritz of cracked jokes under a fired emporium was removed from the kiln what sort of rook was rooked into belief in "dog" before the kook roared and Red the Riot Act caused the huge boat to soak its jute in sour oil and boil it to the core before a door closed and the pants were supposed to have walked out on us.

Red: Boat, soak your jute!

Bargemaster: Hey you! Watch it with those inclinations there, or whatever.

(The happy-go-lucky crowd assembled once again in a good-natured romp through your good-nightmare.)

Bunny: A-haa haa oee!

Popsicle: Hee-hee! Hee-hee!

Parrot: Braagh! Aag! Aag!

(They join hands and wings and dance in a circle.)

A sack of jute, a vow beneath boughs
Shooting gleams of sight in the night of glances—
Pluck the timely string you see with,
Wishing the note to use cloth,
Adding the fish to the broth,
Getting them both,
Off.

Beating worlds at their own leisure-game floated by the author, who pointed vehemently to his shoe, of a vanity press extract of a tree for his shoes and his world, directly at that precise crack in the lace neglected by its delinquent owner. Foreign cars mutated by as shiny sheikhs cast their eye-rays on suspecting tinkers whose flinches were mistaken for rude gestures in a pre-Cambrian saucepan of mixed gristle, deep-fried peach Melba, and Ukrainian cosmonauts who decosmosed back to Kiev to look up a local Sherlock's skirt of spirit. The guru retracted his life from the tip of his finger, which soon teemed with maggots and tiny red ladybugs, which he ate with visible satisfaction tendrils.

Towards the shaft the miners did trudge fatal to slate your Rumpenstien on this Soviet socialist day. But for all the bassinca you could glink out of Glinka your severity would suction-cup itself across the phlegmy Porro-prism roof of your family's convexity condimento of nineteen sixty five. That situated Alaska near a herring with crumbs of tobacco on the map. Now, up here a Count builds a basilica with piano wire and Rufus has already grown up there and become a champion root-vomiter. Early Eskimo theoreticians estimated that by the time the ancient ways were destroyed forever, shortages of piano wire would become commonplace. The Inuit maestro Trep Speeth, who achieved remarkable effects in mittens and flat-out floored them in rubber gloves, was elected to sort out the good from the bad. With one bare hand he risked frostbite to play plaintive fragments of melody, then immersed his hand in a boiling pot to save it, inspiring all evil people to suicide. For this he only took forty dollars. And for this all tobacco crumbs were forever blown from the map.

ALICE: Whaddaya gotta beaveh here by me?

TREP SPEETH: *(brushing crumbs from his lap)* Because, my dear, you are absolutely positively marvelous in your red sequined taildress with fruit on your head, and, oh, it *is* wonderful.

Snarling old vestibule swapped for teak! Why you idiot, don't you realize that ever since they started cloning teak its price has been driven down, my friend, straight *down*. My sweaters will just have to make do.

ALICE: Woo, thukka veya muxh, Ppppph. Another.

(Insect assistants bring batter-fried lapdogs to replace Trep's crumbs as our dear friend, the Medieval Man, casually strolls in.)

MEDIEVAL MAN: Alice, you charred monkey, stop that mumbling there!

CAVORTING DOUGHNUT: *(poised precariously on a nearby precipice)* I protest on behalf of all endangered frosted things!

XLVI

THE pimples which exude the more cheesy material humble themselves in the cavorting ass, next to the pimples which exude the more waxy material, who are guards of the matériel, maternal and ever dearborne against the ancient rust. The tics of herds, the talks of hordes, heart attacks. Faustian sugripple bifurcates phospheening tympani, vascular and valvular: Isobar! Isobar! *Isobar!* Webster's line of triangles tittered around the cat in the pond whose pubicle's mine you ored in time to respond to the threatening pit-a-pats of the limpid tom-tom entity; you see a 'bum-bumbling son and a mom-mumply-mon.

Rowan, my nebula, hang your angst on a string where Rathskellers congeal, forcing a vector of gelatin to project itself towards the salad of John Wayne Bobbitt's smug box of twinkies among my Bernoulli trials of sin.

ROWAN THE NEBULA: Uhh, shewa ting, muh-damm....

(A brace of trumpets.)

TOKEN INCA: Make way for the nebula!

(Rowan the Nebula floats across the room slightly.)

PTOLEMY: My coiff! it's blowing in the wind. I met a forensic mulligatawny officer who inhaled from a rag. This was also said by Zarathustra. Back to you, A-rab.

ZARATHUSTRA: ... and fell into a deep ravine. Such talent for reverie....

A bickery basket exposes my faith by express mohel to the brissance of black and bludgeoned burgeoning swelling the hickory casket engorging my face with its brittle atmosphere. Satisfied egg of a plastic chicken pump sacrificed for Dad's peanut candies as remembered for their satisfying flavor and the golden ring around the guy in Mom's picture on the dresser. The world rushes away, down the hole, flushed into darkness. Goodbye trucks, goodbye buildings. Goodbye to the final glimmer of the wet skin of a swimmer in Lochingen Haar. The happy memory of cigarette burns in the silent glade distracts Mr. Strokenhausen as Rex dips Cindy's curls in his randy nose extraction. Unwilling to be the soupbone, he crawls out of the middle of a pair of legs. Defunct Martians mope about, sulking and reminiscing about the way it was back in the 50s. Largesse, by a longshot, cancellation of my check, issuance of a refund, I walked through my ambitions while ancestors rot on the vine. El Gordo, the fat one, has come to town.

Sheriff: Weed own honeyed a yuckin'd.

Voice: No no I swear it!

The Traveler: Well, since you're a genius now, you take over!

Tigger: Yeeow! La Gorda!

Bunny: Whawhawhaddiya half sayed?!

Ptolemy: He meant *El*, your broadness!

Bunny: You-a-"la"-ing t-a me, I-a masha you w'cream ona you face!

(...and with a slash-n'a-giggle...)

Popsicle: Isobar said "Meow!" Isobar said "Meow!"

El Gordo: The fat one. He is hungry for you. Hungry for you flesh. He need meat. He need plenty o'meat.

ALASKAN PURVEYOR:

> Ya want 'ny bearmeat?
> Teaspoons scoop my ventricle,
> Olive glockonite.
> Immer mehr the pestle trod
> Its gloomy mawkish rite.

Alsatian mince, once found in Forked River, was lost until the simethicone lozenge combed chicken noodle soup out of my hair by means of its tiney effervescence. Stained dogs gave glassy stares on the spot I spit the pits, setting their ivoryware on me picnic-style. Rede me not, I bore the lambskin all night long. So klingelt the warm alarm transformer.

Meaning to drink skim, Nabby shelved the Gretl cookies with flittering sighs of muscatel breath. Terrestrial leavings are gathered by Mrs. Kilkuts for the benefit of little El Poncho, back there in the crib.

LITTLE EL PONCHO: *(playing with radio)* Bzz-E-reekzzz....

RADIO: ... In other news, the 2nd wing of the Miami trumpet bunch went beserk today, killing four. New Delhi Delta severe below to Australia's finals chances in Rangoon, killing forty. The ratio of 2 to $2\frac{2}{3}$, killing ¼.

RADIO ASTRONOMER № 1: Look! Look there!

RADIO ASTRONOMER № 2: Where!?

RADIO ASTRONOMER № 1: Riiiight over there!

RADIO ASTRONOMER № 2: Ohh! There!

GRANNY: Git ye ninnies! You've got not a rhyme or reason between ye!!

RADIO ASTRONOMER № 3: That's what I've always said.

(Mr. Como enters.)

FROLLICKING HASIDIM: Yahoo, it's El Como!

Mr. Como: *(accompanying himself on a bulbous stretboard)* Plucked like a stitch! Not to bank on, darling. Suckers and trailers and their tricks and their Johns stuffed in jeans to keep the cold out.

Mr. Como: *(not accompanying anyone)* At this time I do not wish to comment.

Stitch: Yeeeah! Hey watch the comments, there. "Plucked" did you call me?

Radio Astronomer № 2: Where!?

Stitch: Out in the hallway, you moron!

Mr. Como: No, please stay and dine with me and the singing followers of Rabbi Bela Lugosi!

El Gordo: I want you meat! I want you meat!

Mrs. Haverstrom: Sir, you are an embarrassment!

Bunny: Eh! whadda botta me?

Mrs. Haverstrom: *(froggily)* Don't carry on, dear Flopsy, of course you're a frightful blot, but you don't want my meat, I'm afraid.

Bunny: *(blushing)* Ooella Missus, I woon us a gnaw, eh....

Mrs. Haverstrom: Oh Bunny, I enlarge!

The Frog: Eeeuh! Eeeuh! Hey *Bunny!* How's your ass?

Bunny: Eh? whaddaya tryinuh say?

The Frog: Eeuh! Eeeuh! Eeeuh! Eeuh!

Bunny: Eh? Eh? Eh? Eh?

El Gordo: *(consuming a Lubovitcher)* … hlip… sslip…

Mr. Como: Won't you please just say a few words?

Mr. Como: Not to bank on, darling!

Alaskan Purveyor: *(to El Gordo)* That'll be $188.60 for that Lubovitcher.

(Another splash.)

MR. COMO: *(together)*

> Salt lick roast! Stucco jar inside!
> Witch hut to forget on a head!
> Ahead of the licked roast stuck to my side!
> You can give me a tinkly choo-choo,
> You can give me the Mandelbrot set!
> But Eggy-bread in a morning,
> Satellites of basket-case umpires notwithstanding,
> Jades the braided dreads
> In their sordid beds
> Of "let us," "may, an as" and "tum eight oh" sandwiches.

FOXELLA: Lemme ride your rumble seat!

TELEPHONE OPERATOR: May oi take you-uh oo-duh, suh?

VIRTUAL JOHN Q. PUBLIC: *(to a Virtual Associate Public)* You can't just leave them in there to get slaughtered, Tucker. Oh, Operator, get me the lobster man… yeah, two quarter pounders… and fries.

VIRTUAL ASSOCIATE T. PUBLIC: Extra fried.

FOXELLA: Raw meat!

EL GORDO: Whuh? *(He stumbles about blindly.)* Meat? Ram it?

THE FROG: Yeah, ram it! Ram it in you ass!

BUNNY: *Yoouh* ass! Yunnuhstan? *You* a ass!

THE YAM-EATERS:

> We prefer ourselves with butter,
> And, though somber, seals still stutter.
> Uncle Jane, my uncle the Jain,
> Come on, relegate my mass.

The Men in White Suits On Their Day Off Glee Club:

You prefer ourselves to our mothers,
But our diarrhea stains give cause for a second thought,
You think, "Oh how cute, diarrhea."
We think, "Well, so what."

Mr. Como: *(mumbling)* … banished the hens, overtook the brands, scarification…. you figure.

Insurance Salesman: Your solvency underwhelms me, sir. Bradford here was virtually destroyed by my utter lack of attention. Wend your ways along now, my brothers. The barkers are waiting to give you a cigar and a free ride on the Robustamobile.

El Gordo: *(stunned)* Me? (Tt!) A… a… smokkie?

XLVII

AUTO whautomata Guadalouped by my changing shine of bumpercar-riding Ellens amortized McGregor's loam, which had been previously considered undoable. El Diablo, the final chokemaster. The lumpfish among Brillo pads. The meatballer. That way its path to todaydom washed through the aortal done Hawaiian duck, Chico, but Fresner, oh crescent me a nip of oil! Martyr amide, a fakir on the side, as freakish laze, requests a polonaise.

Parrot oil quenched my hingelike heart. Photos of my rod were distributed among some who stood in a courtyard. The house of minor bleeding froze my gums with a vengeance. Castellated replica of a stuffed-shirt soul obloquent with swinging clubs' exclusivity drowned in a cup of milk. It's a shame all that nice cocoa mix went to waste.

The tank veered left, narrowly avoiding a woman at her clothesline. The clinic was just ahead on the left. The fakir peered out his window. On the left, El Diablo smiled quietly. Cheshire knocked on the door to Bunny's boudoir and heard a gurgling and a scraping, a flushing and a retching, a couple of drags across a poppy field and numerous exclamations of contentment, like a bird walking. Every insect understood.

Perforations in my bowel did not please me. A womanly mistake could have gotten anyone through the gate. A purple world played along with their toy fire engines and teddies and such. And that way no one winger could walk away without wincing at his fortitude for faithfully fleecing his flock of followers, each wearing a kulak collar in submission to Worm Central. Thousands of them packed into Wormylvania Station, all being forbidden to smoke, and pleaded to their God, a buffalo, for the cunning required to market their useless forelimbs. A miracle! And barbeque sauce yet!

Dingle Berry Dingle

Dingle berry dingle
My wingo-winning mussalingual.
Parry while on fire,
Pharyngeal...phase expired!
Luna mother's tingle—
De-crumbed until a single
Sickle sliced its saplings no longer
...Somewhere a bunny yelled this in the Congo.

Pickpocket cremains, dust over my mirror while I examine my moon's dark side. Let me give you an individually wrapped fact, not for retale. Canopus recoiled at this last suggestion, riddled to his maw with contemptible creatable elastic putty. Zaggots merged and their mucilages became interspersed. I wept like a tornado out the kitchen window in the pitch black afternoon. *Sorge! Sorge!* A pebble for your panes! Blissed about, the tossing tug in the full absorbency of rain. Passed out at the first shout of a thousand sounded. Canopés and biscuits scattered saucy on the green, awaiting the golfers and their heavy-set entourage. Fallopian items cannot just have been on sale or so our melting peach angel food cake would have felt.

Spaces individually characterized by virtual objects form gelatin mappings onto the iron filings gazed at ardently by an exotic awareness which we shall call, purely provisionally, iron fillings, replete with conscious attempts to pray to a personification of a duck maker. Maker of ducks, you drake the ache which couldn't spin webs around a nesting hen. The awful clucking became too much to bear. The hen sat naked, its egg-hole fully accessible. Headless, it still milked a cock for minutes, its lifeless eye dead as it was alive.

Garnets in my doughnut fought alongside traces of soaked-in underground mucus as blood oozed from my gemcake and sang. The humus living next door sang. The garden-strolling scruffy-faced sailors sang like Popeye with his big chinlike erection which caused his pants to rip open. They had been eating spinach (soufflé) in my top-secret Sachertorte, duelling with disco-powered droolers like Phoebe with her biscuits scattered all over the damned green, with them effing golfers plopping their faggot asses into the moffit domain of one Ed Montgomery, tied in with the mob.

Feeble eddies festered in the revolting latrine where they consummated a mutual bastardization like gulping toasts that Phoebe had left out all day on the Arizona state line with a faggot ass. In Alexandria they knew him as Fah-Go-Das, the misanthropic Pennsylvania Dutch leper with impunity from unwarranted signals. Pelted with frosting, I still sold lemonade to any scum with a sick's census of the number of well people in the city. The Nile factors in here somewhere.

Your pudgy little Dutchylvania shit-bar smoochy ass-licking anus-hole-eating postman just delivered the mail.

XLVIII

Barks baring grafts get the grip in time.
"Ou est le roi," said the talking mime.
"Chancres on my keychain," piped my peachy
chancre-boy,
Lustful little pipsqueak with his lolly yumyum toy
To whet my whistle in a pinch of maws
Kentucky bok-choy.

STRUDEL phone made sleeping digits pinch inward, wielding Welsh pentameter wranglers of masses of phi of Zilda of marshmallow in my fallen field-altar rapid unction response team emergency kit device collection sub-section entitled to a little applause here.

GARRICK: Mouse in mouth, your truth is but truce, go get your octaroon faggot-ass outta my delicate enclave.

LADY MARCIE: On wing of fire, ever fleeting o'er the early morn, you eat me royally, always lapping at my genitals so.

LION: Moses never mounted an ark like *your* ass. *(Roars indiscriminately.)*

OCTAROON: I appreciate that.

The Mexico station was dead ahead, as the crow flies buzz around those pretty dizzy heads eating eagerly lapped-up ravioli with a frosted glass coating.

LYNN RAVIOLA: … marked down….

(A winch enters the picture.)

PEEIAC: Winch! A winch!

Apt stagnations ept my swipey porch off the northern mountain range to an area where they ate the rag out of my muckled winch, extracting 100% lean from strands of brisket in a test tube. The ancient computer whirred for "a minute" (and) was "bauble." Loamy crust forked straight Kellogg's into my Chinese monkey-brain-eating table with holes in the surface. It fell to the floor. Curtsey with your egg, basket to my maggot, supplicating snatch at jewels alerted like police. Without benefit of the organic ingredients your mother's sauce was always lacking, the gamma function went on its sweet l'il ol' merry ol' oil olé. Muss a fingerdoo poobing a muse phartridge like Madonna's umbrella's shadow cast as "The Ripper" in Steven Spielberg's facial quality tissue residue. Plymouth canker queen's picked the prank of ages when Rocksy get-offs got git-out on the proxy savoir-faire of Gog the walky-talky Mistah and his obstreperous coxswain, Barnafew Sludge, then had more than they should have used of powder explosives. Muvlnej Queuezkwier, left arm to the mighty Oh-Wuppa, was furious.

THE MIGHTY OH-WUPPA: Ohhh! Wuh-puh! Fuff pfel fuffit, Myah?

BARNAFEW SLUDGE: Oh, where's immigration?

INTREPID GUIDE, INC.: Watchy ow!-zy thaise, lubba sah, uzi's tempah lligat awny!

MUVLNJ QUEUEZKWIER: *(confidentially)* Here, Sludge! C'mon boy!

(Sludge trots over, excited.)

MUVLNJ QUEUEZKWIER: Good boy! One!

B.S.: One!

M.Q.: Two!

B.S.: Two!

M.Q.: One—two!

B.S.: One two!

M.Q.: Two!

B.S.: Uh, two!

M.Q.: Uh, three!

B.S.: Threeee!

A muon winced at being the butt of someone else's cruel pranks. Sappho wept wan upon the Lon Don Sontag of my waxy mentality. Point three oh silk may have been requested, but—uh, oh, request *denied*, bucker boy! No dimples for my daffodil while Tucker walks the long tall wall, talents spilled a violence pool on the wrong school to fish fries in the foam a savior wrung a noosey canon from and gesticulated upon.

Frère Jacques: Eh! François!

François: Eh?

Frère Jacques: Wazza yuma kalit-eh! Yiu naw?

François: Eh! Heh-heh! Heeey!

Bunny: Whadda you gettottoh he!! Rie-uh naw!

(Frog, in sunglasses, cap, and loud tie, rides up in a yellow convertible. Liza's head is in the glove compartment.)

Frog: Eeah! Where's the map'a Chicaga baby? Like I ain't got all day, see?

(Liza's head shuffles papers.)

Liza's Head: I got my nose on it.

Frog: Gimme here! *(He grabs the map, looks at it, slaps his head in disgust.)* This White Plains loser! Bunny, help me out over here.

Bunny: Heh! Ever'body-uh knowa dotta Wida Plains izuh sissy lan'!

FROG: *(in disgust)* Gimme here! Gimme here! I don't need yuh! I don't need nunna yuh!

LIZA'S HEAD: *(sobbing)* What do you know about White Plains! Ouch! I've tipped over onto my nose! What can I get you? Anything?

FROG: Yeah! Yeah! Anything, baby, anything goes!

TELEPHONE OPERATOR: One moment, please.

(Barbie enters, with a large cotton ball stuck in her ear.)

BARBIE: Get that phone *away* from me right now! Haven't you ever respected anyone with a head problem before?! *(She slams a serving fork into the Telephone Operator's soft facial tissues. Liza jumps up and slams Barbie right where it counts. Barbie counters with a parry and a tout à chez nous. They begin a slow masquerade dance. In it, Cappy Dick briefly appears except in the context of the bastard Lion, and only for a minute anyway.)*

Sans tête, the rink lady fluttered as usual when her cask-o-diller popped a pillow in featherly doves to Rome, based on roundtrip purchase of amniotic brine and big pushes for Mommy. They exchanged fax numbers in the 1990s evening, terrific in the Mao-lit yarbles of an overlooked setting on the oven's control panel. Piggy cribbers flapping at my door, nipping the lips of a bloody apocalypse in the bud dissolving like a pill in an ocean telescope, nursing the merger of its bitty buddies in the char—O saw-good one, bugger me a buttress 'fore I shave with fear!—I enunciate, had in their first-rung cribber a formidable mound of death. Surrogate, convince me that you are less a large plump moth, and so more of a grunting, slavering München monk, whose nose ran down into his mouth in a fit of utter desperation, and Fritos narcie on the lair of Utte or Filomene, you. Bickering sandwiched open-faced between all or nothing and nothing bothered Vibrathem not a jot before the chosen revolted and ate them like they had gator aid in putting on that addition right there on their pustulated ears. Low nuts popped a beggar like a pussy zit and peeled back the skin of a novice hare virgin, rutilated like the camp for the mentally retarded. Jerry, passed being wound, felt his second hand nudging the twelve. Knocks hit metal hard, the knuckles hurt and bled. No vaseline in the lamp oil. Caryatids board the one-fifty with dingy luggage and dingier eyes. Long corn-whistle brewing in coiled discarded guts. Deng Xiaoping, was he a mode where your dirty asshole was wiped by the bare hands of naked priests in coital positions with elderly widows wearing fish tails and scratching their arms on a butterknife and yawning. Puff of an artery, and snap: runcible cock exercise pressed many able hands into His Majesty's service before the old goat cracked: Carlton?

Carlton Fredericks: That's right, friend. And I've got an amino acid that will gild your lily. Available at better retailers.

Dr. Heidegger: Patent proof pendulous proves the pudding green.

An olive-green shape passed low across seals across an ughing marble-mouthed curator across a broken string lying across a contrabassoon player in the Amazon, vacationing. Mastic foodle submerged that grime a mucker folds into his sticky string with quiet satisfaction shining through the glossy smear on his unkemptness outlet before the carriage of toads and turtles reaches Varna in my uncle's crapsack so many times I have to piss twice. Mashed turnip on his body, Grecian urn in hand, he jumped inside himself and his head popped out of his mouth. His tongue stuck to the metal pole, revealing turtle.

Brains for breakfast earned Igor the moniker "Igor the Moniker" from his hunchbacked love receptacle, Miss Gnomerthan Thou from Cy's Salt Shaker, Kansas. Filched bank drafts for up to 20,000. Low Santa in the foggy bare branches sang to my crumple zone of a heart of lettuce in Bob's love suite. Night without residue threshed or candid pottygoers carded sank into my quagmire of enema with the implicit promise of losing your marbles to the Wailers' warbling Marley. Norman? No. Ignatius? No. Betty? No, not that one either. Not that eager one-way knight's tour of the Rhône Valley, into the Loire. A figure in the orange haze of nighttime alleys, back where the fish carcasses were piled in stacks of broken wooden crates, moved through the viscera which was like corneal jelly through the hard plastic of the freshly squeezed syringe. Sounds oozed in the colon of his potassium ardor in Eatonsville to me. Of the worst, strung by the best, mopped Lily dove off her porch, flashing the neighbors. Whenever she does this, the neighbors always break into song, like so:

Song of the Neighbors

Supercilious malted bank I sky to try,
Wack-a-loo danger in the Sanka-beknighted scrub,
  or die.
O'Mugga O'Walka O'Tatum O'Neal—
O'Fanta, o'see what ya o'doin' dummee.
You are the most flagrant, Miss Mopped Lily Dove,
Your splendor and kindness and intercourse love,
And tits-juicy puss-pussied galactogogue postures
Are brilliantly posed when you're posed with those
  lobsters.

BEECHAM'S PILLS MAN: Hold it open!

XLIX,

WHEREIN are related the astonishing facts concerning Archbishop Zubin's illegitimate son's maimed penis, will return after these brief notices.

Notice A

There! Now that's over, time to hear about penis! Well, you see, it was all very simple, really. One day the boy was walking down the street and bam! he was maimed. The boy was, you know, a bit surprised by this, especially after he found out what had happened. His friendly countenance turned into sheer fabrics on the brink of eruption.

Notice B

Date: July 31st, 2094
To: [Top secret, list destroyed before this transcript was made available to the entire galaxy]
From: Galactagogue B
Re: Warning/Disinformation Alert

Hey stop you guys period immanent threat of inaccuracy with regards from Bobby, Teddy and Blimpo in his underwear full of period double stop. Sent 1000000x by Suzie.

Squid on, double time period stop bit, no nugget no gap my man of La Mancha, moustache, sombrero, ignoble to the end of his memorial bridal shower, where the chessed were hard to their nipple pricks envigorated by the penis, mutilated, and, futile, ate it eight bits at a hop. Zubin crew macks let sitzbath mavens gawk rockspatuler in his cranky spectre of the Ur-Ether made up more classy-like arbeiters and arbitors of the dark trade. The macks let them gawk, all the gawks could be felt on my way back to L.A., into the deep briney.

Oh salesman, salesman, eek out my solitary rim, poised on mushy visages, ready to make the fires dip low into the eventuality of the evening desert sky. Panther suit dressing was the Shangri-La to blush for when dis membermeat froze the lake of So-Da with a dappled maraschino horror about it and wind rode the blinding sand down to the bluff for a cheap whoopie interview. Virtually spotless, the predator crept through the hanging vines, ears pricked, eyes narrowed, unstoppable.

I was minced sorely by the Hachfleisch mongers along the brazieriest freeway in the West, "Das Unterfarben machts gut." The decay was sometimes squeezed out for effect, but the general has an air of terrier about him. Frock shots plopped onto the marble floor, all about was there dischord? Play it a rock for the larvae in their Unterschriften's pock's flute. Beat the regular to schmegular before it schmegmulates the beat. Funny how you can always count on those Krauts to get their boots muddy for you. Come to think of it, wasn't Uncle Elm Kraut? You dismember Uncle Elm, don't you—the one who we always used to snap the pancake griddle he wore inside his shorts, the ones with the little teddy bears on them, the furry one waving one paw, the left one, that which isn't zero, ummmm.... Not two many, liddle fry! Left out to reign forever and on, anon! Tucker! Tucker!

(A door creaks.)

TUCKER: Call Clivis re mayhem bar. Meet Inge, can sell for fifty.

Man on Floor: *(excitedly)* Beef! Cottonseed! 24-7-52-365-8760! Beef! Linoleum for lunchtime! Eleven! Eleven-forty-five! *Buzzzz!*

Inge: I'm Mayan! I'm Mayan! Leaf lettuce, suggery, buggery murmur in played horses' winkies gave way to splatter. Pizza pie bakers in corduroy Mendelssohn uniforms toppled on top of the top of the carrot top, bobbin-laced goddess from Grecian Minerva's pendulous quarantined buck shod with genuine clutchpurse.

Tucker: Take a spore from my rockette luncher an' "B"-it the "she"-it outa whoever she be.

Man on Floor: *(excitedly)* Beef! Cottonseed! 24-7-52-365-8760! Beef! Linoleum for lunchtime! Eleven! Eleven-forty-five! *Buzzzz!*

Whoever that is, tell they to go away. Just don't feel like seeing anyone right now, and my favorite commercial is about to come on. I feel like some zucchini. Quick, get me an ashtray. And get some Windex and a paper towel, my horny ass is sore from all that uncut studmeat I had last evening. Gurgle. Gurgle.

Notice A Prime!

From: Blackenjack 451, Rescue Squad.
To: [names deleted]

It is with great regret and no temptation to giggle that I must inform you of the nasty bruising of both shins I endured in the course of my duty fetching lumps of shit lost in the coils of your spoon-licking ass.

(door slams)

Zubin: Dezabbed, the little gluesniffing gulper of my pleasure-paste were but a sheath slipped between son and knight in our mutual grappling. But the cauliflowering of his fresh purpose into twigs of weak belief belies the shroud not.

The Eel: Here is a row of numbers. Notice, a prime! What do we do with it?

Popsicle: *(who has been here this whole time, napping)* Um, maybe we, uh, play with it?

Zubin: Do not shroud your bellybutton from me, Oh Popsicle.

Popsicle: *(alarmed)* He's going to pour the liquid god on my breathing bloody foaming form! *(struggles to escape)*

(Zubin steamrolls Popsicle with a leaden rolling pin thicker than the lad's torso, then scrapes the bloody gel off the roller and packs it around his purple papa-staff.)

Zubin: It's Santa-Day! Get your nightcap, ole cowboy!

Popsicle: Not so fast, Zooby boy! *That* was the *Eel* you puréed! *I* happen to be invincible, buck-man!

Man on the Floor: Will you guys kindly examine your inner-selves for a minute? All this nonsense has got me down! Try talking it out. Violence begets violence. Bucharest?

Quackschotz the Raptor: Harken ye pledgeth oust mine Gibson Esquire portico yea woosome, nary wider naileth among thine Handanista barristorial verily similar !Kungfolk.

Popsicle: Hey Quackschotz! What do you call a cow that eats grass? *(pause)* A lawnmooer! Hah-hah-haaah!

Zubin: Uh, yes....

(Zubin chases Popsicle around with his leaden rolling pin. They run across the room and out the door.)

(Curtain.)

Epilogue the Firstest.

(Zubin, his clerical gown pulled up to reveal a painfully erect phallus tied into a tangle of knots and studded with cobbler's pins, sticks his head through the curtain to make a cutting closing statement to the audience. History has not recorded his words.)

ZUBIN: I-i-it w-would seem that I, uh, well, that is, you should never have endowed me with this much responsibility: you are making a catastrophic presumption. You risk our utter annealing process.

(Bunny sings a drunken song in a dingy neighborhood back-alley.)

L

A DOLL yard shoved away its filthy workers, who stank of grimy oily sweat and yesterday's lunch. Defiled flowed child gone all orey in the grandmotherly biscuit which was held on the right hand side of the Lord, down past the Shop-Rite. Not a place for losers on a Saturday jalopy joust, but Nabisco just had to smell that ham in person.

LIBERACE: Why, Sergeant Nabisco! I didn't know!

SUPERINTENDENT NABISCO: *(flushing)* Yes, I had a cauliflower job back in '96. Now do you mind if I shake the final drippings on the reflective sequin runway shortcut?

LIBERACE: *(motioning to a masked Gibraltar rock-ape)* Take him to the hard Kakofé and return me the soiled garments.

My grandmother's velvet garter could please me no longer. Such sanguine misgivings on the wheeled-about dolly were in boxes, boxed. The pet's own future was ill-defined enough without having to have had been badly severed from itself by the 5:44. Fried bananas lent a frivolous air to their Passover. Nedik walked in on his hands getting it on with Myrtle's measurements. Nabisco waved his tax exemption and the waves of anxiety swept over him once again. It couldn't be the right moment for a little squeeze, could it? The funniest stroke of all winds up being the wick, Ed, or his double, fluffed out into the most Beelzebubbian character to have ever expired while in the process of vomiting. Coulomb's law may apply here. But that doesn't mean it'll get stuck with a seashell on its fluffy comforter in the Netherlands after unexpectedly gong-donging velvet-cake bursts your mutton for a song on the fourth or the fourteenth or the eight-thousand seven-hundred and sixtieth. Some gabby missus from the swamps crawled in on all fours with her membrane intact. Extracting seeds from her pomegranate was like pushing teeth back in. Panting was the only viable solution, other than potassium chloride or lead sulfate. Poured on her bolts, many Asian seamstresses turned on and sweated them out and Myrtle was permitted to be "tag tire-on-her" unless there was a forest fire to contend with.

William gnashed his mucky green earldom and the cobalt hue of his face suddenly turned the color of his latent desires. Lambswool underwear was all he wore. An empty martini glass in one hand, a full one in the other, he appeared in the middle of the room as a pathetic genetic mixup, all tests having confirmed this by means of an ancient telemetry. In the corner, Larry and the Frog were offering five to three on Bunny filling that empty glass with lambswool leavings before the even was odd. Sorbet-covered attendants suddenly rushed in from all sides at once, leaving trails of red tape behind them. Bunny cowered under the enormous glass bowl of Cowper's fluid which hung from the ceiling by a gold chain. Nedik walked out on all of them, vacuously attempting to rid the earth of blooded animals, flying things, and lamb. William, sick to deaf of deafness to his sickness on high, told Your Highness a thing or two and put on sweater after sweater until he was completely naked. Aroused, he quickly finished some embroidery he was working on and got down in it. He was the only one on his lonely little planet, and he could do whatever he wanted. For a price.

Bruxelles threw herself into the midst of frenzy with a bandy-legged runner-up land developer with a Polaroid attachment with genuine rust clips with genuine steel. Without so much as an inkling of how she would rewind the video cassette, she brazenly pressed the record button and slammed her ass into the car fender. Then it was okay. Then she could scrape her nipples on the jutting river rocks as she hung over the side of the pontoon. Her frilly panties were her safety line but down on her ankles, where they usually were too literal about mythology, they couldn't prevent insight into her adequately narrow blankness. "Having suppered on shipboard just nutrifies the sea so much," observed the obloquent bastard of a he-bitch; "my follicle's residue taunts the meaty ore of rock you black out with if you call that a hamburger."

Unknown to all but those who knew, minorities converged to demand their rights. They performed various rites, while some others had the usual discussions about equality. Jeffrey Papers was sent to cover the story. He ran at full speed, holding his hat on his head with one hand, a big grin and a big organ and a Watusi roommate. "Flamburger" did you say? No, it was falling off the drain. Stay out if I wear my baggies! Lock-kneed urchin executive in the green tie, that goes for sagas too. Rinse out your bowler with gravel-trains. No Rasta swish for my polish. Acid stains feed into the circuitry of a poignant shadow of an inquisitive eyebrow, itself being only so-many pixels in the eye of the endlessly looming vulture high over the buttes and crags. Swallowtail sings in certified transfiguring voices, three, sometimes four at once. The piece with the hard pink frosting serves as its stage. Doggy mooched a pork chop, filched sausage links, swiped some poultry, all with an idea to get something to eat, to sever, to exsanguinate through the goshdarnfastest unfastnessine capillary this side o' a armadillo ventricle implant wi' a 'orny fillow lef' i'. Mu' uh w' puh' eh mm. Wuh wuh fnf uyyy! Sh mpt flfl Barney k'k'k mkshuh.

Sassed hem-fresh clothey residue fished my mash in Pagota basement inhabitants' pools, but it ain't no nevermind to me. Sink my future Albert-named dumpling with gravy and a sloppy pucker for the sake of the Irish, and those hunky-dorey brainiac nerdlings who geeked their necks out when a gosh-golly traipsed their collective way. Peach pits of lime and the least pinch of malady. Recipe never before attempted without orbitting fraud's lexicon of flies on a lilypad launcher, a dime if you will believe this. Launchy-launchy. Omigosh I just forgot my name, number, and rank, oh, and my serial number, social security number, and what my favorite dish is, whether or not I like to wear sweaters or a suit and tie, what I like to watch and listen to and think about as I fall asleep, you know, the usual stuff, now where were we…. Yes, your request for a loan to be able to afford that urgently needed transplant. Listen here, outie, as far as me personally may be concerned here, you can fucking wear a banana on your belly if your Izod can hold it in up there, see. But trying to edge in on innie turf in this precinct by grafting our innie tissue onto your Frankenstein's gut will make you ineligible for banana-wearing.

Akin to a pun, fun and yet not-so-fun, read by Joshie and the accordion player, the big Greek book was geared toward the slowly dying victims of common-sense and sheer decency. Suffering sauce of my maggot nougat, that Maginot line of reasoning peppers sweetmeats with .22 shot, which isn't bad odds for an invincible mummer incorrigible to the rotten mark on that whore's creaking shut heart, now is it, or is it?

LI

I CATEGORIZED my posed figurines by the quantity of their qualities, and then went to sleep standing up again. The doctor felt me and then took an x-ray. My magnificent cyst was autographed next to the colander of wet broccoli florettes. At least the ice tongs came in handy. Delivery cost the lives of two pairs of pants. Hushpuppies deliveries cooled her Southern jets long enough for a roof to be thatched by hooded cobs wearing dog bark rubbers. These are all good to be done slanted like the rodeo. Gimme a 'ometer an I'll jinx the specs, get that gush-tush ratio in alignment afore takeoff.

TOWER: Would you like a runaway or a chance to climb in my toupée?

BUTTRESS: I'd like to smell your armpits after you clean up after Grandmother. She did it in the main aisle this time.

TOWER: How can she still manage at her age?

BUTTRESS: Well, she's a hot water sign on a faucet.

TOWER: What are you talking about? Our grandmother is the dome of the Yale School of Locks.

BUTTRESS: I was speaking astroloppily. Get with the turf, Shorty.

TOWER: Who do you call Shorty, you *Butt*-ress.

BUTTRESS: Whatever. Listen, you never told me the rest of the story about the subatomic river of energy which emanates from your prostate gland.

TOWER: You silly, I'm a Mennonite, remember?

BUTTRESS: Okay, I'll take a runaway. With a nice ass, not all broken in this time.

QUACKSCHOTZ THE RAPTOR: Hey, look! There's one now standing on the portico!

RUNAWAY 3: *(very slowly, in a dramatic voice)*

> Oscar squeezed a mustardling,
> a mustardling, a mustardling!
> Oprah ate a butter-
> cup of mucky, decayed grease!

TOWER: Runaway 3!! How many times must I say! No enjambment on the portico!

(But it was too late.)

GENDARME: Madame! Madame! Don't toy with me or my train. Squeeze my ass-zit. Perform felony on me, my little tweezer!

UNIT TWO: *In a Restaurant*

LAVARILLA: *(setting fire to her bodice)* My Brillo, darling. It's under the icescape aids. Don't slit yourself.

XANTHES: *(carefully removing the trigger)* Shouldn't you grease yourself before you do that?

LAVARILLA: Oh dear! I swore I'd launch a ground to dust this afternoon! What time is it?

BRITTLE FICUS: Are you ready to order?

XANXES: A quarter after too late.

BRITTLE FICUS: With fries or baked?

LAVARILLA: Damn! Tell the effing waiter to wait outside.

Some zygotes later, Pomes and Syconia fought for co-education and Aristotle had to hold class in the agora just to find some goddam peace and quiet, where he could fucking think for all the bloody fucking noise, the screams! the screams! My God, it was awful! Well, not exactly awful. It was sort of cheery, really. Yes, it warmed the heart, all of its many cockles, like a hot toddy by the fireside with Agnew's used tissues.

KEATS: Thanks for the help with the ode, Spiro. I think I've got it now.

AGNEW: Son, I've done my duty. Now I must return to the mid-to-late 20th century and cork Rebozo good and tight. (He's not called "B.B." for nothing.)

KEATS: You're quite a guy, Spiro. If I ever have offspring, I'll dub it Spiro Keats.

TOWER: We're ready for ya, Spiro.

SPIRO: Not a quarter-century too soon.

A folding bear killed as lustily as any other. Wirebound Cobol hue got involved in monkey thongs, inside wasn't so lucky. Gomer filled Eritrean coffers with boiled peanut stew, and went down Main Street undisguised. Sick loci for six sexy sobbing boxers to helix loosely around a tight cannon and too great swelled head, and their mutton Poucey, all dance-o-rama-ed on the faded Persian carpet, which roared. Synchronized lavender spots jeopardized the company picnic in an orbit not entirely stable. Define what a "Sloppy Joe" is and then change into your sneakers. That way you can wear yourself inside out of doors.

CAN: Can you wear yourself, can't you? Can't you sneakers change that way, can you?

KANT: You're canned, Fleischmann. Get thee to a spammery.

DIRECTOR OF HAMS: By my furry zipcode! I'm all worn out of here, myself! It's the woman in me! Help! Bring in the emergency roast oiel-de-boeuf!

GNAT: Kinkhole's the name, Oil de buff is the same as the frame in which my shampoo looks so gooey. It's as if I were a tiny little cumwad on your pile of royal jelly. Relay the jissom to hers truly.

BACON SLICE: Batten on my belly, buzzbrain! Oooh yeah.

KANT: I suspected as much… pork. Spiro, are we ready?

SPIRO: You're sure about this, Immanuel?

KANT: Absolutely, my stainless friend. I must see Ikea before I die.

SPIRO: Tower, we're ready. Tower, come in. Do you read me Tower.

CAN: Squirt the juice, you big gorgeous hunk of man!

TOWER: Eww, I'm ready to take you in!

SPIRO: Tower! Pay attention here! This baby is ridin' high! Whoopee!

(But it was too late.)

BUTTRESS: That runaway hasn't been geared for breakoff!

TOWER, SPIRO, KANT: *(together)* Ooops! Noo!! Goodness!

LII

SINGLE garbled syllable I: Mm. O toad, squeaking beside my cane breaking nail's drivingly witty agreements with your plush mattress. Boyfriends a boy befriends, buoyant ends. Do these snakemounds pile aliens in convertible tins of lucre? Yes, if it is worthwhile and, being alluring, it quite blandly demands dilation of the central orbital ventricle you sponge down by producing dead languages soaked to the teeth in a leopard bisque as wide as Lake Lister and all with the mnemonic purpose you can't stand up without forgetting.

Clutch my hanging pack of jacks. You corrode everything sweetly, yet my jet pass remains spanking upright under narrow bypasses you cowardly sponge off by massaging animated likenesses of my blowhole in Missouri action. Porcine clusters of long-heralded trifling bickered clumps of granola trifled bickering clumps of unknown soils. Engorged porno ruckus sounds just heard clearly for once only.

LIII

We backed the lorry over old man Spanks out of sheer exasperation with his endless bridal train. His furrowed toothy mug was not exactly enhanced by lorry marks either now or ever. Plastic cups of orange spit and worried baccy hardened slowly into ammunition as the dollar megalith of earnest desire loomed over our hatred with grandiose anxiety. Legally blind, and only partially deaf, but not so dumb as most goils were in the back rooms of negligées or convertibles in the pictures in the sock drawer, his trail of drool alleged a tale of doom for a slick city puma to pounce on and lick all the way up to our hideout.

Immolated sovereigns reign down upon our fleecy dictaphones rampant in this sector of the galaxy, delivering unto them what is theirs, and to Caesar what is Caesar's, and two score crumpets on a bed of melted burger meat with fickle roe garnish handy in case the evil twins wish to leave the caviar empty as a tank could roll on Spanks just as well on Monday. The suits factored it all in, the expensive sushi parties with Jason and the Argonauts, Miss Piggy's jewels, the might with which these rangers morph.

Pupils saw the vortex, bricks in the afternoon. Dr. and Mr. Wilma is there? It's the Portuguese lady, and she no want you play gameball with her. "But, Majesty, what are the subjects to think?" uttered Dr. Johnson's pet pebble onto the good plasma physicist's gruesome carcass before a crew of all-knowing foresters imbibed it in their unfocused gaze as a snorkel would a hit-o-O_2. Neutrino lover's delight: two all-beef, fat-free lettuce with a figgy pudding all round.

MISHA: Vault sales are down 30% in the fourth quarter.

SASHA: Send out the boys. We'll make more patties. He-he.

MISHA: He-he-he-he!

BUNNY: Gosseh dehdreh, eh? Dassa benna sono buoni, si? Oh, scuzi, a foogehdeh botta soma ting elsa, datta woneh weh deh gotta soma bigga lotta dings datta day sayuh atta serta time. Lika wohne guy deh sayuh "moocha bella" walla nudduh guy deh sayuh "Missy coma home widda mea?" Yeah?

SAMMY THE GIANT NINE-YEAR-OLD: *(appearing in the distance)* Oh Bunny, my little bunny floppy with some wiseguys! Gather round, eensy critters! I have here the trippy text of Hank's Hopping Tale of Dread, and read it I shall! *(He ruthlessly prevents their escape.)*

(Here is included the complete text of the Tale.)

Hank's Hopping Tale of Dread

One day there came to be a simple photocopier repairman named Hank and his family of three other relatives, his wife Hanky and his daughter Hank Prime (hereafter "Edith") and his son Ankle. That was enough for that day. One day a day later it was the next day, not the same one, and then Hank noticed as he was undressing Edith in the afternoon after school that she had three recent bite marks on her inner thigh, euphemistically speaking. She claimed that nails in the gym horse had wounded her, but Hank took care that night to watch her through his special peephole. And this is what he saw with an amazed eye. She extracted from beneath her pillow a long yellow fang, encrusted with blood. Pulling up her skirt, she drove it deep into her pink flesh. Immediately a purple mist began to issue from her vagina; it formed a cloud, and then condensed into a turbaned but otherwise naked genie. She stabbed herself again and he became aroused and did his job in her three times. When she had had her fill, she sighed and stabbed herself a third time, and the genie returned into her womb as mist.

LIV

Part Three: In a Pink Box

RAVISHING RONALD: My pediatrician recommends kerosene.

MAY IN GRAY CANDY: Burnt obtuse relics cast impressions from the land of gnomens where the fozzy and the chomp ring a vestibule playing monolithic chords on a Pompeiian complexity set interspersed with conic selection.

NAKED BAPTIST WITH SICKLE: Wheaties again this morning! Already my bristling members dwarf their overalls!

Part Four: Hank's Addendum (Safely In the Box)

The next morning, Hank noticed that time had advanced. He snuck into his daughter's room and found the bloody fang. "I need my own inner genie," he said to himself as he stuck the sharp bone into his testicle. No mist, nothing came from the tip of his cock. "Must live in the other side of town," he thought, and bravely speared the second testicle. Still nothing happened. "Very well," he said out loud, "one last try." And he then stabbed his remaining testicle with his daughter's fang.

LV

AM-FUGSTA, telstar ventrilator, marma*lade*, taffy, fruity pulls, softener-enhanced drills select telephony on a circuit with a line, minced *clam chowder*, claw chowder. Nothing else. Sticks on the elf line based homily grew like rope in a duckaroon's hands. And fair wood sold for fire wouldn't catch a fly without wincing in unfamiliar celebrity. Solo cartwrights melted Vaseline onto waiting staff-members in a circumlocutious marmaladultory miggot-playing faggot blowing nukka, casting her nudnik eyes up and down over carried kings of Old Calay. Rapid response teams dribbled and served like live flesh sizzling up wrapped particulars' members' delectable kibbles in its own juices and vomited paisley all over hide and hair; several parsecs of intermittent angst within a molded crusty patina of years, no, generations of forced vomiting. Pine Sol saint of the year drove the crafty into hiding tents where mildew said "Morning" to the milkman and Purvis lit the Lionel train with a horselight.

Malthusian sugripple played felgergarb to the movie script specialist's sister Nutto. Mind azure dots of the cold totem fazz inkling along where we're where we were wanted, once, along about the time we merrily-we-stroll-alonged in a conceptual polyanny plot among your Huxleyan hedgerow. Sax-skinned bramble willy-o-nither captivating clouds of down in its force-field puff. Shades of Kleenex you feared to contact remain mismarked as to size and quantity. Closing your fingers around the idol like the feeling of a Taylor polynomial clutching at your soft underscored maverick on the couch with bad breath, a beer, and a Norton's under his arm was an involuntary reaction. Blessing the blood and the meat seemed like a good idea at the time.

Pander-plenty™ was out of my ass. Get in line.

KELLY: So how's your ass, Doc?

DR. VADAPALLI: I am a doctor! You do not ask me about my ass!

Get in line. Kiss my ass. My millionth asset won me wide acclaim in photojournalism bake-offs where we all had to get in line. Cliff train of Santa's dessert topping the Mensch-Pudding with bake-on-bits where we dispersed ourselves into fragments. Sneezes were easily obtained with the proper form of I.D. You wind up being a qualifier in any simian landscape foot-and-mouth painters contest you care to enter. Your daughter wins the beauty pageant and everyone winds up winning at least second prize. Chalk one up to experience, one less for you to worry about. Bankrupt skates, sneakers that had lost the confidence of the people. Das Volk submitted to the doctor's rifle butt while in the next office Dr. Wang had a terrible responsibility.

PATIENT: Well, Dr. Wang, how was my extract? I mean, how were the results?

DR. WANG: *(burping a little)* Wait till this Xenakis is finished.

XENAKIS MUSIC: Yosef! Come to the table! Your efforts have gone unnoticed, and no one cares.

YOSEF: Zinc mining! That is the subject of my predicate. Thank you for the inspiration, although the inscription predates my ever having had my way in matters of the heart.

SINGED NEWCOMER: Peaker cloming ack the fouth ock ald pipons abown aire feese-nakings!

Unsung Haircomber: My silly sensibilities underwhelm you. This is only confirmed further by your several new out-buildings I see around the yard here.

Yosef: Oh, no no, you've got it all wrong, that's for the conveyor belt things the zinc ore goes around on.

Constable: Sure, sure. You can tell them all about it downtown. I'm taking you with me to the Royal Academy. Sargeant?

Sargeant: Honey?

Constable or no Constable are con-stable together. Your co-NP way of life makes the most drenching soaking shower of dough of yours a possibility. Your bridge, I'm sorry to say, is out.

LVI

HARNESSED fort, a rink of cinches, a lecture-bordello for incorrigible regressors, blaze a tripwire through a maze of sweaters with the signature of no certain sign but within of noble thread and breeding, a mile from the gas station at Wellings, Nebraska, long about well nigh of 6:30 PM. The instrument of drapery conjugates well within its melonophone underpinning. Marked dawn-indicator's repeatedly issuing the rabbit-sound signed a gaseous sphere over to the bean-counters male-4-male scat. Brandied cordiality was strewn with reckless fecality by servile amateurs of sicklied amity, the feckless wrecks, yet at intervals alternation breathed the eye-spirit into their collapsed singularities and bit a nipple of ice cream from the friendly biker.

Frederich spelled quickly, and left early on the flying stain. Lanthanum fractured ringlets off into over-the-limit globules of Mecca Manna. Nipsy Russell took the pussy naval corps to mean a pussy navel chord, and that's why your grandad's prized Scotch is sopped into his crotch with maple syrup and tomato sauce. Hot eyes were wanking as the infectious projectile penetrated our rough blistery solace and vaporized all future effects of what inert residues of cause still remain on the morgue bargain table. 451° F for 20 minutes, refrigerate, and serve. She talked about wanting to have babies, all without leaving the context of the topic of vitamin supplements. Was it the Hall Institute? Was it vitamin pills or, like, in vegetables? All the cough drops in Danbury, Connecticut wouldn't start to flavor Mom's flaky menthol Melba peach cherry-popping plate of pie without a stout drink to begin with. To begin with, take a load off your feet and half a box of loose filling pudding smeared on the bathroom floor won't seem so much like shit as it used to seem like Japanimation stains. Regard your Sappho-image in the Pompeiian nectar jar mirror for a keen eyesight effect. Radiating right from the lump of rosin in the luminous kettle's very rump of loss is a spigot spouting motocause insanity, just because Ross's red ass stank all up and down the turnpike during the Revolution. Some were out of rotation, while others' Sunshine-Boy mentalities earned them the moniker "Nixie Knox," in tribute to Aristophanes' *The School of Hard Knocks*. Extra red ass was to be had from Nipsey the Turtle by lowering white ass and asses of color over its shell. Pungent rippers of the curtain of flesh stroked the nugget in their webcrawler's way of having things done. Microabsorbent Baskerville Comtesse sketched a rink for the male assistant in the Polska reflex measurement bake-off. No wonder so amazed them as did the Colossus of Rhodes. Well, Lighthouse of Alexandria wasn't too bad, and Six Flags Hanging Gardens was pretty awesome come to think of it. Not, it must have been Mother. I've never found a plastic dish quite like her.

August Voice: Say, Sally.

Sally: Ice! Snow! Cones! Bake-a-muffin barnacly Job to boot! Dogs! Sleds! Rice Krispie beignets deigning to pop and chatter!

Denali's atmosphere in longitudinal elbowed mackerel torsion does not deny fleabites from infecting the host with one of the flesh-eating diseases. This is an emergency. If you are reading this, please save me. Urgent communiqué from central station, distress signal now in effect. The voice of denial was Denali's, and though Denali was not denied a voice, his voice was denied retroactively for 6 months and the bank in the Cayman Islands he visited once a month foreclosed on his scuba-gear and bathysphere and rumble-seat and gun for potting squabs, whice and wheremits. Myles Davis gave it all up in the next moment.

Porcupine incidents between Bally's and Trump made a salad for M. Jèlide seem like Salaam in Thebes on Fat Tuesday. Bind me, Mother. Cream-cheesy cheesecake act for your impatient spouse. The chokecollar he makes you wear is none of my business. I called Myles about my transmission but he wanted to know where the spines came from. I think I put his mind to rest for a little while, but Mr. Davis is an inquisitive, not to say intrusive transmission specialist. We should continue to indulge a paralyzing noxious fear that he is creeping up on us with a suit of tails and power tools. If we should suddenly stop indulging that fear then we'll all be written out of Mr. Sondheim's otherwise generous will. I don't care how many people die, it's too late to say whether or not it's possible to save the famous busts from pulverization. The cabinet did a striptease. Today we begin working for ourselves. See to it, Cindy.

SALLY: My name isn't Cindy. *(She produces an assault weapon.)* Now, old geezer. Pull 'em down all the way.

GEEZER: *(pointing)* What is that thing?

SALLY: Keep your long arm away from my firearm, short arm!

GEEZER: Doesn't look like any firearm I've ever seen. There, I'm naked and ready.

(Sally fires.)

BARGEMASTER: Whoaaa there, Nelly. Your purity and virtue are at stake here. I'm heterosexual, you know. *(He collapses on the deck, bleeding profusely.)*

GEEZER: You've got it backwards, Cindy. How could it ever go in that way, ha!

(Sally fires again.)

JELLYBEAN: There, Popsicle, that's exactly why I could never get turned on by a girl. They're always firing their gun or farting or leaving the toilet seat down.

GEEZER: Thank the Lord I had that laser surgery.

POPSICLE: I just got a telegram. We've both been fired.

GEEZER: Gimme that! That's my birth certificate you idiot. And that's my peanut coupon over there.... Say, have you chaps been going through my drawers again? Any gems?

JELLYBEAN: None larger than a stone.

BARGEMASTER: Drop anchor you incorrigible twits. Can't you get a certain thing straight there!

POPSICLE: Stop being so overly sensitive to my favorites.

JELLYBEAN: We'll talk about this later.

BARGEMASTER: Popsicle, I entreat you!

POPSICLE: Get off me with your strawberry sauce!

GEEZER: Grapes in a jar! All mine!

JELLYBEAN: Okay, you want doldrums, you got 'em!

(The dolorous sound of drums arises from the deep waters.)

SALLY: My master is calling. Quick! Someone book me on the nearest talk-show. My leather chafes are finally healed.

MONTEL: From trade battles to budget battles, stay tuned for the next issue of House Plan!

POPSICLE: Alright, I'll let you use strawberry sauce if you turn that knob to a firmer setting.

(A drummer seven tall stories tall emerges from the sea.)

BARGEMASTER: Derrick has come! Earl, accept these humble offerings.

EARL DERRICK: I'll just have a nibble. *(He picks up Sally and Montel with tweezers and puts them in his mouth.)*

SALLY AND MONTEL: *(in ecstasy)* Ohh! God! Oh! Mmm! Oh! Ahh! *(They both come in his mouth.)*

EARL DERRICK: *(spitting them out)* Ohh! Yuck! Guys? You're disgusting, you know that?

BARGEMASTER: I tried to warn you.

BUNNY: Derrick, a-my-a-fa wren, yucca nah-ah lemaya commee you noblah unnawa-a moustache lika so.

FAT HAPPY HAWAIIAN: Unna wa-a pineapple o-ee o-ee nookie nookie le maya Malaya laya commee o-wana moustache lika so.

FAT EGYPTIAN MERCHANT (WEARING A FEZ): Gnaw! Gnaw!

Bargemaster and Bunny look over at the raft which has floated up and are temporarily blinded by Sally's ex-husband, Morton the Munificent.

BARGEMASTER AND BUNNY: You've blinded me! Mya blickas! Oy Mama!

MORTON THE MUNIFICENT: Next time there won't be a next time. Now watch closely. My hands are empty. What do I find here? A coin! Madam, it's for you!

SALLY: Creep!

(Everyone gets down on their hands and knees and crawls slowly.)

LVII

Wonder and gravy and moist towelettes,
under barged skies with a series of regrets,
faded to, fated to stare at the sky,
lectures by lecturers, poopy my, aye, my
telephonic game, with the letter H *on it.*
A single hut with a simple mouse on it, pointing
out my gimmick glinting on mighty Mount Glinka,
pointing pictogogue loci of phlegmatic scrape
in the specialist's office, while chewing some crèpe
by the nape of the neck of the lid of my eye,
by Tinglenut's glory days awash with twinkly meer to drink
and foamy soap of male delight
forgotten in the drains.
Unwashed it yet remains,
maintained in accordance with the stone of Ptolemy's
throne,
which, unlike a ruined ruin fallen in the Rhône,
commands "Dry." Swirling Dakota coast,
Haggard the Decathalon-Hearted carefully stripped
layers of old linseed. His coat shone a bony menace.
Boxers fiery drew the sun
and minced the juicy discharge
from Sonny Bono's wound.
Victoria Principal went to see
if a beauty from Key Biscayne could float
shards of moist Shakespeare in the shrubbery
and sprain a neuron by pasting polka dots
until Casablanca's hoighty barranca rots
and there are no I's left in spots.

BUNNY: Amy, affa, you wren witta yucca na alla maya come witta Grenoble witta marra wanna ehny gotta moustache daddy lika.

AUTHOR OF [TITLE]: Must you forever spoil everything! How am I ever to find the right angle for your carrot if you persist in twiddling your mouth with this twaddle!

BUNNY: *(bashful)* Iza knocka mya fowlette! Itta dah speechawrita!

PORTRAIT ARTIST: Halten zee shticken all way it up to me, chatty tail! Or zis interview never finish mitout red sticky Blut....

MARIO: ... comin' from yuh ass. Quick! Calla Doctuh who made that cuttin yuh ass.

BUNNY: Hey-a! Maya fluffuh tail izza gotta stay snow-white-a.

SPEECHWRITER: Don't just stand there, comb it!

BUNNY'S GROOM: Yaaaah-sirree, suckie!

GOON (FREELANCE): *(sings)*

> Sweet, sweet, Jesus, come here,
> And sanctify my spirit with thy thighs!
> Come hither and I'll rip off your Jesus image,
> And I'll lay you in the middle of the road.

GOONMOSELLES IN GOONMOBILES WITH TUTUS AND WITH BOAS: What a roar for Franz! Edy, I mean you Ghandi drain with all the other and saw dot it was gumme.

LVIII

I LAPPED until I laughed no more, then lapsed. Mundial voids later, transversed or subverted (but then lapsing no more until laughing I lapped up, not across, and I was full of the void in my fiery belly), the shortcuts through the thicket fell afoul of Fate. Pink poodle dinnerware could have had the image of Queen Elizabeth, but it had several pictures of pink poodles and petals and it was plastic and there were several examples of it.

FICUS ALI: Un da rising sun yacht, Seine floating in the makes bigga splash, it. Cooks, it. Mine, it is!

Pink plastic mistook a secret underwater ventricle or port- or cubby-hole or cave or entrance or any shadowing opening at all for another similar any sort of submerged door or cavity or auspicious spot for passage-people or -plastics but not the same one anyway at all. In the way, the large person, a woman actually, continued to stare far into the distance at the exit for Gates 83–90. No one could get by. In a sandwich, one man was reported to have attested to the opinion that red-onion degauss buttons were not a feature of software. Colonoscopic peepholes were soaked with saliva. Aye Pannerbrake, I hugged the donkey and wept while slowly it roasted to death, but today, today I'm gonna warsh my sin-suds away sans slentando. Survival is dirty with my sanity.

My meanderings take me to a place where I meet Dr. Ilogu. He and Dr. Garcia would beckon with that come-hither look to each other for hours. It would be the twilight of my mentality before I won twenty thousand in the casinos at the IQ-test tables. I might have just been able to make nineteen as a has-been, but my gas-ring took me out to the jetty to pump up some Getty the third and, swivelling, see the jet-black purple streak whimper and suffocate between my ermine booties and Carmine con tutti. Rodeo January spliced into your marginal Fuquay-Varina cable station's busy schedule made no difference to anyone.

In the languorous chamber off the north end of the Bridge of Size, the young misty hugged her spaniel and wept into the first rays of the morning sun. She was about to be rudely butchered by a man in an overcoat, and the next day that man—her mourning son—would get his first raise wet without soaking it. Drip-dry disgust at feats of self-abuse made him the type who would woo like a train whistle whenever the sun was nigh. Tin Lizzies made a buttload of smoke when the crap-fry was not cancelled. Cock doody, sang the chipster, cocky doodie poopy. Little tiny furry mouse rears up on its hind legs and there before you stands this 9-foot hulking giant, massively calling our countrymen to their duty.

COUNTRYMAN № 1: What was that, some sort of rodent?

COUNTRYMAN № 2: What?

COUNTRYMAN № 1: That scratching sound. It goes like *tzzzsk tzzzsk tzzsk*, and then it stops, and then….

COUNTRYMAN № 3: Yeah yeah, I know which one you mean. But you've got it wrong, its not the same one I'm hearing. It's a bird on distant gravel.

COUNTRYMAN № 1: No, it just sounds like a bird.

GIANT MOUSE: My fellow American cheese-lovers, in this hour of greatest need I call upon each of yous—to your country and to yourselves and to each other. Kill!

COUNTRYMAN № 2: It's definitely more than *gnawing*.

COUNTRYMAN № 1: It *is* gnawed!

The Chipster: Well, I wouldn't say "gnaw."

Giant Mouse: *(to cheese)* Oh, my target, my goal, the light at the end of my tunnel, as a Swiss some may think you perforated, but Mayan neighs imply Mayan horses, and Mayan nurses were expert in setting fractures.

LIX

And curses, forces, raptures, glaze
The sullen mulch of laundry days—
And barren mornings loose their stays
In nakedness, and not in praise.

Do locked-beaked bitters howl, but sharply
In descent they mock thee, harpie.
Moo gutch to generations of primes,
And vulgar boys' spit drying up our sombrest times.

More gassed than papery in mere raised arms of light,
Increased in both height and form-fitted lengths beyond
        our sight.
Moon-morphed dolls stoop to dupe the mirrored forms
        that night
Envelopes with its check and scutches the rooster's tight

Pastures. Not in the 1903 glypted loon of Servitudor,
But a butter packet smeared on a capstan of the Studer.
Inkily not the cudgeon, nor the budgie-wooer
To his extravenous blackened breath triply assure
The golden lox mounted up on the veals of azure.

Campo magnified Moishe in a Cagean slip
In which was lost the crimper and the scissors
Until—flourish—Bunny in a hatta themma fown.
Haunt down the wet harness, rope of flame,
Carcass of our might-be God; rip-slip
Of wealthy tit-nip petty do and knots to be,
That is the bastion, unser fester knuckle bandwidth.

Much that society, Xang calliope, ingress to my cam
Could pull couth from tasture, farl from a cock,
A two from what a wonny tuna-swirl Ike Anna telnet
Too bravely switches for the shard of prey's ungodly
Tale. Then some more.

Announcer prey fall victim to they who
Forfend all too harshly.
Lucky are those, to whom their own clothes
Might just as well be parsley.

LX

APING bickot, urcoddle me fry-colore monto-prop in August Paris! Brand of beard I sought to ensky, reply. Weak agent was a certain type of entity of substance, xor. Lone surrounded the form, as if queueing up a second force of natural ore behind the first thirsty saw-good to needle π in its fidgety course towards madness and sanity and death. A shady veteran was host to many albino flies, much like madness, sanity and death could offer what the meat market could bare, its eternal flame pissing off the tenants upstairs by the basement. This was the toast which, when scraped of its charred exterior, was patently edible. What a nummy mixture—he oiled his flesh. Siva threshed the pleasure from weather's navel in a sit-down evening of pleats and scandal in the sheets on the Thames by the quay where the veteran's darkness grew like an umbrella telescoped like a star shot in the sky fell like a balloon. And he saw it wasn't any good. In fact, he thought I farted. But I didn't fart, no, I measured Harry Dildo's pet turtle's head when it stuck its head stiffly out of its rock-hard shell to which reference is made in the Blythe television ads of yolk (yore) for the Eggsoakleteria Titanica's tight little New Zealand gap-ventricle and zap-supplement. It, kind of, reminds me of the time Czechoslovakian croakers forced umbilical cucumberine appendages to penetrate the underlying meanings of Posken and Downey Boy crouching in the good vet's crapacious flywheel until it happened. He took a crap right out from under Granny's nose, so she pissed her panties soaking wet.

Gorman Tito expressed his capacity like this. Once encapsulating fissures were pronounced, a foreman in a square bunion hat sat like a cat on a bag, exclaiming, "Ruts!" and pulsing body language communiqués through the open window of the old tower. Tito, instantly alerted by his special headgear, bit hard. "Ruts!" the cry was heard again. Open Tito's mangy obsequious sea creature, foraging for Monday bank loans in a sailors' sly, darkly folding ventricles into obstacles over and over in the sailor moon. Birds fell limp from branch to ground as chipmunks accelerated screaming into the clouds. It rained Maalox in June as swarming Philistines bumped against the dock the day Thomas Dolphin landed Liberty and Morton's ceased to flow. Noise reduction stopped dead in its 8-tracks and Gimmowmere wove bracelets from demolished C.B. radios.

MASSES: Cecil?

CECIL: *(tying knots in polyester twine)* Yeah?

(Silence.)

BUZZ: Hum, you stupid dinger. What do you think of my nagging robot's voice?

CECIL: You'll have to ask them. *(He points to the Masses.)*

A band of clots was covered with fresh soil and colorful rubbish. Later everything was found in my sock to the left of my foot, above the trampoline that sings Bandoliera and rinses gardenias carefully under the hose before the final rebellious outburst of flying crab delight. Back in the old days, when the wayward trampoline had not yet refined its skills, gardenias were often left torn and raggedy on the eclipse of evil nocturnal transactions in the endless fields of aluminum foil. But not any more would bills crispen and tear glands smart under a tenuous five-year plan, not while Lieutenant Céline Portes-Monbourgnondiesses de Croqueduerre-les-Dames sat plumply on the john, his white folds purple at the contact perimeter. She decided to save the skull as a trophy.

Comfy air-conditioned fireplace seats bored me when I thought of the difference between luggage and luxury. The townsmen concurred. Greg Potsdamer from the Philipsburg Mountain Gazette was embarrassed to be found wearing spats and a feather in his cap and the leather vest didn't help matters. No one asked him what he thought about it and he was satisfied to creep by, unseeing, unknowing, wreathed in a cloud of pipe smoke Corky had released from a pressurized capsule along with a nitrogenous frogman.

LXI

CHEESEMOUTH velva mung chafing oren flyswatters ambled King Shats within Grecian ganji methods in transcribing valve data from Mexican into a Scottish curling tradition equid amphispheres enpa occupine empfid nungly sapatine turquiescents awig on uplit speaktures angstrophize loftopical screeds whereon errant nonicals mungsulight. Walis of young wedges nickel-plated ortangular sparking genitalia is what I'm trying to make you understand: wetness counts up to one.

> Slipper shape, shot lead thou crease,
> Anchor at you landing, lateral at you locked
> In courageously ending late. Really, do you
>   Luxembourgeoises
> Even know what an American smells like?
> Think again when you do the misdeeds of your
> Fates, in seldom seen Encino landmarks
> Shown off so brazenly.

Illness harbours Vanna's scrammed-in all-on-ice-'n-niceness, muddles in "Is it of Ruffles, did Samantha doing no-ness gawk?" Loin in the corded model, mottled and brazen in the soon-to-be heat was taken as fully cooked and served as such throughout most of the South as hard times fell upon us and the welcome wagon ceased to make the rounds. Stillborn on the brie, Zima flowed like Zima in a harsh climate for any refreshment.

Admirable Snowburne pulled into his driveway and admired his wife through the window. How I need her to love me, and love her to need me. How I know her—her knowing that she loves me to know that I know to need her to love my knowing it and that I see her through the window, knowing I need her there, loving her through the window, and her needing to know it to love me, needing me to put love through the window into my knowing and needing her and her love, needing to put her through the window all the while she knows I need to. But actually I was just admiring her new hairdo and her tits. Love, schmuv, just give me them Goldilocks and them tits there and I'll come in from the front.

Prancing principals flapped and gawed, but who knew their birdness or needed it, only the swans knew, and who are they and who needs them? Discipline, get hold of yours today, for Mog's sake contort yourself for the pity, the swallow, the strainer, the bog! B-nutrient, homage to your complex! Now!

Admirable Snowburne cast a long shadow all the way back to his days in Tripoli-coated laminate sales, of which he knew something. Angular velocity was the reason why the orbiting ball pulled on the string, as was discussed in vibrant college talks where it is always cool. Bursting me a sucker fudger won't harken my bark to the goodle dais and King Cudgelwup and his sixteen ounces of cyst. "Quartz obliges, mistal sea! Repent of bliss, noble one!"

Normality: Oh Hedgewig's a sacred carrier of the ridge, oh bound noblesse martyr flea-ball from a fans-of-Benjamin-Franklin yearbook photograph, oh liver, bladder, bowels, and spleen, okay.

Normalcy: Kaolin nails pock my transient affectation with lipid droplets yeasty with mildew and thunder, sackbuts not with full measure.

Normalinda: You say vitality but I know the real reason is your desire to dominate me intellectually and sexually, with your gnasher in my masher, your tubulesence in my protrudescense, your flavoring in my wanderings, oh calabash of my velcro visage.

(He knocks three times.)

GERMAN ANNOUNCER: Why Snowburne, why, Snowburne?

(Jürgen and Jocasta in their den. Jürgen takes up the remote and presses it against Jocasta's recently licked navel.)

—Where are they?

—Right there, above my navel.

—I don't see anything there.

—No, a bit higher.

—Oh! There they are!

(Jürgen once more fits in his dentures.)

JELLYBEAN: *(from the far distance)* Actually don't you mean "once more fits"?

(Footsteps. A gun is cocked. Normality and Normalcy exit.)

BARGEMASTER: Who were those weirdos?

(Jürgen replaces his dentures with a Cracker Jack/popgun amalgam.)

JÜRGEN: *(grins, exposing painted metal teeth)* Veer not veered, an I dink du shotz a noise up.

BARGEMASTER: Lock on phasers!

JELLYBEAN: I'm getting all jiggly sir, pass the ketchup!

POPSICLE: *(from inside a refrigerated compartment)* You'll never believe what I saw on the news—your prostate imploding.

GANYMEDE: *(gnashing Jürgen's discarded dentures)* Poor boy, the sensory deprivation is depriving his zwieback from being a biscuit.

POPSICLE: Not at all, the temperature in here is just so. Mark your territory on my links, Jelly-boy!

JELLYBEAN: *(smiling)* Anchor's away... *(A stream emerges.)*

BARGEMASTER: ... Make it sew!

(Popsicle forces Jürgen to crochet something.)

JÜRGEN: Hereby I frankly ejaculate my seed on Jocasta's exposed square feet, suitable for framing.

NORMALINDA: Waiter! Bring me my check! I want outta here!

GANYMEDE: Hold your labia there, lady. Who do you think I am, Rockefeller?

BARGEMASTER: Okay, now that you're all nice and down at my level, can we get on with this barge trip I've got planned? There's blood oozing from that lady's navel vessel already!

(All suffer him to get on with it. It goes on. It goes on again. It goes on and on, and on and on it went.)

LXII

I'm pumped and buoyant out upon the moo goo guy's plan of record, or that which it represents, the calamine lotion fragrance thing I had to throw in but which didn't quite work. Up in fir country pox isn't a way a life, lumps aren't. Don't doubt me on this, I've finally gotten it straight to be tied up in why nots and wherefores. Isn't it enticing, don't you see it, the chickens and the small cows, and the gruff old men with beards, how they'll spoon it on at the drive in, and then afterwards?

The beezly shifted and perpendicted among the splayed shadow nuisance of a dangling cleft umpta-weening delicate fond tendrils in a land of stringy kielbasa substitutes and fillers which couldn't be perceived for the trees save for slight, nearly imperceptible undulations produced by the gill-like gonadoids affixed to their arching backsides and so forth and backwards. Rod called a starcab DNA, but toys are not applicable to the confluence of everything that deserted the central square at midnight, neglecting to summon reinforcements for a concrete raisin on the moon, and then went for one last round and a solid jolly hula-hula con toute Sonny's energie.

Eyeing the beamed smile of the interloper, Sonny flanked himself in front of a crowd of Muscovites near the corner. The Yellow River compromised its banks that day, the day of Mary, the day of Sonny, the day of spangled oats. Dag the rowboat-eater rained on the Todd-elevating Hoover that morning, and sandwiched between Wasa and a voluptuous Gorgon, Emil became far from realistic. Parsley was the leaf to shield their brüderschaftlich robustiaries from Hosenkrunch and Geldensperm, and their breath was never easier to draw or sweeter to smell. Why not rain on the Hoover? What stops from lifting away stains magically and well? Let's not wordsmith the gollygosh thing to death now, Dag it all. Please let's go see the big rollercoaster and forget how much we hate each other. Then the business with pouring the paraffin under the lidded eaves of the loaded sky of yam's Elvish wight rockery, or is it hawkery. Anyway, it's something to wave your hankie against in your jammies to ward off the salty preserve, may guppy interview us.

Velvet cheating pineapple-faced dictators filled the tiny room. From the efforts of that French phoney to assuage our lust arose the clannish kebob of rapturous yarn. Cambelline crystal Knox expectorated his filth into a lover's triangular area, and the tabloids throbbed in unison. For when the bice on the pica croze a botty dool of marce keece, Lotte canked san griable poltisjunction three miles east of envy's gruesome grasp and what's-it-to-ya bundled his worts into greenful camshaft raised holy to gawk stonky begobbing sunspod. I hope you're glad I told you that, because I felt a certain sense of urgency in relaying it from myself to you.

LXIII

POISSON gas. My beady high. A dispute arising in an inn. How Gaspard and Constance filtered home brew through found crustacea. A pact. A learned discourse on the salting of severed remainders. Tender cuts, come flay my double-jointed awareness. Fork my child, oblong sumptuous gleaming herbalescence of Penobscot dunk flan rightfully. Fonder my condor poll-risket at the precise bonder Lowell Farghtet of my dearest consquatulence. Prefer ring to marble slat, as I do before a breakfast of molten tungsten, and I'll dredge your bulk in flour, and lock you into the guest bathroom to dumplingify. In essence congratulation begot melted jarred opulence, but that wasn't imported. Flimsy valvy texture golded my ear and happy was I-Am, Bic though pentagons went fleeming down bulbous wear, ready tot to tote.

Sammy smote Sally Sangria where it hurt her shirt to sloak. Other than that, the old grey house walked about the dark forest in its bathrobe and left no visible signs or markers and was sparsely commented at that. Sometimes a light bulb is not enough, even at 3 for a dollar.

Utter sheer dismissable Pez scrambled velcro umber dahlias into a flour base steeped in boiling tradition amongst the embedded base of momentary fragments and don't you disrepair to crevice my Art Carney replica all night long and all day deep, and baby! spoke it to my rock kebab! Imperceptible silliness didn't matter to anyone's mother or alter ego. Legalese jinxed the dirty diaper container and, in so doing, the baby's dirt bomb lasted in our memories till gloryhole day.

Wan roasted barnacle proffered a used fortune cookie fortune by way of excuse as no purple urgency cloaked its mandate in puissant rebuttal and the toilet couldn't swallow my present. Brainy decent guy smiled awkwardly at my Elven nanny and spoke also to Zarathustra in this way.

BRAINY DECENT GUY: You're funny. That's my speech.

(Zarathustra, in lab coat, paces and strokes his beard.)

ZARATHUSTRA: Ach, Herr Graumass, Sie haben der innersten Nexus gebißen! Und nun?

(Z. manipulates the controls.)

X-TRA VOLT: Uhhhh….

BRAINY DECENT GUY: Packa Parliament 100s … and degauss my imitation crab-on-the-double!

ZARATHUSTRA: Jeengle my diphthong, as they say?

BRAINY DECENT GUY: You got it, Meisterbrau—now saw me some brainmeat, and hold the prions!

LXIV

Fun-covered twitterdale kaded my jeolepathy
Hard as simple Erb was a fella.
Rank as coda, death delayed.
Orange razor, snappy stays,
Pole rotating in the haze
Car lot jiffy, oo.
Came cleaning,
The Igory rebellion,
And the umber icing, too.

Hugo Glandez and Emilion Saliva rode into Albaturkey as the scum's last cleanings fell to but a bloody ragged incision in the mountains a hundred leagues hence. Yes, like the National League, the American League, the League of Women Voters, *20,000 Leagues Under the Sea*, and so forth. Oh! Their name is Legion. And Balboa spoke unto the riders, saying, the coherence of the document is hereby bespoilt all over da place here! Sheriff, my buzzard's twitching something awful!

Balboa: Hey Sheriff, the coherence of the document is hereby geschticht all over the place!

Sheriff: Hey, uh, you meant "bespoilt" there, didn't ya?

Balboa: No.

Sheriff: Oh… okay….

{long period of inactivity}

A brand, heated up in the marketplace, still seared at home, right where it counts. Filled mallards webbed openly, not unlike Chantilly lace and all the feldspar gone careening openly into a spittoon gone url, recedivist receptacle from another cosmic entity on Astor Place Nine. Balder, dashing man lacks article, does not appear in newspaper but wears clothes like a regular S.O.B. Hijacking ethernet packets, mission being, well, lan' sakes if I was a mudskipper's eye. Lounge act does my bog in one single-chambered dragon snort of a chemo-jalopy's worth of bicuspidae.

BALBOA: Uh, great, now what do I do?

GLANDEZ: Is that falafel you have there?

BALBOA: No, meatballs.

SALIVA: *(grabbing Balboa by the collar)* Never call the Señor Meatballs!

BUNNY: Thassa right, yonly calla da Señorita Meat-a-Ball!

POPSICLE: *(astonished)* You mean, all I have to do is dial ten-ninety-four Aquitaine of Eleanor and I won't be creamed into a turnip?

ROBERT HUGHES: That's right, Billy.

POPSICLE: I'm not Billy, I'm astonished.

(A hawk looms overhead.)

GRANNY: Ok yeah good, now get ready with the obstacles and projectiles and make it reek like bad funk.

The slobbering was audible for miles and for years, if years was within miles. The rinsers got up and moved slowly towards the well. Ever so casual-like, Saliva reached into his trouser-pockets as it thickly dripped from his mouth.

SALIVA: *(tasting himself)* Mmm, I am sweet, aren't I?

GLANDEZ: *(shuddering ever so slightly despite himself)* Emilion, smooth the waters!

(Gusts of liquid fire reduced the folk to wisps of blackened crackle.)

LXV

WITHOUT stopping I could not pick up Hank. … One more time, Miss Williams.

MISS WILLIAMS: Seven!

… And, so, I just really could not pick up Hank. Oh, once again, Miss Williams.

MISS WILLIAMS: Eight!

I had the definite impression that Othello was playing Iago, or vice versa, or that I was playing chess but was going to be playing Go with Mr. Wushy-pants over there … OK, hit me.

MISS WILLIAMS: Eleven! *(She wins plush hog.)*

EAR OF KORN: Please return your water moccasins to the front desk and thank you from the very bottom of my soul!

LORCA'S GULL: Mug my moll if I'm not Trellis the Tooth.

MOUTH OF KORN: Get out of there, I don't want a corn on my sole!

GALLOPING GOURMET: Too late, it's been shredded.

CABBAGE: *(talking through his "Cabbage-Device")* Hey, shut your bad mouth, you!

Julia "Not-From-Tulsa" Childs sank deeper into her couch and switched her elemental dexterity modulator to "High." Rubbery thrills fast forwarded too far to catch were collapsed as a missionary collapses his sphere of influence into a quantum singularity. Lasker's rook fell into Eggs Benedict as a missionary tried to do that.

Lasker: I wouldn't try that.

Missionary: Try telling that to your Eggs Benedict.

Eggs Benedict: Hey, leave it *alone* Clarence!

(A Macy's-Parade-sized Julia Childs looms over them with a knife sharpener in her hand muttering "Butter, butter.")

Knife Sharpener: Get back on your heels, Childs, I know your game!

Macy's-Parade-Sized Julia Childs: Stop it, you're not fluffy enough! Not enough for my buttery nougat of love!

(She sharpens her knife on the knife sharpener.)

Clarence: I'm not Clarence, *he's* Clarence!

(Clarence points to empty space.)

Empty space: See diagram:

Diagram

Hank missed being picked up and disposed of in the back seat. But I could not stop. How was I supposed to know? Look, my back seat's still empty, the water still pure and dribbling. Minerva triggered my muscle cell, and low-burned lucre swam around my coral enclosure, whose erection had engrossed a team of engineers for six months, give or take a year.

Vying wildly towards being very offensive, his acrid air fouled the entire restaurant. Dishes of nuts felt it the most. Gesoin mezzo-mastered the wunderbar Geschmutzigzeit. The abnormal social context became too great a Frito to lay upon his ample laurels. Then Ritz cracked and the sky lay back on its heels, as if to wank, but right at the last minute it sat up, looked around, and shot a one-liner clear across the clearcase ratchet cabinet and hit Clarence straight in the nads.

(Julia swats the Frito with the flank of her sharpener.)

CHILDS: Take that! You're not for breakfast any more!

FRITO: Hey waja piknin me yold sowwipe!

(The Frito unmasks and strips off his Fritotard to reveal his true cotton-tailed identity!)

BUNNY: Hey, watsa dis hee-uh widda dat? Ha!

(He o'erpowers her and trusses her with onion slices.)

BUNNY: Nah I geeva you buttah! Buttah dess en buttuh dat! Now I hidda you widah base-a-bow bat!

(D'Artagnan, Porthos, Aramis and Buzbee drive up in a sedan.)

BUNNY: Sinsa when you'a drive a me crazy, I canneven remembuh. Butta wenna you wasuh leetuh boy, I tella you Mooma tuh putta pasta oneh table. Buttua you knowah whatta she do?

CLARENCE: She put the pasta in a dish, then put the dish on the table.

(Bunny glances reprovingly at him between bastes.)

JULIA: Mmmpf! Mmpf bhhh!

SHARPENER: That hurt me too you know.

JULIA: Mpf?

SHARPENER: When you hit the Frito with me.

JULIA: Mpf!!

CLARENCE: C'mon, Pop, let me give her… the thermometer! Yeah!

BUNNY: You a sicka liddle boy.

LXVI

DONNY Osmond used a cheese slicer in the kitchen as the twins Wilhelm and MacGiver throttled the family pet. Egbert the Gecko was disappointed to see his whole family waiting for him by the riverbank.

Part III

Idylls of the Chicken

Chapter One

Idylls of the chicken a lá Rodney were mailed to select
Poles with sockets wrenched out of their arms
by jammed jellied marms of untamed felicity
in abject complicity with sirens and the fowl they pecked
with fair bushel and chainy strands of cork and Cindy.
Meanwhile Bjork, in Hindi, nattered praisefully of his
true homily grit
to whit, to woo, Mr. McGood in shards with much frail
ladybug tendered
gratefully on his bed of cheese-scented Egyptian cotton.

EXCEPT for the time when the bulemic middle-aged Goatse (last kenned by mid-city astronomers letting earwigglers crawl into his unshaved mug of stout foam round about the soda siphon tween Atlas and the seasonal ice scrapadiddle where he carried great big Tiny Tonks on his flankton and spilled him jolly in the precipitation) was rebuffed seeking to trail his nosecurls in still-soft fondant, it was a lovely evening. Corn-charged and ready for the pandemic, the big hulking blond waxed his tractor and killed a few hours sifting through the old photos of Whitsun Terrace where Aunty's bodies were carefully summed and sucked by means of a pipette into somebody's little hardened Chesterfield. We sailed over TCP seas to where, max or min, latitute went ashtray-in-the-pocket and little men with dark mustachios sold marble torsos for a song in the back of cheap restaurants on Tuesdays.

Some of the more pornographic accountants threw their circular saw blades out of windows and into people causing them to ooze deductions and writeoffs in such a saucy way so as to cause the sympathetically oozing temple monkeys to raze a racquetball court and build a Jamba Juice in its place. The wireless at Jamba could only drink until their batteries ran out, but the wired could doppio until midnight with the shambling dereliction of the damned spotting their pajamas had to take in the crotch.

Stale marble cake and all, the entire contents of her junk drawers spilled out and upon the floor, addressed to one Cindy McGood, appeared the following of Bjork's Fundamentalistan guru, Mahatma McGoodji, so nattily attired in not-so-mauve homespun that pork couldn't chew peelings off the nattiest rind which ever dreaded being unfried into a simple pellet. To give back, in Spanish, came to be known as that which was behind the shiny chrome grille adjacent to your extant cylindrical mouthpiece, but it would be another Ding entirely zweimal unter den Linden eines kleines ungeheueres Beatnikchen zu fressen, and to rob the little senile professor emeritus on his way to the luncheonette of his denture container. Creme de canard cascaded down the drapery in huge head-lopping dollops that enveloped all the ladies' taut cotton floral midriffs with that special paté Aunty used to serve drifters on coasters well before her time. Among the lesser-known species, Aunty became well regarded as one of the more prominent busts in the greater good of mankind.

Enter Loony Lyricist.

Loony Lyricist: In the event of her dropping of a busting dropping becoming prominent, in the event of her busting of a dropping becoming busting well regard, in the event of her regarding a busting of her dropping, in the event of her bust regard welling a bursting of her busting droppings, in the event of her coasting on a prominent drift, I see the Daimler coming to drive her away on smarting camshaft or brie.

Enter Abstract Apologist.

ABSTRACT APOLOGIST: Sorry folks, he is a bit loony, after all.

Enter Fenwickle.

FENWICKLE: That wasn't very abstract.

Glimmerglass looked in himself and made final adjustments: pomade-cementing his parefully carted rig, wrist wriggling into Wolex while his bowwow stwaitened owt into a cawtioo-styoo bow-weh-wo wiff subboo westewn twaits. Seminary never suited him, he reflected as a thorny red one perforated his buttonhole; whereas the Walmart gave him that warm runny feeling that he could never get off his mind. Nevertheless, the Master of Divinity had come in handy once or twice. Take, for example, the time he sang duets with Eilert Pilarm in Malmö, or how about when Yvonne Goolagong hit one straight between his frock and a hard place.

GLIMMERGLASS: What wasn't airily vacuum-fact, Penwiggle?

FENWICKLE: *(dry cough)* Permit me to stwaiten your bowwow, sir.

GLIMMERGLASS: I say, what wasn't airily vacuum-fact, Penwiggle?

ABSTRACT APOLOGIST: Not having heard you ….

Glossy Extremist runs in.

GLOSSY EXTREMIST: I'm sorry to interrupt, but my chocolate cups aren't working!

Glassnikoff's snarch ears, whether stort, farboard, or pull frontal, doorways pissillusioned the simpressikoffs while naptivating ceophytes in tortoise mode. He oggled l'assembly in preft tofile, flossing the while.

GLIMMERGLASS: Cocklette chups? Rully, Glossia, one's phasor's out. Cat in the bunny, chapnik!

Fenwickle: Your mildew, sir.

In rushes the The Rebar Dixit.

The Rebar Dixit: Nuh nuh nuh nuh nuh nuh nuh. Deezhuh huh mmmm nubbly! Pootar venga wooo! Mupple fuss twist witta tootoo occurlz.

Chapter Two

IRA ROTH: Gimme your Ruben Sammich, and make the Pastriani sing like a cappella on a toasty January morning next to the radiator with grandma's bottle of Vick's within noseshot.

ABSTRACT APOLOGIST: I … I … just can't! I mean, not only have I already eaten it, but it was made with pastrami not Pastriani, and I assure you that the fennel seed in the rye tasted not like the Vick's in grandma's lap all those long nights ago.

ENRAGED SPONSOR: How dare you disparage our formula. Bunny!

Bunny swings in, hanging from a chandelier.

BUNNY: I be givin you one bigga karate chop-eh!

Abstract Apologist hits the deck, hard.

IRA ROTH: *(looks around, concerned)* What the fuck was that?

A head pops up from below deck, it's Ginnie Mae.

GINNIE MAE: Lan' speed record! Can't a body catch a body drinking the rest of the rye down here, below decks an' all? I don't go commando for nothin you know!

Enraged Sponsor becomes enlarged.

ENLARGED SPONSOR: Um, heh heh, well! *(blushes)* May I accompany you down in the … what do you call it … the holding bay or what have you? I wish to sit upon the tall stacks of burlap sacks and drink your rye and make you cry.

A toad in tweed puffs up like a Yorkshire pudd on the f'c'stle.

Tweedy Toad: *(swinging a golf club menacingly and spitting hot gravy)* Take your cotton-pickin eight-by-ten off my mini-jay, Shopin-pay!

Ira Roth: Waiter, two more jugs of immoderatium!

A Waiter swims over from a nearby island.

Waiter: *(dripping wet)* I'm sorry sir, we're fresh out.

Ira Roth: Then just get me some fuckin' vermifuge you… you drip!

Tweedy Toad: *(gurgling hot gravy)* Peh-ha-ha-hah! Good one there, I.R.

Waiter jumps ship.

Concerned Sponsor: *(pouring thick syrup into a disposable cup)* Ira, don't do this. Think of the mucilage. *(hands Ira the cup)*

Ira Roth: *(eyes rolling back in his head, at last persuaded he is Cleopatra)* Oooo eeeee oooo ee oooooooo eeeeeee ooo eeee eeeooo eeeooo ooooooooooo!

In waddles a rotund Eskimo.

Rotund Eskimo: That's nothing compared to the whoops of joy exhibited by ancestors upon slaughtering of the whale god.

Enter Mike Redd.

Mike Redd: I was not appointed Vice President of Cake Marketing by accident, Clara Lou!

Clara Lou appears from around the corner.

Clara Lou: Oh, okay then.

A cat, Dogma, and a dog, Catma are beamed down to the surface.

Dogma: Woof! Ahem I mean "meow."

Fenwickle: *(looking down his nose at the new arrivals)* Will your meta-pets, sir, be staying for tea?

Glimmerglass elegantly wallops Fenwickle with a breakaway wine bottle.

Glimmerglass: You've made a mess on the carpet again, Fenwickle.

Fenwickle: Right… I'll get that spiffed up straight away. Oh Waiter!

The Waiter swims back from the nearby island.

Fenwickle points at mess.

Waiter nods and produces a tiny dustbin and broom from his pocket, and hands it to Glimmerglass.

Glimmerglass stoops down and humbly sweeps up the mess in abject silence.

Rotund Eskimo: Yohohoho! Now that's a nice scene isn't it? Whitey's ass bent over picking up the schmutz. Ancestors say plenty on that a one. *(He drops a cigarette butt in front of Glimmerglass's dustbin for him to sweep.)*

Glimmerglass: *(his boyish face prettily tarred with coal-dust, sings)* O Withmoth Twee! I coo to thee! Stwike down the Eskimo wwathfully!

The Eskimo is knocked to the ground by a pantomime SCUD missile, and transforms into a valuable fossil skeleton.

Pantomine SCUD Missile pantomimes a look of gleeful surprise, followed by an explosion.

Fenwickle points at the Pantomine SCUD Missile.

Waiter scurries over and defuses Pantomine SCUD Missile, which moans softly, perhaps with pleasure, perhaps with disappointment. Perhaps jam doesn't like to be spread, but there you have it. Jam.

VALUABLE SKELETON: Do I directly or indirectly sense jam? Did someone say something about jam? Or see or otherwise perceive jam? Does my sudden skeletal intuition of jam correspond to some external jammy or jam-relevant object or event?

Glimmerglass sweeps up the skeleton into his dustbin. The skeleton creaks softly, perhaps with understanding, perhaps with puzzlement. Perhaps he has finally figured out about the jam, or perhaps he is still stuck on it. Jammed.

VALUABLE SKELETON: *(from inside the dustbin)* I heard or imagined that, and I resent it!

BUNNY: *(brushing away some extra jam)* Wadaya yaya mama odda knowa whadda …

Waiter sweeps up Bunny into Dust Bin.

DUST BIN: I'm gonna be sick … ohhh … I don't feel so good …. *(bursts)*

BUNNY: *(emerging from a cloud of ambient particles, grabs announcer's microphone)* Dusta inna—busta din toa stunna bidda, like ayou knowa, dusta to a nice adinna and whaddy youa fine, usta busta allovada rigatoni, musta to muster, sa snap get clap. Olé, boys!

Ponies, clowns, and dogs form an enormous can-can line.

THE REBAR DIXIT: Ok ok ok ok ok lookit. Now that we've got the 1Q projections, corporate is going to have a field day on our smooth supple ass if we don't get it in gear, people!

CLARA LOU: Oh, okay then.

Everyone who has ever appeared now leaves, only to be replaced by Mildew.

MILDEW: I cannot tell a lie. It was all about popping my cherry. And now, there is nothing left.

Chapter Three

As the Count of T. awaited hungrily the strip of raw chihuahua meat he knew Y. would eventually fling down to him, he tried to thread a rat's tooth between the leg irons and his skin to ease the terrible itching of sores he could not otherwise scratch.

His likeness was dimly reflected in the tin foil smoothly covering tomorrow's Salisbury steak. Barney grafted a deb onto mum-mum widgets and burned his corneas on the Rex Subtlebar. "Apt-get a baguette, a Lecour '61, and hold the thou," thought the Count as he regretfully witnessed Barney, his cellmate and sometime conquistador, defrocked sysadmin of the cult of St. Yahoo, rubbing runny balm that would never ferment into little bugsacks of further Barney into the layer of dirt that lay atop the dirt beneath it. Barney was cashew turtles all the way down; the Count eschewed hurdles all the way up.

Finally realizing that ass can smell good at times, he brought his Snickers bar upside her Caramello only to find that the nut was reverse-threaded and would require the opposite of what he had planned. Big pain in the arsenal, exploding warm syrup, subterfuge with an opera mask unlike any seen to date on ebay dot com. It went for tree fitty. Reserve not met. Damn Black Shoes! Why'd I spend this time preening my green and yellow feathers all these empty days along the brown fudgy river. Polly's barbed insights into the frailty of crackerbearers corroded my zinc insides.

Camberly loved to pretend someone important loved her girlie ass. It was a perfectly loveable ass, but it just so happened to be the same ass from which she expelled waste. However, Camberly asserted vigorously in our presence that the waste she expelled was not her waste, that it did not belong to her ass, and that any revulsion accorded her girlie ass on the basis of that waste was a misapprehension as objectionable as her cousin Seymour's, when he beat an old lady on the subway with his umbrella just because the bum next to her smelled. Camberly furthermore suggested that masses of other substances, such as violet-scented sherbet, mahogany ornaments, rich cloths, great cucumbiform braccioli, etc., were as likely to dwell within her blessed ass region as the homeless shits who may illicitly squat there and are righteously ignored save by Ass Police. Persuaded by these arguments, we tied her down against the radiator next to the Boss.

Now the Boss was a man, and a very upset little man was he. He had just given up on Rogaine, and the market was down 45 points. He could smell his bum Fagin from down the hall as he shuffled between the john and the trickster in slippers and an old bathrobe drenched in hair, blood, spit, and acrid perspiration.

Fagin relished being the Boss' bum. His filed teeth and thick gobs of mascara glistened in the dark as he left a small present behind. The Boss's hips soon succumbed to the deliciously moist music of Fagin's sticky viscera endlessly coiling out from themselves, and swayed hurtling down on his fellow prisoner's protruding hillocks of irritable flesh, which responded with a triple-creme cheesequake of enthusiastic frottage.

Chapter Four

OUT from the cadaver flew the Winged Spectaculars. Shiny and smiling, slim and versatile, they felt confident in being. Uniforms all, swarming, smarming, ushering forth from the decayed wound, filling the secret room with their mass. Ribbed grubs with Sousaphones blaring Varèse clung to the pink torn skin edge, wriggling with each blast, while tiny clarinetists in patent leather boots stamped up and down in the bloody marsh below them, occasionally stooping over to retrieve their fallen parts so that firelight sparkled on their stretched leather tights.

It was around this time that maggoty bums arrived with violas and osophones. They struck up a great phony caca amongst the other insects all clamoring for the attention of their captive audience. In strode the grand Mesmer upon his trusty coackroach steed. Baton in hand, magazine through armpit, Gunther at his tail, he calculated the risk and decided to proceed with a confident nod and narrowed eyes.

MESMER: *(appreciatively to a prostrate and besmeared figure)* That's one pretty patty in your Danskins. *(wrinkles his nose at a grub who seems to be dilly-dallying with a long fork, then passes on to a tapeworm who has settled roll-like into a fruit dish)* Here's one bug who knows how to compote himself on a spittlefield.

PROSTATE AND BESMEARED FIGURE: *(They pull out folded scraps of paper from their pockets and read together, both squinting, and slightly out of sync)*

large big fat huge obese massive enormous penis.
gigantic overweight,
small.
ginormous heavy humongous ugly cock.
giant chubby fatass.
tiny big boned dick.
dumb little pig,
sexy stupid woman,
asian ass beast.
fatty gigantor lardass.
nose sex.
short an abnormal, a bigger.
black breasts,
car chick,
chunky crazy extreme food freak,
freakish.

Tapeworm: No, turn 'em over.

Mesmer: He's right. It's Lucky Numbers! We're saved!

(The Besmeared Figure notices something crawling along the floor and goes off to see it.)

Prostate: *(looks up at the interruption with great annoyance, rustles his paper sharply, clears his throat, and continues more loudly than before:)*

nuts! balls!
testicles.
crazy scrotum sack.
insane penis,
testes dick,
gonads nutsack.

mad nads!
sex ass!
bollocks
ball ball
sack family.

jewels nutz teabag nut!
sac bonkers,
loco mental.
psycho cock pain,
stupid wild cum.

testicals!
testicle—anus—asshole: kick.
loony poker,
silly sweat.
whacko ballsack,
Bitch Blue Balls.
butt damn.
fuck gay grundle!

GUNTHER: Die Nutzen, die Kügeln, die Fischbölle, sagt er. Sollen wir mit viele panzerartige erotische Tanzen die Muschbar zum Nullheit vermischen werden?

WILLIAM F. BUCKLEY: Mhm.

TAPEWORM: Oh gosh darn it, I'll go with Door Number Three.

The Varèse bleats maddeningly. Mesmer shows off his toothpaste and turns, pointing at the vast door, which opens with a slow creak. The prostate gasps.

PROSTATE: Daddy!

GUNTHER: Heil, die grosse Kuhauster!

BESMEARED FIGURE: Hooray for the big boss hermaphrodite. *(weeps)*

Chapter Five

By a certain time in the morning, or the night, Feinberg can usually be found sitting quietly by himself in the corner of a dockside tavern called L'Ammonia, drinking from a greasy labelless bottle, a blank or almost blank piece of paper in front of him, a pen open and leeching ink in his hand, staring as if his indemnity policy was one of the facts that colored the early morning light dappling his thick glass of fruit juice in the window seat on the main street of this raped village. It took three bumblebees to wind up floating stinger down in the nectar cup for him to be reminded of cousin Beebee and the raisins in Mama's porridge, all those years ago before they moved to the Institute at La Jolla.

The creamatorium pumped out another 50 gallons of the good stuff. Wanderlust enveloped the strawberry jam mountains with a frozen green spritz of lime and cilantro. Finger met berry, and plucked its delicate sweetness from the softly bleeding branch. A breeze feigning soughness got Feinberg in the eye with a randy whiffle of spritzer, making him twitch with sudden desire to squeeze Charmin, the dock's Alcibiades and Brando rolled into one package of ineptitude and misrepresentation.

Chapter Fünf

THE bitch was Chow on my pussyboned obstacle and made the English give up their war on my Mommy. Einstein Moomjy. Yeah that's right. Einstein Fuckin Moomjy with a side-salad of sodium silicon dioxide and bifurcated jabber giblets. Turkey fucker—that's what everyone knows you are. Feinberg might dazzle you with those patented contorted bun sculptures, but in the back room the Mexicans will always look at you with heavily lidded stockpots, and thick wads of spit will hit the griddle next to your home fries.

Too bad your deQuervain's syndrome prevents you from fondling the handle bar moustache attached to the burled Glock with tacticals hanging down on the trophy wall in the den; not the old den, the new one with the faux-Ionic columns and surround-sound and shag. Your wireless repeater keeps saying "Bouncing," which is not honest-to-goodness good company, but it will have to do.

Looking back I'm a bit flabbergasted at the thought that I may have given one the impression that I perceive some kind of dichotomy between "The Mexicans" and "The Jews." I mean, take "Jaime" "Escalante" for example. Well wait; okay. He was Bolivian. And I don't know WHAT'S going on with his religion, or mine for that matter. Especially since Bolivar sidled up to a busy-ladling compatriot in the kitchen and offered to share his toque under certain, shall we say, conditions, not the least of which involved drilling multiple holes in Feinberg's torso, conveniently divided on the attached illustration into concentric zones. Zone 1, the bullseye, is worth 100 points. A day pass for zones 1 and 2 will set you back 3 quid; or do you have a sensitive constitution? Splattering commuters on the Tube with Jew blood not part of your plan for the day? Shortage of small talk, not sure what to say afterwards? Understandable reservations. You can always continue to ladle soup with your remaining arm.

ANNOUNCER: …and on the sax, Mister Willy La …fon …TAINE….

ON THE SAX, MISTER WILLY LA …FON …TAINE: Well, I've never had a reception like this one. Thank you. Thanks. *(laughs)* Thanks. Thanks so much. Thank you. … Thank you. Wow. Thank you so much. I'm flattered. Really. Ok, thank you. All right. All right. Heh … thanks. C'mon now. Aw, thanks. Ok, really. Enough is enough. Haha thanks, ok? Thanks. I get it ok? Good good, ok … applause sounds; I get it. …getting a bit impatient now. All right, all right. Please, everyone. Please. Really, thank you. Ok, I want to um say something now. All right thanks. Can I have a turn? Ok, haha, thanks. Thanks so much. Really, I mean it. You're all so wonderful. The way you give it up for me. Give it up for me. Give it up for me. Okay!

FINIS

About the Authors

J.F. Mamjjasond

J.F. Mamjjasond (1964–2014) was a musician, artist, writer, filmmaker, sound engineer, medical answering service phone operator, telecommunications systems analyst, collector of useless objects and useless degrees, and a Senior Fellow of the Institute of Krinst Studies. Reclusive and idiosyncratic, he had difficulty in establishing relationships or finding lasting solace in anything. He possessed a conspicuous intelligence, a profound understanding, and a sardonic wit.

Fafnir Finkelmeyer (1964–), a Senior Fellow of the Institute of Krinst Studies, is the author of *Ex Nihilo*, a biography of the legendary Icelandic Nihilist poet Samwise Mallorn. Equally credible is his long-expected "recovered memoir" *Alternate Lives*. He lives outside Cincinnati.